Six Triple Eight
The Novel

By Mary McCallum

Based on the Stageplay and Screenplay
"Six Triple Eight" by Mary McCallum

Dedication

To Mary Emily Arrington, my beloved mother, whose unwavering love and support have been the guiding light in my life.

To Isabella Jackson, my precious daughter, whose presence fills my heart with joy and inspires me to be the best version of myself.

To the talented actors who have breathed life into the characters of "Six Triple Eight" on the stage over the past decade, thank you for your dedication and for believing in the power of this story.

To Shannon Wood and Darkhorse Theater, thank you for your invaluable support in nurturing new works and helping bring this story to life on stage.

To Dawn C. Mallory, thank you for believing in my script and believing in me and my work.

To Molly Breen, thank you for your friendship, words of encouragement, and feedback.

And to the brave women of the 6888th Central Postal Battalion, whose courage, sacrifice, and resilience continue to inspire us all. Your legacy will never be forgotten.

TABLE OF CONTENTS

Chapter 1: Sadie and Andrew 5

Chapter 2: Mary McLeoud Bethune 10

Chapter 3: Sammy 13

Chapter 4: Paige 18

Chapter 5: Cleopatra 22

Chapter 6: Sadie 26

Chapter 7: Mary McCloud Bethune 29

Chapter 8: Sammy 32

Chapter 9: Sadie 36

Chapter 10: Nathan 45

Chapter 11: Paige 50

Chapter 12: Sadie 54

Chapter 13: Paige 60

Chapter 14: Sammy 63

Chapter 15: Cleopatra 68

Chapter 16: Sadie 74

Chapter 17: Paige 78

Chapter 18: Cleopatra 82

Chapter 19: Mary McLeod Bethune 85

Chapter 20: Major Dixon 88

Chapter 21: Cleopatra 93

Chapter 22: Sadie 96

Chapter 23: Major Dixon 103

Chapter 24: Paige 109

Chapter 25: Nathan 112
Chapter 26: Sadie 116
Chapter 27: Cleopatra 122
Chapter 28: Mary McLeod Bethune 126
Chapter 29: Sadie 132
Chapter 30: Nathan 137
Chapter 31: Sadie 142
Chapter 32: Major Dixon 150
Chapter 33: Sammy 156
Chapter 34: Paige 170
Chapter 35: Sammy 177
Chapter 36: Nathan 184
Chapter 37: Major Dixon 189
Chapter 38: Sammy 194
Chapter 39: Paige 203
Chapter 40: Cleopatra 210
Chapter 41: Paige 219
Chapter 42: Cleopatra 225
Chapter 43: Sammy 239
Chapter 44: Sadie 246
Chapter 45: Sammy 254
Chapter 46: Paige 260
Chapter 47: Sadie 269
Chapter 48: Major Dixon 274
Chapter 49: Sadie 282

CHAPTER 1:
SADIE AND ANDREW

July 17, 1944

The evening darkness enveloped Peoria, Illinois on a hot summer night. Amidst the shadows, Sadie Lewis's hopeful figure emerged into the dim glow of the streetlights. Sadie radiated a subtle beauty and quiet grace as she made her way down the street, softly humming a tune to herself. The moonlight cast a warm glow on the rich brown of her skin. She tried to shake the uneasiness that had hung over her like a cloud all day. She usually would not be out so late, but Lauren had insisted she come for dinner to get her mind off of Andrew. As if that were possible.

As Sadie strolled past the rows of shops, everywhere she looked she was reminded of him. She stopped in front of the restaurant where they had celebrated her thirtieth birthday. She closed her eyes and for a moment was transported to their table and Andrew's goofy smile as he sang *Happy Birthday*. As she continued down the street, the signs in the windows stirred up reminders of the ongoing war effort: *Are You Doing All You Can?, Together We Can Do It, Carry On, Buy War Bonds*. She wished Andrew was walking beside her and not thousands of miles away. He had bravely shipped off to serve his country, leaving her to carry on in his absence.

As she climbed the stairs to their apartment, the bag of leftovers that Lauren had insisted she take weighed heavy in her arms.

Even though it was late at night, out of the corner of her eye she saw the window curtains belonging to her downstairs neighbor move slightly.

"Good evening, Mrs. Jones" she called out.

Suddenly Mrs. Jones appeared at the window. "Evening Sadie, out late I see." Sadie smiled and nodded as she continued up the stairs.

Mrs. Jones, sensing that Sadie was not going to provide additional details regarding her whereabouts of the evening called out "I'm sure that husband of yours wouldn't approve of you being out so late. When did you say he was coming home?".

"Soon I hope. Have a good night."

Mrs. Jones let out a disapproving "humph" and disappeared behind her curtains.

Sadie entered their modest but tidy apartment and set her bag and purse down on the wooden table by the door. On the table sat two framed photographs: the wedding portrait featuring herself and Andrew, both radiant and hopeful despite the looming war; and a more recent portrait of Andrew dressed in his naval uniform.

Sadie gently lifted the wedding photograph, her fingers gliding over the smooth glass as she gazed at her husband's muscular frame and soulful brown eyes. A wave of longing swept through her body. "Andrew are you thinking of me?"

Across the country in California, indeed he was. Andrew toiled below deck on a naval cargo ship with his friend Nathan and a group of fellow black sailors. The humid air hung heavy as the men hauled heavy boxes of munitions to be loaded for transport, their shirts damp with sweat.

While Andrew paused to catch his breath and wipe his brow, Sadie's face floated to his mind. He couldn't help but smile. Nathan teased his lovestruck friend. "You just going to stand there while we do all the work?" Nathan joked.

Andrew blinked, drawn back from his vision of Sadie's face. "What?"

"Stop daydreaming about some girl back home and get back to work!" Nathan said with a laugh.

Andrew's face broke into a proud grin. "That's my wife, not just 'some girl'. You know that."

Nathan glanced over at the white naval officers standing watchfully nearby. "I know she's a looker," he said in a lowered voice. "Let me see the picture again."

Andrew shook his head firmly. "I don't want them coming over here," he muttered. "Let's get back to work."

But Nathan persisted mischievously. "Just let me see it!" Before Andrew could react, Nathan snatched the treasured photo from his pocket.

"Woo-wee!" Nathan whistled as he admired the portrait. "I can't get enough of looking at her! You ever seen a woman like that?" He showcased the picture to the other intrigued sailors nearby.

Andrew swelled with pride. "You wish you could land a woman like Sadie," he retorted, reaching out to reclaim the pilfered photo.

One of the other sailors chimed in cheekily, "He wishes he could land a woman at all!" The men erupted into laughter.

Nathan grinned, dancing out of Andrew's grasp. "If I had a wife like that, I'd be daydreaming about her too. And night dreaming, afternoon dreaming..."

Nathan spotted the corner of a letter peeking temptingly from Andrew's pocket. With nimble fingers, Nathan captured the envelope and held it triumphantly.

"Mrs. Andrew Lewis," Nathan read aloud in a dramatic tone. "What's it say inside? Let me guess..." He smacked his lips together loudly. "Oooh Sadie, I miss you soooo much!"

As the other sailors guffawed, Andrew once more scrambled to reclaim his stolen possessions. But suddenly, the mirth was cut short by the sharp bark of a white naval officer.

"I don't want to be in here all night!" the officer snapped. "Stop messing around and get back to work. You boys should have had twice as much loaded by now." He signaled brusquely to Nathan. "Wilson, come with me. I'm moving you down to the railroad for unloading."

Nathan shot his friend an impish glance as he sauntered off. "I'll give them back tonight!" he called over his shoulder, letter and photo still in hand.

Andrew started to protest before being silenced by another officer's warning glare. He swore under his breath as his treasured mementos disappeared from view. "Dammit."

Back in Peoria as Sadie tidied up her humble kitchen, she suddenly froze. An ominous chill crept down her spine as she was possessed by an unshakable sense of foreboding. Her eyes drifted to Andrew's portrait on the table, so handsome and vital in his uniform. As she reached out to clutch the frame, her hands began to tremble violently. The murmuring wind whispered foreboding premonitions that sank into her bones and blood, chilling her to the core. Something terrible was coming; she felt it as sure as the sun rises each morning.

As Andrew's weary muscles protested, he stopped to catch his breath. Suddenly an earsplitting blast filled the air, a blinding fireball mushrooming toward the night sky.

Sadie shrieked as the wedding photo slipped from her grasp, crashing to the floor in a glittering rain of glass. She collapsed atop the shards, sobs wracking her body. Her worst fear had come to pass - she felt it in her marrow. Andrew was gone.

CHAPTER 2:
MARY MCLEOUD BETHUNE

Mary McLeod Bethune strode with purpose through the hallowed halls of the White House, her regal presence commanding attention. At sixty-nine, her body may have aged, but her mind remained as sharp and fiery as ever. Her keen dark eyes took in the ornate surroundings, noting the staffers milling about on various errands. Most paid her little mind, a few shooting barely concealed looks of disdain her way. But Mary held her head high, unaffected by their bigotry. She was on a mission of grave importance.

Stacked neatly in her arms were numerous file folders crammed with paperwork and proposals. As she navigated the winding corridors, her stride never faltered despite the precarious mountain of documents. She offered a congenial nod to Isabel, one of the young black maids dusting the antique vases in an alcove. Isabel's eyes widened at the sight of the esteemed Mrs. Bethune roaming the presidential halls.

"Good morning, Mrs. Bethune," Isabel greeted in hushed awe. Even many whites who worked in these halls lacked the privilege of addressing President Roosevelt directly. Yet here was Mrs. Bethune, spine straight and gait unwavering as she embarked on her vital errand.

"Good morning, Isabel," Bethune returned warmly before continuing onward. She did not have time for pleasantries, not with so much at stake.

At last Mary arrived at her destination - the stately wooden door to the Oval Office. Beyond the polished oak, she could hear the drone of male voices locked in serious discussion. She did not bother to knock but swept right in, fixing the room's occupants with her piercing gaze.

Seated around an oblong table were President Franklin Roosevelt, his wife Eleanor, Chief of Staff Howard, and various other high-ranking officials and advisors. Their conversation died abruptly at Bethune's bold entrance. All eyes turned to her in various shades of shock, curiosity, and thinly veiled contempt as she strode to the table's center. With an air of utter authority, she deposited her mountain of folders atop the glossy wooden surface.

Finally breaking the tense silence, she announced, "Negro women can make a difference in this war."

The men gawked at her, none immediately leaping to voice agreement. Bethune's unwavering poise did not so much as waver.

Chief Howard was the first to find his voice. "We are in the middle of something," he stated brusquely, a clear order for her to leave.

But Bethune would not be deterred or intimidated. "This is important," she insisted, her honeyed voice both elegant and commanding.

Howard's lip curled derisively. "We have a Negro mutiny taking place at Port Chicago. Now you want to add Negro women to the mix?" His disdainful tone left no doubt as to his bigoted opinions.

Again, Mary stood firm, unintimidated by his attitude or rank. "Is it a mutiny when they have every right to be concerned about going back to work?" she challenged. "Three hundred and twenty men died. But what I want to discuss now is how to utilize our women."

Howard opened his mouth to offer further protest, but Mary continued undaunted. If he would not willingly hear her, she would make him listen. The stakes were far too high to be turned away so easily. She began distributing folders around the table, launching decisively into her meticulously prepared presentation.

Eleanor Roosevelt, one of the few allies Bethune had in the room, spoke up in her support. "Let's make time." The President remained silent but attentive, his expression considering.

As Mary took command of the meeting, Eleanor nodded her encouragement. Here was the leader they needed in this dark hour - fearless, relentless, and utterly devoted to her cause. The men could ignore her no longer.

CHAPTER 3:
SAMMY

The Alabama sun blazed down from its throne in the cloudless blue sky, beating relentlessly upon the dusty farmland. The already scorching morning was made even more stifling by the foul odor coming from the pigpen. For Sammy Love Bonnet, the stench mingled with the sweat dripping down her neck made for miserable work. But it was a chore that had to be done, just as it had been done every day since she was old enough to lift a pail.

At nineteen years old, Sammy was weary of the backbreaking routine on her daddy's farm. She longed to break free somehow, to find adventure beyond these fences that seemed to hem her in more with each passing year. But a young woman didn't have many options in rural Alabama, especially one without a husband.

As she slopped another bucket of slop into the feeding trough, some of the putrid contents splashed onto the bib of her faded denim overalls. Sammy grimaced. She couldn't wait to be shed of this awful task for the day. At least then she could scrub off some of the lingering foulness.

Over by the barn, she noticed her two brothers, Danny and Rammy, laughing and scrapping as they always did. Though older than Sammy, the boys still loved nothing more than juvenile roughhousing. Sammy shook her head. She couldn't comprehend why the two lugs found amusement in pinching and shoving each other every blessed day.

Watching their antics, Sammy paused to wipe sweat from her brow, leaning on her slop pail. "There has got to be more to life than this," she muttered under her breath.

Reaching into her pocket, she pulled out a folded piece of paper - an enlistment flyer for the Women's Army Corps that she'd found in town. Smoothing it open, she devoured the words hungrily:

Your Country Needs You! Women can serve too! Join the WAC and embark on the adventure of a lifetime.

Sammy's heart quickened as she envisioned herself wearing the tidy green uniform, marching smartly along to begin her military training. She imagined all the glorious places she might travel with the Army, the fascinating people she would meet. She might even make it to California! This could be her ticket out of dusty, dreary Camden. Imagine the men she might meet.

Lost in her daydream, Sammy didn't notice Danny and Rammy sneaking up behind her until it was too late. In a flash, Danny snatched the flyer from her hands.

"Give me that!" Sammy blurted out, lunging fruitlessly as the boys danced away.

"Come and get it!" Danny taunted. He and Rammy laughed as they played their cruel game of keep-away.

Sammy's cheeks burned, the sting of humiliation only increasing her anger. "Give it to me right now!" she demanded. But the boys were quicker, tossing the flyer back and forth over her head.

"Take it, if you're bad enough!" Rammy yelled.

The comment made Sammy see red. She had suffered the boys' teasing her whole life, ever since they were children. When would they quit tormenting her just for sport?

"I'm telling Daddy!" she finally threatened, on the verge of frustrated tears.

Danny paused to scan the crumpled paper in his hand. "What is this anyway?"

"None of your business!" Sammy huffed, making another futile grab for the flyer. "Just give it here!"

Before the taunting could continue, a stern voice rang out. "Are you working or playing?"

The siblings froze. Their weathered father stood surveying the scene, his face set in a disapproving scowl. He had clearly noticed their antics from across the property.

The boys immediately dropped their mischievous grins. Sammy seized the opportunity to explain. "I was working, and they took something from me," she told her father, glaring indignantly at her brothers.

"It's just a piece of paper," Rammy muttered.

But their father was having none of it. "Give it to me," he ordered gruffly, holding out his calloused hand.

With a sigh, Danny surrendered the flyer. As their father scrutinized the print, his brows drew together in a thunderous look. Sammy's heart sank. She should have known better than to bring such a thing onto the farm.

"What's this?" he barked. "'Join the WAC NOW'?"

He skewered Sammy with an angry look. She squirmed under his harsh gaze but willed some courage to her voice. "I was thinking that maybe...this could be my chance to travel. To do something important."

At that, her father's nostril flared with rage. "Absolutely not!" he bellowed. "You're not joining the Army!"

Sammy's gut twisted, but she had to make him understand. "But Daddy, I ain't never been nowhere or done nothing," she pleaded. "This could be my chance."

"You're a gal," he lectured gruffly. "You don't need to go nowhere but from here to your husband's house. If you ever find one. In the meantime, you're needed here."

To punctuate his authoritative words, he crumpled the flyer into a ball and flung it to the dusty ground. Sammy watched her dreams scatter just as quickly.

"Now get back to work, all of you," her father commanded. He pointed a stubby finger at Sammy. "Them pigs ain't gonna feed themselves, girl."

As he stormed off, Danny and Rammy resumed their snickering and whispered taunts. As soon as their father was out of sight, Sammy swung angrily at them. With her vision blurred by embarrassed tears, she missed her mark and instead lost her footing. She landed face-first in the mud beside the slop pail.

The boys howled with laughter at her misfortune. "Look at clumsy cry-baby Sammy!" Danny jeered.

As they scurried away before she could retaliate, Sammy sat up slowly, coated in filth. But through her misery and anger, she remained resolute about one thing: she would find a way to escape this place, no matter what her father decreed.

Brushing off the mud as best she could, she carefully retrieved the crumpled flyer. Though stained and worn, its words yet held promise. She just needed to figure out how to seize this chance without her father stopping her.

CHAPTER 4:
PAIGE

Paige Thomas zipped up her faded, worn suitcase with trembling hands, taking a deep breath to steady her nerves. The early morning Kansas City sun filtered in through the crooked blinds of her tidy but cramped apartment, glinting off the prominent brass cross mounted on the wall above her sofa. Its presence was a small comfort in this moment of upheaval.

At thirty years old, Paige considered herself a devout woman, conservative and dutiful in her Christian faith. But devotion had not made her current path any less daunting. She was about to leave behind all she knew - including her dear son, Joe - to join the WAC. As a single mother, she had to make the best choice for their future, no matter how it tore at her heart.

"Joe!" Paige called out, her voice echoing through the sparsely furnished rooms. "It's time to go, sweetie!"

A few moments later, seventeen-year-old Joe shuffled into the front room, followed closely by Paige's mother, Gloria. Joe had shot up in height this past year, all gangly limbs and sullen expressions as he navigated the tumultuous transition into manhood. Paige often wondered what had happened to her sweet little boy who used to proudly show her his finger paintings and help bake cookies. Now he barely spoke to her except in mumbles and grunts.

"I think I have everything packed," Paige said brightly, trying to mask the sadness in her voice. "My bus will be here soon."

Joe just stared at the floor, shoulders hunched, as if hoping it would swallow him up.

Gloria clicked her tongue in disapproval. "Don't just stand there. Give your mama a hug goodbye."

Reluctantly, Joe shambled over and half-heartedly put his arms around Paige. She clung to him tightly, tears pricking at the corners of her eyes.

"You know I'm only doing this for us - for you," she murmured into his shoulder. "So you can have a better life someday. I wish I didn't have to go."

As soon as she loosened her grip, Joe quickly pulled away and took a few steps back, giving a small nod without meeting her gaze.

Paige sighed, her heart aching. She longed to connect with him like they used to, but he had put up so many walls. "Make sure you go to church every Sunday," she said firmly. "And listen to your grandma. I don't want to hear any reports of you giving her trouble, you hear?"

Joe shifted his weight and jammed his hands into his pockets, still avoiding her eyes.

"I love you, Joe," Paige whispered. Joe nodded and left the bedroom.

Gloria stepped forward and put a hand on Paige's shoulder. "I'll make sure he helps get your bag downstairs," she said with an encouraging smile. "He'll come around eventually. I'll see to it."

Paige managed a small, grateful smile. At least Joe would have his grandma here to look after him. She pulled the older woman into an embrace.

"Thank you, Mama," she murmured. "Please give him my love every day."

"Make us proud." Gloria replied as she left the bedroom with the suitcase.

With a brave nod, Paige stopped to stare at the cross on the wall. She paused at the door, her eyes lingering on the recruitment ad tucked into the pages of her worn leather Bible. This opportunity represented hope for the future. She had to cling to that, even if it meant leaving all else behind for now.

With a shaky exhale, Paige wiped away a stray tear and headed for the door without looking back. The advertisement crinkled softly as she tucked the Bible securely into her purse. She refused to allow regret to take root in her heart.

Down on the curb, the bus idled noisily, sending up plumes of exhaust. The driver helped load her bag into the cargo hold while Paige stared up at her apartment window. Joe's silhouette was barely visible behind the grimy glass before he turned away. Swallowing down the lump in her throat, Paige climbed the bus steps.

As the bus lumbered away down the street, she settled into her seat and watched the city buildings gradually transform into open fields and farms. The farther they traveled from Kansas City, the lighter her heart felt. She was pursuing her purpose. This was the right path - the only path.

Everything would work out exactly as God intended. The coming days may be difficult, but Paige knew the sacrifices would shape her and Joe into the people they were meant to become. Their lives were only just beginning.

CHAPTER 5:
CLEOPATRA

Cleopatra Laurier strode confidently into the quiet theater, her heels clicking rhythmically on the worn wooden floorboards. Though the cavernous performance space was empty, she carried herself like a queen entering court, chin lifted and shoulders back. Her embroidered purple dress swished around her knees as she made her way down the aisle to the front.

At a table sat the director, a middle-aged white man with thinning hair and an air of impatience. Beside him was his assistant, a young white woman with her blonde hair tied back in a tight bun. Neither acknowledged Cleopatra's entrance, their heads bent over paperwork.

Cleopatra cleared her throat. "Cleopatra Laurier, auditioning for the role of Miranda," she announced, her resonant voice projecting to the back rows. "There shall be no night there: They need no lamp nor light of the sun, for the Lord God gives them light."

At this, the director and assistant finally glanced up, surprise etched on their faces. The assistant's eyes widened before she quickly gathered her papers and hurried from the room without a word.

The director's lips thinned as he surveyed Cleopatra. "I believe you are in the wrong place," he said coolly.

Cleopatra clasped her hands before her, undeterred. "I'm here to audition for the role of Miranda."

"This is not a Negro production," the director snapped. His paternalistic tone grated on Cleopatra's ears.

"It says here that Miranda is 'the American-born wife'," she countered, keeping her voice even.

The director's eyebrows shot up condescendingly. "Yes..."

"I'm American-born," Cleopatra said pointedly.

The man let out an exasperated sigh, as if addressing a child. "That's not what it means."

Cleopatra pressed on. "It doesn't say she has to be white."

At this, the director bristled, his neck reddening. "I would assume it to be understood that she is certainly not a Negro!" he blustered.

Refusing to be intimidated, Cleopatra squared her shoulders. "Well, you know what they say about ass-uming things," she retorted, allowing a hint of steel to enter her tone.

The director's face purpled. He shot to his feet. "I'm going to have to ask you to leave now."

"If you would just listen to me do the scene-" Cleopatra attempted.

"There are no roles here for you!" the man bellowed. "Please leave at once before I summon the police."

At that moment, the assistant scurried back in, a police officer in tow. Cleopatra recognized him as one of the beat cops who was often patrolling the theater district.

The assistant pointed a trembling, accusatory finger at Cleopatra. "There she is!" Her voice rang with exaggerated panic as if Cleopatra had threatened her rather than simply walked in seeking an audition.

The officer turned his stern gaze on Cleopatra. "Is there a problem here?" His hand rested casually on his holstered gun.

Cleopatra held her head high, refusing to show an ounce of fear or shame. "No problem," she replied crisply. "I was just leaving. It's their loss. Not mine."

With all the dignity she could muster, Cleopatra swept from the theater, the officer dogging her heels. She heard the director making exaggerated soothing noises to the sniffling assistant behind her.

As she passed by the waiting area outside, she noticed a young blonde woman sitting anxiously on the edge of her chair, script in hand. Likely there for the part of Miranda.

"Break a leg," Cleopatra offered kindly. After all, it wasn't this naive girl's fault the role would undoubtedly go to someone like her.

Once outside, Cleopatra leaned against the brick building and fished a crumpled cigarette from her purse with slightly unsteady hands. As she lit it, the acrid smoke burned in her lungs. Sucking in a long drag, she slowly exhaled through her nose, regaining her composure.

From her bag, she retrieved a newspaper listing of local auditions. With the end of the cigarette, she decisively crossed out the one she had just left, marking it with a bold X. No use dwelling on closed doors. As she perused the remaining options, an advertisement for the Women's Army Corps caught her eye.

Perhaps it was time to broaden her scope beyond the stage. Cleopatra had honed her skills these long years for a greater purpose than landing roles laden with demeaning stereotypes - if any roles at all. She was destined to make a difference on a grander scale.

Squaring her shoulders once more, Cleopatra ground the cigarette under her heel and strode purposefully down the street. The spring sunshine glinted off the metal recruitment signs lining the sidewalk. Her earlier humiliation burning in her heart, she now saw them as beacons lighting her way.

CHAPTER 6:
SADIE

Sadie lay curled in her bed, enveloped in a heavy despair. Shafts of morning light attempted to pierce the closed curtains of her bedroom, but she had not opened them in days. What was the point of letting in the sun? It only reminded her of the light that had gone out of her own life.

Three weeks had passed since her husband Andrew's death at Port Chicago, but time may as well have stood still. Sadie moved through her days in a fog, barely eating or sleeping. The outside world held too many memories, too many places they had been together, now forever changed.

On the bedside table sat a stack of letters from Andrew along with her tarot cards in their embroidered cloth wrapping. When she had first received the terrible news, she desperately turned to both these links to her departed husband, drawing a strange comfort from their presence. She had slept for days on end curled around the letters, his words haunting her dreams.

But this morning, something in her had shifted. A restless anger simmered beneath her grief. With sudden violence, Sadie swept the cards off the table. They scattered across the worn floorboards, their once-mystical illustrations now meaningless.

Breathing hard, she stared at the chaos she had created. But the outburst brought little relief to the howling void inside her. She sank back against the pillows, fresh tears carving trails down her hollow cheeks.

Sometime later, the muffled sound of mail sliding under her door roused Sadie from her stupor. The mundane reminder of worldly routine resurrected her anger. With jerky movements, she slipped from bed and gathered the small pile of envelopes.

The first was from the government, containing official notice of the death benefit payment headed her way. A paltry sum of $3,000 for the life of her husband. She tore the letter to bits and let them fall like confetti over the cards and letters on the floor. Money could not begin to fill the hole Andrew had left.

The second envelope contained a letter she had written to Andrew months ago, before this awful numbness had overtaken her. It had been returned unopened, stamped with the cold declaration "DECEASED - RETURN TO SENDER". The harsh finality of those words was like a punch to her stomach.

Sadie's hands trembled with the force of her heartache. She had thought herself all cried out, but the injustice of losing him so senselessly brought stinging tears once more. Though the battle had long ended, she was still in the trenches of grief.

Blinking through blurred vision, she reached for the third envelope. As she extracted the contents, the logo on the letterhead gave her pause. It was a recruitment advertisement for the Women's Army Corp.

Sadie sank slowly to the edge of the bed, gripping the crisp paper. She traced a finger over the proud image of a woman standing at attention. A glimmer of purpose kindled inside her like the last ember of a dying fire suddenly exposed to a rush of oxygen.

Andrew had sacrificed his life for their country. Could she do any less? If she could not fight beside him, perhaps she could fight for him and the ideals he cherished.

In that moment, Sadie knew she would join the WAC. She owed it to her husband to carry on bravely when he no longer could. She was not only his wife, but his legacy.

CHAPTER 7:
MARY MCCLOUD BETHUNE

The morning sun streamed through the tall windows of the White House, casting long shadows across the polished wood of the conference table. Mary McLeod Bethune sat with perfect posture, her keen eyes taking in every detail of the room and its occupants. To her left, Howard fidgeted with his pen, his brow furrowed in concentration. Across the table, Eleanor Roosevelt's compassionate gaze met Mary's, a silent understanding passing between them.

President Franklin D. Roosevelt sat at the head of the table, his weathered hands clasped before him. The weight of a nation at war seemed to press down on his shoulders, yet his eyes remained sharp and alert. Around them, staffers shuffled papers and exchanged hushed whispers, the gravity of the situation palpable in the air.

Howard cleared his throat, breaking the tense silence. "The low morale is hurting us, especially in the European Theater." His words hung in the air, heavy with implication.

Eleanor leaned forward, her voice soft but firm. "Those young men need word from home. We can't let this continue." Her eyes swept the room, challenging anyone to disagree.

Mary seized the moment, her voice steady and determined. "This is the perfect opportunity to engage Negro WACs." She held her breath, watching for the reaction her words would provoke.

President Roosevelt's eyebrows raised slightly, a mix of curiosity and skepticism playing across his features. "Do you think enough of them would be willing to go overseas? That's a big ask."

Mary's spine straightened even further, if possible. Her voice rang out clear and confident. "It's no bigger ask than what other soldiers are being requested to do."

Howard's pen clattered to the table as he leaned back, disbelief etched on his face. "You're saying a group of Negro women can do what white male soldiers have been unable to do for the past two years?"

The room fell silent, all eyes turning to Mary. She met Howard's gaze unflinchingly. "That's exactly what I'm saying."

Howard's face flushed red, his voice rising. "Not to disparage Negro women, but that's simply not possible."

Mary's lips curved into a small, determined smile. "Watch them."

Eleanor nodded emphatically, her voice cutting through the tension. "I agree. It's time for Negro women to have a role in the war overseas."

Emboldened, Mary pressed on. "And to use them in meaningful Army jobs."

Howard's fist came down on the table, causing several staffers to jump. "Those Port Chicago men are preventing munitions from making it to the Pacific theater. They should be locked up for life and never see the light of day again."

Mary's eyes flashed, her voice taking on a dangerous edge. "If you feel so strongly about it and believe it's so safe now, why don't you go to California and volunteer?"

Howard's glare could have melted steel, but Mary refused to back down. The two locked eyes across the table, the air crackling with unspoken challenge.

President Roosevelt's voice cut through the tension like a knife. "Put together the proposal and let's review it later this week."

Mary and Eleanor exchanged triumphant smiles as Howard fumed silently, his face a storm cloud of barely contained rage.

As the meeting adjourned, Mary strode purposefully through the White House corridors, her mind racing with possibilities. She found an empty office and slipped inside, closing the door behind her. The weight of what she was about to do settled on her shoulders as she picked up the phone, her fingers dialing a familiar number.

"I think it's time for you to get involved with Port Chicago," she said without preamble, her voice low and urgent.

The sun had begun its descent as Mary left the White House, casting long shadows across the manicured lawns. She paused for a moment, taking in the grandeur of the building behind her. The enormity of what she had set in motion washed over her, a mix of excitement and trepidation churning in her stomach.

As she made her way down the street, her mind wandered to the women who would soon be called upon to serve their country in ways they had never imagined. She thought of their strength, their determination, and the barriers they would have to overcome. A fierce pride swelled in her chest, tempered by the knowledge of the challenges that lay ahead.

CHAPTER 8:
SAMMY

The old Chevy rumbled down the dusty Alabama road, its worn suspension creaking with every pothole and bump. Inside, the air hung heavy with unspoken words and simmering tension. Sammy sat rigid in the front passenger seat, her fingers twisting the hem of her best dress - the one she'd chosen for this momentous day. Her eyes darted between the passing landscape and her father's stony profile, searching for any sign of softening in his hardened expression.

In the backseat, Danny and Rammy fidgeted uncomfortably, the silence pressing down on them like a physical weight. The boys exchanged worried glances, unused to seeing their vivacious sister so subdued.

Sammy's heart pounded against her ribcage; each beat a painful reminder of the rift she'd created. She couldn't bear it any longer. Her voice cracked as she broke the suffocating silence.

"Will you please just say something? I can't stand the silence."

Her father's hands tightened on the steering wheel, his knuckles whitening. When he finally spoke, his voice was low and gravelly, tinged with disappointment.

"I needed you on the farm."

Those six words hit Sammy like a punch to the gut. Tears welled in her eyes, threatening to spill over. She blinked rapidly, desperate to hold them back.

"I'll undo it, Daddy. I'm sorry," she pleaded, hating how small her voice sounded.

Her father's jaw clenched, a muscle twitching beneath the stubble on his cheek. "It's too late now Sammy. You in there now."

The finality in his tone sent a chill down Sammy's spine. She turned to stare out the window, watching as familiar landmarks slipped away. The city loomed ahead, a world away from the farm she'd called home her entire life.

As they approached their destination, a flurry of activity caught Sammy's eye. A bus, packed to the brim with young women, was pulling away from the curb. Panic seized her chest as she realized what was happening.

Danny's voice piped up from the backseat, a mix of alarm and excitement. "They leaving without you."

Sammy's body moved on instinct. She scrambled to gather her meager belongings, her hands shaking as she fumbled with the door handle. The car had barely rolled to a stop when she tumbled out onto the sidewalk.

"Bye, Daddy," she called over her shoulder, not daring to look back and see the expression on his face.

Rammy's voice rang out behind her, a familiar mix of teasing and encouragement. "You betta run gal!"

And run she did. Sammy's legs pumped furiously, her lungs burning as she sprinted down the street after the departing bus. Years of farm work had honed her body into a lean, powerful machine, and she ate up the distance with long, determined strides.

"Wait! Wait!" she shouted, her voice hoarse with exertion and desperation.

The bus continued its steady progress down the street, oblivious to the girl chasing it with everything she had. Sammy's chest heaved as she pushed herself harder, ignoring the curious stares of passersby.

"Please! Wait for me!"

Her legs finally gave out, sending her sprawling onto the unforgiving pavement. Sammy curled into herself, hot tears of frustration and defeat spilling down her cheeks. She'd come so close, only to fail at the final hurdle.

The rumble of an engine cut through her sobs. Sammy looked up, hardly daring to hope. The bus was reversing, inching its way back towards her. She scrambled to her feet, hastily wiping away her tears with the back of her hand.

"Thank you, thank you!" she cried, gathering her scattered belongings.

Sammy climbed aboard the bus on shaky legs, her heart soaring even as a lump formed in her throat. She turned to wave at her family one last time, catching sight of her father's car still idling at the curb.

"Bye Daddy! Bye Rammy, bye Danny! I'll write you!" she called out, her voice carrying on the warm Alabama breeze.

Danny and Rammy waved enthusiastically, their earlier discomfort forgotten in the excitement of the moment. But it was her father's reaction that Sammy sought most desperately. He remained motionless behind the wheel, his gaze fixed straight ahead, giving no indication that he'd heard her parting words.

As the bus lurched forward, carrying Sammy towards her new life, she couldn't shake the image of her father's impassive face. It burned itself into her memory, a bittersweet reminder of what she was leaving behind and the uncertain future that lay ahead.

The interior of the bus buzzed with nervous energy as Sammy made her way down the narrow aisle. Young women from all walks of life filled the seats, their faces a mixture of excitement, apprehension, and determination. Sammy felt a kinship with these strangers, all of them embarking on a journey that would change their lives forever.

She found an empty seat near the back, squeezing in next to a tall, willowy girl with skin the color of rich mahogany. The girl offered Sammy a small smile, which she returned gratefully.

"Cutting it a bit close there, weren't you?" the girl asked, her voice tinged with amusement.

Sammy let out a shaky laugh, the adrenaline from her mad dash still coursing through her veins. "You have no idea. I'm Sammy, by the way."

"Evelyn," the girl replied, extending her hand. "Pleased to meet you, Sammy."

As they shook hands, Sammy noticed the calluses on Evelyn's palm, similar to her own. "Farm girl?" she asked.

Evelyn nodded. "Cotton fields of Mississippi. You?"

"Farm in Alabama," Sammy replied, a wave of homesickness washing over her.

The two girls lapsed into silence, each lost in their own thoughts as the bus rumbled on. Sammy pressed her forehead against the cool glass of the window, watching as the city gave way to rolling countryside. With each mile that passed, she felt the ties to her old life stretching thinner.

CHAPTER 9:
SADIE

The Georgia sun beat down mercilessly on Fort Oglethorpe, its rays reflecting off the dusty parade ground with an intensity that seemed to mock the gravity of the moment. An army truck, its olive-drab paint dulled by miles of travel, rumbled to a stop at the base's entrance. The vehicle's suspension groaned under the weight of its precious cargo - a group of Black women arriving for training, their faces a mixture of determination, apprehension, and barely contained excitement.

Among them sat Sadie, her fingers gripping the edge of the wooden bench so tightly her knuckles had turned white. Beside her, Cleopatra exuded an air of regal composure, though the slight tremor in her hands betrayed her nerves. Sammy fidgeted restlessly, her irrepressible energy at odds with the solemn atmosphere. Paige sat ramrod straight, her eyes fixed on the world beyond the truck's canvas cover, as if trying to memorize every detail of this pivotal moment.

The driver, a white man whose weathered face spoke of years spent behind the wheel, called out impatiently, "What are you waiting for?"

His words hung in the air, unanswered. The women exchanged uncertain glances, suddenly acutely aware of the height of the truck bed. It was a long way down, and none of them wanted to start their military career with a stumble or, worse, a fall.

Colonel Davis, a man whose short stature and sunburned complexion gave him the appearance of a garden gnome, strode towards the truck. His clipboard, clutched tightly in one gnarled hand, seemed an extension of his authority. "Jump!" he barked, his voice cracking like a whip in the stifling air.

The command galvanized the women into action. One by one, they began to descend from the truck, each jump a leap of faith into their new lives. Some landed with grace, others stumbled, but all felt the weight of history in that simple act.

Sammy, her enthusiasm overriding caution, leapt with gusto. Her landing, however, left much to be desired. She sprawled in the dust, a tangle of limbs and embarrassment. The other women winced in sympathy, but none dared offer help, sensing that this was a test - one they couldn't afford to fail.

As the last of the Black women found their footing on solid ground, another truck pulled up, this one carrying white trainees. The contrast in their reception was stark and immediate. The drivers moved to assist each white woman down from the truck, their hands gentle and solicitous as they guided them to the ground.

The two groups of women stood apart, separated by more than just the few yards of dusty earth between them. The white recruits, including Betty Clarke - a blonde vision of high-maintenance beauty - watched the Black women with a mixture of disdain, curiosity, and ill-concealed amusement.

Colonel Davis's voice cut through the tension. "Negro girls, line up," he commanded, his tone leaving no room for hesitation or question.

The Black women hurried to comply, forming a line that was more enthusiasm than precision. Colonel Davis regarded them for a moment, his expression unreadable, before jerking his thumb towards a nearby building. "Negroes, that way."

Their gazes followed his gesture, landing on two figures waiting by the indicated building. Sergeant Carter, a Black woman whose no-nonsense demeanor radiated from every pore, stood alongside her Squad Leader. Chanel Washington, a petite light-skinned woman whose stature belied the force of her presence.

As the Black women moved off in the direction they'd been pointed, Colonel Davis turned his attention to the white recruits. His voice, noticeably softer now, carried clearly across the parade ground. "Welcome to Fort Oglethorpe, Company 7."

The clipboard in his hand came up, and he began to call out names. "Anna Elliot. Ruth Kinney. Mildred Finley..." Each name was a summons, each woman stepping forward as she was called, her posture straightening under the weight of her new identity as a member of Company 7.

The Black women, now clustered near Sergeant Carter and Squad Leader Washington, couldn't help but glance back at this display. The disparity in their reception was impossible to ignore, a stark reminder of the challenges that lay ahead. They had come to serve their country, to prove their worth, but it was clear that the battlefield they would face extended far beyond any war zone.

The Georgia sun continued its relentless assault, but the women of what would become Company 8 stood tall. They had taken their first steps into a new world, and there was no turning back now. The real test was just beginning.

The supply room at Fort Oglethorpe buzzed with nervous energy as the new recruits filed in, their footsteps echoing off the concrete floors. Sadie took her place in line, her spine straight and chin held high. She surveyed the room, taking in the rows of shelves stacked with uniforms and equipment, the harsh fluorescent lights casting everything in a sickly pale glow.

Sergeant Carter stood off to the side, her arms crossed over her chest as she observed the proceedings with a hawkish gaze. Her eyes flicked from recruit to recruit, assessing each one with a practiced eye. Sadie could almost hear the gears turning in her head, already deciding who would and would not make it.

At the front of the line, a Black female supply clerk efficiently handed out items to each recruit. Her movements were practiced and precise, betraying no emotion as she went about her task. Sadie watched as Cleopatra, a statuesque woman with high cheekbones and an air of elegance, reached the front of the line.

The supply clerk thrust a neatly folded uniform into Cleopatra's arms. Cleopatra held it up, her nose wrinkling as if she'd just been handed a dead fish. Her voice dripped with disdain as she asked, "This is what we have to wear?"

The supply clerk didn't even bother to look up, her voice flat and disinterested. "Next."

Cleopatra opened her mouth as if to protest further, but a sharp look from Sergeant Carter silenced her. She stepped aside, still eyeing the uniform with barely concealed disgust.

As the line inched forward, Sadie's attention was drawn to a petite woman with a mop of unruly curls. Sammy Love Bonnet, as she enthusiastically introduced herself to anyone within earshot, seemed determined to befriend every recruit in the room. Her Alabama drawl carried easily over the low murmur of conversation.

"Hi, I'm Sammy. Sammy Love Bonnet. I'm from Alabama. Where're you from?" she chirped, her smile bright enough to rival the harsh overhead lights.

Sadie watched as Sammy worked her way through the line, leaving a trail of bemused smiles and hesitant conversations in her wake. The girl's energy was infectious, providing a much-needed distraction from the gravity of their situation.

As Sadie finally reached the front of the line, she accepted her uniform with a polite nod to the supply clerk. The rough fabric felt foreign in her hands, a tangible reminder of the new life she was embarking upon. She allowed herself a moment to run her fingers over the sturdy material, imagining how it would feel to wear it, to truly become a part of something larger than herself.

The scene shifted abruptly as Sadie found herself in the fort's infirmary, the antiseptic smell assaulting her nostrils. She stood in yet another line, this one moving at an agonizingly slow pace as each recruit received their inoculations. The room was filled with a cacophony of sounds – the snap of latex gloves, the clink of medical instruments, and the occasional sharp intake of breath as needles pierced skin.

Sadie watched as the women ahead of her received their shots, each reacting in their own way. Some winced, others bit their lips to keep from crying out, while a few managed to maintain stoic expressions throughout the ordeal.

When it was finally her turn, Sadie rolled up her sleeve and presented her arm to the nurse. She fixed her gaze on a point on the opposite wall, her expression impassive as the needle slid into her flesh. She didn't flinch, didn't even blink. Years of facing far worse had steeled her against such minor discomforts.

Behind her, she heard a sharp gasp followed by a whimper. Sammy Love Bonnet, it seemed, wasn't quite as prepared for the experience. Sadie resisted the urge to turn and look, keeping her focus straight ahead as the nurse applied a small bandage to her arm.

As she stepped away from the inoculation station, Sadie allowed her gaze to sweep across the room once more. The majority of the women bore expressions of grim determination, their jaws set and eyes forward as they endured this latest trial. It was a stark reminder of the challenges that lay ahead, of the sacrifices they would all be called upon to make.

In that moment, standing in a room full of strangers united by a common purpose, Sadie felt a flicker of something she hadn't experienced in a long time – hope. These women, from all walks of life, had chosen to serve their country despite the obstacles and prejudices they faced. They were fighters, every last one of them.

As she made her way out of the infirmary, her arm still tingling from the injection, Sadie squared her shoulders. Whatever lay ahead, whatever challenges they would face, she knew one thing for certain – she was exactly where she needed to be.

A day later, the Georgia sun beat down mercilessly on Fort Oglethorpe, its early morning rays already hinting at the scorching day ahead. The line of Black women stood at attention, their new uniforms crisp and starched, a stark contrast to the dusty parade ground beneath their feet. The air hummed with tension and anticipation as they awaited inspection, each woman acutely aware of the historical significance of their presence.

Sergeant Carter strode before them, her face an impassive mask as she surveyed the recruits. Her voice, when it came, cut through the morning air like a whip crack.

"Welcome to Company 8. I am Sergeant Carter. I will be your basic training officer for the next eight weeks."

She paced slowly down the line, her eyes boring into each woman as if trying to pierce through to her very soul. The recruits stood ramrod straight, not daring to move a muscle under her scrutiny.

"Let's get one thing straight. I am not your mama. I'm not your daddy. I'm not your meemaw or your peepaw. I am not your best gal pal. I'm not your pal at all. I am not your babysitter. There are no children here. You are grown women and I expect you to act like it."

Her words hung in the air, each syllable a hammer blow driving home the reality of Sadie's situation. This was no social club, no gathering of friends. This was the army, and they were soldiers now.

"I am here for one purpose," Sergeant Carter continued, her voice dropping to a low, intense growl. "To train you for service so you can replace a man for duty closer to the war."

The weight of responsibility settled over the company like a heavy blanket. They were not here merely to wear a uniform or play at being soldiers. They were here to free up men for combat, to play a crucial role in the war effort. The enormity of it all threatened to overwhelm them, but they held their ground, faces set in determination.

Sergeant Carter began her inspection in earnest, moving down the line with meticulous attention to detail. Her eyes missed nothing, from the shine on their shoes to the set of their caps. Sadie watched from the corner of her eye as she approached Cleopatra, her steps slowed, and her eyes narrowed.

Cleopatra stood out from the rest, and not in a way that would please any drill sergeant. Her uniform had been subtly altered, tied at the waist to accentuate her figure. Her hair cascaded down past her collar in defiance of regulations, a silent rebellion against the uniformity demanded of them.

Sergeant Carter's voice dripped with displeasure as she addressed her. "Your hair is touching your collar, and I don't know how you are wearing this uniform, but that is not regulation. I want you to fall out and do something about it before we move."

Confusion flickered across Cleopatra's face. "Fall out?"

The sergeant's patience, already wearing thin, threatened to snap entirely. "Go back to the barracks and get yourself together. We'll wait."

A giggle, quickly stifled but not quickly enough, erupted from further down the line. Sadie knew from the sound, it had to be Sammy. Sergeant Carter's head snapped around, zeroing in on the source of the sound. Sammy stood there, her face a mixture of horror at her own outburst and amusement at the situation.

"Did I say something amusing?" Sergeant Carter's voice dripped icily.

Sammy shook her head vigorously, all traces of mirth vanishing from her face. The sergeant held her gaze for a moment longer, ensuring the message had been received, before turning her attention back to Cleopatra.

"Faster!" she barked, and Cleopatra broke into a run, her non-regulation hair streaming behind her as she dashed towards the barracks.

As if to underscore the contrast between what was expected and what Company 8 had delivered, the white women of Company 7 chose that moment to march past. Their formation was perfect, a testament to discipline and training. At their head marched Betty, her face set in smug satisfaction as she caught sight of Cleopatra's retreating form.

The members of Company 8 watched their counterparts pass by, a mix of emotions playing across their faces. Determination, envy, frustration, and resolve warred within them. They had known this wouldn't be easy; had known they would face challenges their white counterparts would not. But knowing and experiencing were two very different things.

As Cleopatra's footsteps faded and the last echoes of Company 7's march died away, a heavy silence fell over the parade ground. Sergeant Carter's gaze swept over the remaining women, her expression unreadable.

Sadie knew this was only the beginning, the first test of many. The women of Company 8 stood tall under her scrutiny, each silently vowing to prove themselves, to overcome whatever obstacles lay ahead. They were pioneers, trailblazers, and they would not be found wanting.

The Georgia sun continued its relentless ascent, promising a day of sweat and toil. But for the women of Company 8, the real heat was just beginning to rise.

CHAPTER 10:
NATHAN

The stale air of the Port Chicago Naval Base cell block hung heavy with despair and injustice. Nathan lay on his thin, military-issue mattress, his eyes fixed on the faded photograph of Sadie taped to the stark white wall. The image, creased and worn from countless hours of scrutiny, served as both comfort and torment.

The sound of footsteps echoing down the corridor snapped Nathan from his reverie. He sat up, his muscles tensing instinctively as he awaited yet another interrogation or accusation. But the man who appeared before his cell was unlike any he'd seen since his confinement began.

Thurgood Marshall stood tall and proud, his presence filling the narrow corridor with an air of authority and hope. At 36, he carried himself with the confidence of a man twice his age, his eyes sharp and penetrating as they took in Nathan's disheveled appearance.

"I'm Thurgood Marshall," he said, his voice steady and reassuring. "I'm here to help you."

The words hung in the air between them, a lifeline thrown into the murky waters of Nathan's despair. For the first time in weeks, a flicker of hope ignited in his chest.

The scene shifted, the oppressive confines of the cell giving way to the slightly less claustrophobic setting of an interrogation room at Mare Island Naval Yard. Nathan sat across from Marshall, the metal table between them cold and unyielding. The lawyer's presence, however, seemed to soften the harsh edges of their surroundings.

Nathan's voice was low and gravelly as he recounted the events of that fateful day. "We could feel the explosion at the railroad. It was so strong, the boxcars full of ammunition caught on fire."

Marshall listened intently, his eyes never leaving Nathan's face. He flipped through the file before him, his brow furrowing as he read. "It says here you helped put the fires out."

Nathan nodded, his fingers unconsciously tracing the raised scars on his arms. "That's how I got these burns."

Marshall's gaze flickered to the scars before returning to the file. He began to read aloud, his voice taking on a formal tone:

"Ensign Charles Brooks, Ensign Walter Farrow, Ensign Matthew Gray, and Seaman Nathan Wilson, broke open the burning cars, walking on top of them, and played hoses through the holes made by falling fragments, continually exposing themselves to danger until the flames were extinguished. They contributed materially to bringing the flames under control, thereby averting further explosions and possible loss of life."

The words hung in the air, a stark contrast to Nathan's current predicament. He nodded silently, the memory of that day etched into his very being.

Marshall's voice softened as he looked up from the file. "You're a hero."

The word 'hero' seemed to ignite something in Nathan. His posture straightened, his eyes flashing with a mixture of pride and indignation. "Then tell me why only the white sailors I was with are getting medals and I'm locked up here? I wasn't even there for the so-called mutiny. I was watching from the infirmary window."

Marshall's expression remained neutral, but a flicker of anger passed behind his eyes. "It says they're holding you as a witness."

Nathan scoffed, his hands clenching into fists on the table. "They'll say anything to cover their asses. After it all went down, we asked for our survivors' passes to go and see our families. They are supposed to give you 30 days. They said no leaves. I asked to speak to the Commander. They told us he was on leave."

He paused, taking a deep breath before continuing. His voice took on a softer tone, tinged with a mixture of awe and sorrow. "When they assembled those boys and they heard the orders -column left- and -forward march- to march toward the ammunition loading dock, they just stopped. They all stopped. Wasn't no mutiny."

Marshall leaned forward, his eyes intent. "Why do you believe they stopped?"

Nathan's gaze grew distant, his mind clearly replaying the horrors he'd witnessed. "Imagine having to retrieve the body parts and corpses of the men you worked beside out the ocean, your brothers. But for the grace of God, that would be us getting pulled out the water in pieces. Nobody wanted to end up like that. If I was out there, I would have stood there right with them."

The weight of his words settled over the room like a heavy blanket. Marshall nodded solemnly, understanding the gravity of the situation. "Thank you for speaking with me. I assure you, this is the NAACP's top priority right now. We're going to do what we can to get you out as soon as possible."

Nathan's posture relaxed slightly, a glimmer of hope returning to his eyes. "Thank you, sir."

As Marshall stood to leave, Nathan spoke up once more, his voice hesitant. "One thing. Do you think you could get me a pen and some paper?"

Marshall paused, his hand on the door handle. He turned back to Nathan, a small smile playing at the corners of his mouth. "I'll see to it."

As the door closed behind Marshall, Nathan was left alone once more. But the oppressive silence of before had been replaced by something else - a spark of hope, a glimmer of possibility. For the first time since the explosion, Nathan allowed himself to believe that maybe, just maybe, justice could prevail.

Nathan's gaze drifted to his scarred hands, resting on the cold metal surface of the table. The burns he'd sustained putting out the fires were a constant reminder of that horrific day - a day when he'd acted on instinct, driven by a desire to save lives and prevent further catastrophe. Now, those same hands that had worked tirelessly to extinguish the flames were bound by invisible chains of injustice and racial prejudice.

The irony of his situation wasn't lost on Nathan. He'd risked his life alongside white sailors, faced the same dangers, breathed the same smoke-filled air. Yet he sat, locked away while they received commendations and medals. The bitter taste of inequality rose in his throat, threatening to choke him.

Marshall's words echoed in his mind: "You're a hero." But what did that word mean in a world that refused to see past the color of his skin? A world that could look at the same actions and see heroism in one man and suspicion in another, based solely on race?

The sound of a key turning in the lock jolted Nathan back to the present. A guard appeared in the doorway, his face an impassive mask as he gestured for Nathan to stand. As he was led back to his cell, Nathan's mind whirled with the possibilities Marshall's visit had opened up.

For the first time since the explosion, he allowed himself to imagine a future beyond these walls. A future where the truth would come to light, where justice would prevail not just for him, but for all the men who had been wrongly accused of mutiny.

As the cell door clanged shut behind him, Nathan's eyes were drawn once more to the photo of Sadie on the wall. Her smile, frozen in time, seemed to offer encouragement and strength. He made a silent vow to her, to himself, that he would deliver Andrew's last letter to Sadie.

CHAPTER 11:
PAIGE

The morning sun beat down on the Fort Oglethorpe parade ground as Paige stood at rigid attention, sweat trickling down her spine beneath her starched uniform. Her muscles ached from the unfamiliar posture, but she refused to show weakness. The Bible's warnings about idle hands kept running through her mind - at least marching drills meant they were doing something productive.

The drill instructor paced before them, her face creased with growing frustration. Most of the women had picked up the basic marching steps quickly enough, their movements precise if not perfect. But Sammy Love Bonnet stumbled along like a newborn colt, perpetually out of step with the rest of the formation.

"What in the world?" The drill instructor's exasperation echoed across the parade ground.

Squad Leader Washington's voice cracked like a whip. "Get it together, Bonnet!"

Paige kept her eyes forward, fighting the urge to wince at Sammy's continued struggle. The girl had heart, she'd give her that, but this kind of display reflected poorly on all of them. They already had enough strikes against them without looking incompetent.

"How is it that a Negro girl has no rhythm?" Cleopatra's sardonic drawl carried clearly through the morning air.

Before anyone could respond, Sergeant Carter's sharp voice cut through the murmuring. "Lawry, is that hair I see falling down?"

Paige caught Cleopatra hastily tucking a wayward strand back under her cap, muttering under her breath, "It's Laurier."

A burst of mocking laughter drew Paige's attention. Betty and her group of white WACs strolled past, making no attempt to hide their amusement at the scene. Paige's jaw clenched. Every mistake, every misstep would be used against them. They had to be better than perfect just to be considered adequate.

The morning's frustrations followed them into the mess hall. Paige sat with Wanda Moore, a late-thirties no-nonsense woman with caramel skin. The strict segregation of the dining space meant the white women occupied their own section, a physical reminder of the divide that persisted even in wartime.

Movement caught Paige's eye as Sadie Lewis entered, carrying her tray with careful precision. The woman's presence sent an involuntary chill down Paige's spine. There was something unsettling about her, something that set Paige's spiritual alarm bells ringing.

Sadie stood awkwardly in the center of the room, met with unwelcoming stares from every table. After a moment's hesitation, she chose an empty table and sat alone.

"What's the deal with that one?" Paige asked Wanda, unable to contain her curiosity.

Wanda leaned forward, her voice dropping conspiratorially. "She's in my bunk. We call her voodoo woman. She has these cards in a voodoo box that she looks at when she thinks no one is watching."

A cold knot formed in Paige's stomach. Her mama had warned her about such things - fortune telling, conjuring, witchcraft. The devil's tools, every one of them. "That ain't nothing but the devil," she declared firmly. "You best stay far away from her. I know I will."

Wanda nodded in agreement. The urge to pray rose strong within Paige.

Lord give me strength, she thought, watching Sadie eat her meal in isolation. This was supposed to be about serving her country, making a better life for Joe. Instead, she found herself facing spiritual warfare right here in Georgia.

The food on her tray grew cold as Paige wrestled with her conscience. Her upbringing told her to shun such evil, to avoid any association with practices that went against God's word. But they were all here to serve a greater purpose. The conflict twisted in her gut like a living thing.

A memory surfaced of her last Sunday at church before enlisting. The pastor had preached about standing firm against evil, about being a light in the darkness. Was that why God had placed her here? To stand as a righteous example?

Paige straightened her spine, renewed purpose flowing through her. She would do her duty - to her country and to her Lord. But she would not let Satan gain a foothold through association with ungodly practices. She would keep her distance from Sadie Lewis and her devil cards, no matter what.

As if sensing Paige's thoughts, Sadie glanced up briefly from her meal. Their eyes met across the mess hall, and Paige quickly looked away, murmuring a quiet prayer under her breath. The trials of basic training suddenly seemed minor compared to the spiritual battle she faced.

"Lord protect us," she whispered, pushing her tray away. Her appetite had deserted her entirely.

Wanda touched her arm sympathetically. "Don't worry. We'll watch out for each other."

Paige nodded gratefully, but her mind was already drafting the letter she would write to Joe tonight. She would have to be careful what she told him - no need to worry him about the evil lurking in their midst. But perhaps she could ask him to pray for her extra hard.

The mess hall slowly emptied as women finished their meals and headed to their next assignments. Paige lingered, deep in thought. She would need to be strong, to keep her faith as a shield against whatever darkness might come.

CHAPTER 12:
SADIE

The worn wooden floorboards of the Fort Oglethorpe barracks creaked beneath Sadie's weight as she sat cross-legged on her bunk. Her fingers trembled slightly as she laid out the tarot cards, their familiar faces bringing both comfort and pain. In the quiet solitude of the empty barracks, she could almost pretend she was back home, reading for Andrew before he shipped out.

The sharp slam of the barracks door shattered her peace. Sadie's hands moved with practiced speed, sweeping the cards away as Wanda and three other women burst in. Their animated chatter died at the sight of her, replaced by knowing looks and poorly concealed sneers.

Wanda's hip brushed Sadie's bed as she passed, deliberately knocking her bag to the floor. The contents scattered across the dusty boards like autumn leaves. Sadie remained still, her face a careful mask as she met Wanda's challenging gaze.

"You dropped something," Wanda announced with mock innocence. Her laughter, sharp as broken glass, was quickly echoed by her companions.

Sadie kept her eyes fixed straight ahead, letting their cruel mirth wash over her like rain. She'd learned early that reaction only fed their appetite for torment. Still, her fingers itched to gather her cards, to seek guidance or comfort in their familiar patterns.

Instead, she sat motionless until the women tired of their game and moved on.

Later, during marching drills, Sadie found herself watching Sammy's continued struggles with the basic steps. The girl's enthusiasm couldn't mask her complete lack of rhythm - every attempted maneuver sent her stumbling out of formation like a puppet with tangled strings.

Sergeant Carter's exasperation radiated across the parade ground as she conferred with the drill instructor. "Something needs to be done."

"Yes, Sergeant," the drill instructor replied, her expression grim as she watched another failed attempt at coordination.

The afternoon found them crowded into a stuffy classroom, bent over yet another Army General Classification Test. Sadie worked methodically through the questions, trying to ignore the whispered conversation between Sammy and Cleopatra.

"Why do we have to keep taking all of these tests?" Sammy's whine carried clearly despite her attempt at discretion.

"Shh," Cleopatra hissed, not looking up from her paper.

"My arm still hurts from all those shots," Sammy persisted. "I don't know what I'm worst at--taking tests or marching."

A hint of amusement colored Cleopatra's response. "Nothing can be worse than your marching."

"It's too many tests."

"It's so they can figure out what position to put us in."

"Position?"

"Shh!"

Sadie's pencil moved steadily across her paper, but her mind wandered. She'd known her position, her purpose, once. Back when Andrew was alive, when her gift seemed more blessing than curse. Now she felt adrift, surrounded by women who feared or despised her, serving a country that barely acknowledged her humanity.

The mess hall offered no refuge. Sadie sat alone at her usual table, the empty seats around her a stark reminder of her isolation. She could feel Wanda and Paige's stares boring into her back as they huddled at their table, their conversation carrying despite their lowered voices.

"When do you think we'll get our assignments?" Wanda asked.

"Not until the end probably." Paige's response held both resignation and anticipation.

"I want to know now. So I can know if this whole thing is worth it."

"I'm praying they put me in medical training so I can be a nurse after the war. Make my son proud."

A pause, then Wanda's voice again, tight with pain. "I got a headache from not sleeping. I can't sleep with her in my bunk. I keep thinking about what you said about her doing the devil's work."

Their gazes burned into Sadie's back. She forced herself to take another bite of the tasteless food, though her appetite had long since fled. The cards in her pocket seemed to pulse with energy, begging to be consulted. But she knew better than to draw them here, where every action was scrutinized and judged.

A memory surfaced - Andrew's warm laugh as she'd laid out the cards for him that last time. "You don't need those to know our future," he'd said, gathering her into his arms. "We're gonna grow old together, watch our grandkids play in the yard."

The vision had come to her then, sharp and terrible, but she'd pushed it away. What good was the gift of sight if you couldn't change what you saw? If you couldn't save the ones you loved?

Sadie gathered her tray with steady hands, ignoring the whispers that followed her from the mess hall. Let them talk, let them fear. They didn't understand that real darkness had nothing to do with cards or visions. Real darkness was watching the future unfold like a nightmare and being powerless to stop it.

Back in the barracks, she traced the outline of her cards through her pocket. Soon enough, night would fall. Then she could seek answers in their familiar patterns, could pretend for a few precious moments that she wasn't completely alone in this strange new world she'd chosen.

For now, she straightened her spine and lifted her chin. She was a soldier now, even if no one else saw her that way. And soldiers carried on, no matter the weight of their burdens.

Night settled over Fort Oglethorpe like a heavy blanket, but sleep eluded Sadie. The soft breathing of her bunkmates only emphasized her isolation as she lay rigid in her narrow bed, Andrew's absence an ache in her chest. The darkness seemed to pulse with unspoken warnings, whispered premonitions that slipped away before she could grasp their meaning.

Finally giving up on rest, Sadie eased from her bunk with practiced stealth. Her fingers found her box in the darkness, its familiar edges offering small comfort. As she crept toward the door, she missed Wanda's eyes tracking her movement through carefully slitted lids.

The night air wrapped around her like a shroud as she wandered the shadowy grounds. Her feet carried her instinctively toward the pool, its dark water gleaming under the sparse lighting. She found a secluded corner, settling into the shadows like a ghost.

The cards felt alive in her hands as she laid them out, their faces catching what little light filtered through the trees.

"Why won't you come to me?" she whispered, frustration cracking her voice. The words carried across the still water, unanswered.

She wasn't even sure anymore who she was asking - the cards, Andrew's spirit, or some higher power that seemed to have abandoned her. The gift that had once felt like a blessing now mocked her with its selective silence.

Hours passed as she repeatedly shuffled and dealt, searching for any sign, any message. But the cards remained merely paper and ink, lifeless in her trembling hands. The approaching dawn finally drove her back toward the barracks, her box clutched close like a shield.

Sadie slipped back inside just as the sky began to lighten. She tucked her box away and eased into her bunk, careful to avoid the creaking springs. Across the room, Wanda lay perfectly still, but Sadie could feel the weight of her watchful gaze.

Another sleepless night, another failed attempt to pierce the veil between worlds. Perhaps this was her true punishment - not the isolation or the whispered accusations, but the silence of her gift when she needed it most.

As the first rays of sun crept through the windows, Sadie closed her eyes, not in sleep but in resignation. Soon the bugle would sound, calling them to another day of drills and tests and carefully maintained distance. She would rise and face it all with the same stoic mask she'd worn since arriving.

But in these last quiet moments before dawn, she allowed herself to acknowledge the truth - she was more alone now than ever before, cut off not only from the world of the living but from the spiritual realm that had once been her solace. The gift of sight had become just one more loss in a long string of losses, leaving her adrift between two worlds, belonging to neither.

CHAPTER 13:
PAIGE

The late afternoon sun blazed against the Fort Oglethorpe pool building as Paige walked with Wanda, Cleopatra, and several other women from their company. Despite the oppressive Georgia heat, Paige had been looking forward to their designated swim hour - a rare chance to cool off and forget, for a moment, the rigors of training.

Her hopes died at the sight of the "Pool Closed" sign hanging mockingly on the gate. Again. Cleopatra let out a string of words that made Paige wince - definitely not the kind of language a God-fearing woman should use.

"Third time this week," Wanda muttered, wiping sweat from her brow. "Funny how it's always closed during our hours."

Paige's jaw tightened as she watched a group of white WACs strolling past, their hair still damp from their own swim time. The injustice of it burned in her throat, but she swallowed it down. The Lord taught patience and understanding, even in the face of prejudice.

"Come on," she touched Wanda's arm. "Let's head back to the barracks while it's empty. We need to take care of that... other matter."

Understanding passed between them. They'd been planning this intervention since Wanda's confession about being unable to sleep with Sadie and her ungodly practices in their quarters. As they walked back, Paige's hand brushed the small bottle of blessed oil in her pocket, drawing comfort from its presence.

The barracks stood quiet and empty, most of the women still at evening activities. Paige closed the door behind them, drawing out the oil as Wanda kept watch.

"Hurry, before everyone gets back," Wanda urged.

Paige's fingers trembled slightly as she unscrewed the cap. The sweet scent of the oil filled her nostrils as she began the ritual she'd learned in countless prayer meetings back home. She moved methodically through the space, anointing the doorframe first, then the walls, paying special attention to the area around Sadie's bed.

This wasn't about hate or fear, she reminded herself. This was about protection, about cleansing Wanda's space of any demonic influence those cards might have invited in. It was her Christian duty to stand against such darkness.

"Take my hand," she instructed Wanda, raising her voice in prayer. "Jesus, by faith I anoint this room and declare it all holy unto you. I rebuke the power of darkness and any attempt of the enemy to bring evil devils against Wanda and these women." The words flowed with practiced ease, her mama's teachings rising strong within her. "Lord, we sanctify this space and invite Your presence to dwell here FOREVER, and EVER, AMEN!"

"Amen," Wanda echoed fervently.

Relief flooded through Paige as she tucked the oil away. "It's done. You should be able to sleep now."

She began gathering her things, her mind already turning to the letter she needed to write to Joe. Her son needed to know she was staying strong in her faith, even here among such spiritual challenges.

A floorboard creaked behind them, but when Paige turned, she caught only a glimpse of a shadow retreating from the doorway. Her heart skipped a beat - had Sadie seen them? But no, surely they would have heard her enter.

Still, unease settled in her stomach as she bid Wanda goodnight and headed to her own bunk. She tried to focus on scripture as she walked, reciting Psalms in her head for protection. But other verses kept intruding - ones about loving thy neighbor, about judge not lest ye be judged.

Paige pushed the doubts aside. She was doing what needed to be done, protecting herself and the other women from influences they might not even recognize as dangerous. If Sadie chose to mess with forces better left alone, that was between her and God.

Besides, she reasoned, settling onto her bunk, perhaps this would be the wake-up call Sadie needed. Maybe seeing their faith in action would guide her back to the righteous path. Wasn't that what Christians were supposed to do - help lost souls find their way back to the light?

As she pulled out her Bible for evening devotions, Paige sent up an extra prayer - not just for protection, but for wisdom. The words on the well-worn pages brought their usual comfort, but something nagged at the edges of her consciousness. She couldn't shake the image of that retreating shadow, or the memory of Sadie sitting alone at meals, isolated by the very women who should be showing her Christ's love.

"Lord give me guidance," she whispered into the growing darkness. But for the first time since arriving at Fort Oglethorpe, she wasn't entirely sure what guidance she was seeking.

CHAPTER 14:
SAMMY

Sammy Love Bonnet's lungs burned as she tried desperately to keep up with the drill formations. Her feet, usually so quick and sure on her daddy's farm, seemed to have developed a stubborn mind of their own. Left became right, right became left, and her body refused to move in harmony with the other women.

"Stop! Just stop!" Sergeant Carter's command cracked across the parade ground.

Sammy snapped to attention with the others, her heart hammering against her ribs. Sweat trickled down her spine, and her legs trembled from exertion. She could feel the other women's sideways glances, their silent judgment of her continued failure.

Sergeant Carter's face appeared inches from her own, eyes blazing with frustration. "Do you want to be here?"

"Yes." The word came out smaller than Sammy intended.

"Excuse me?"

"Yes, Sergeant." She tried to put more force behind it.

"I can't hear you!"

"Yes, Sergeant!" Sammy bellowed, pouring every ounce of determination into her voice.

"Dismissed!"

Relief flooded through her as the formation began to break up. Cleopatra shot her a sympathetic glance as she passed, while Paige and Wanda hurried by without looking her way. Even Sadie's usual stoic expression held a hint of pity.

"Not you, Bonnet."

Sammy's heart sank as she froze in place. She watched Sergeant Carter consult with the drill instructor, their voices carrying clearly in the evening air.

"I don't want to see her until she has it together. No food, no bathroom, no break. Stay out here all night if you have to."

"Yes, Sergeant."

As Sergeant Carter strode away, Sammy fought back tears. She hadn't cried this much since leaving the farm, but now her eyes seemed determined to betray her at every turn.

The drill instructor regarded her with weary resignation. "Do you know the difference between your left and your right?"

"My mind does, but my feet don't." The honest admission slipped out before she could stop it.

The Drill Instructor's deep sigh spoke volumes about the night ahead. But Sammy squared her shoulders, determined to prove herself worthy of the uniform she wore.

Hours passed in a blur of commands and movements. "Left face! Right face! About face!" The words began to lose meaning as hunger gnawed at her belly and her muscles screamed in protest. Still, she pushed on, forcing her rebellious feet to obey.

The moon rose over Fort Oglethorpe, casting long shadows across the parade ground. Sammy's throat was parched, her stomach a hollow ache, but she refused to quit. She thought of her daddy's disapproving face when she'd announced her enlistment, of her brothers' mocking laughter. She couldn't prove them right by failing here.

"Again!" the drill instructor barked as she stumbled through another sequence. "What's so hard about this, Bonnet? Everyone else managed to figure it out!"

Tears leaked from the corners of Sammy's eyes as she started over. Back home, she could outrun her brothers, could lift hay bales with the best of them. But this precision, this rigid control of movement - it felt like trying to speak a foreign language with her body.

"Column right! Forward march!"

Her feet tangled and she stumbled again. The drill instructor's exasperated grunt cut deeper than any sharp word could have.

"I'm trying," she whispered, more to herself than to him. "Lord knows I'm trying."

As midnight approached, exhaustion made the world swim before her eyes. Her movements had become mechanical, driven by pure stubborn will rather than any real understanding. The hunger had faded to a distant ache, replaced by a bone-deep weariness that threatened to drop her where she stood.

Yet something kept her going - the same determination that had driven her to chase down that bus in Birmingham, that had given her the courage to defy her father's wishes. She hadn't come this far to fail now.

"Left face!"

This time, miraculously, her body responded correctly. The drill instructor's eyebrows rose slightly.

"Again."

Left face. Right face. About face. Slowly, painfully, her feet began to find their rhythm. It wasn't pretty, wasn't graceful, but it was correct.

The night stretched endlessly on. Sammy lost track of how many times they repeated the same sequences. Her uniform was soaked with sweat despite the cooling air, and her legs shook with every movement. But gradually, incrementally, muscle memory began to take hold.

She thought of her brothers and how they would mock her if they could see her stumbling around the parade ground like a newborn colt. The thought brought a fresh determination to her tired muscles.

"Forward march!"

Step by step, hour by hour, Sammy forced her body to comply with the commands. The moon tracked across the sky, stars wheeling overhead as she marched and turned, turned and marched. Her world narrowed to the next step, the next command, the next chance to prove she belonged here.

Finally, the drill instructor called a halt. Sammy stood at attention, swaying slightly with exhaustion.

"Well, Bonnet," she said, studying her with critical eyes, "you're not going to win any prizes for style, but at least you won't embarrass the company anymore."

It was far from high praise, but Sammy felt tears of relief spring to her eyes. "Thank you, ma'am," she managed through parched lips.

As Sammy stumbled back to her barracks, her legs barely supporting her weight, a fierce pride bloomed in her chest. She'd done it. It hadn't been pretty, hadn't been graceful, but she'd proven she could learn, could adapt, could overcome.

Let them laugh about the country girl with no rhythm. She'd shown she had something better - determination. And in the Army, sometimes that counted for more than natural talent.

Collapsing onto her bunk without even removing her boots, Sammy sent up a quiet prayer of thanks. Tomorrow would bring new challenges, but she'd face them knowing she'd conquered this one. One step at a time, just like she'd learned tonight, she would prove she belonged here.

As sleep claimed her, Sammy's lips curved in a small smile.

CHAPTER 15:
CLEOPATRA

The evening air clung to Cleopatra's skin as she led a group of Black WACs toward the pool. Her feet moved with the grace of a trained performer, each step deliberate despite her mounting frustration. Three weeks they'd been trying to use the pool during their designated hours, and three weeks they'd found it mysteriously "closed."

Tonight, though, something felt different. Maybe it was the barely contained anger thrumming through her veins, or maybe it was the way Betty and her gaggle of white trainees had smirked at them during dinner. Either way, Cleopatra had convinced a group of women to accompany her for one more attempt at their rightful swim time.

As they approached, voices carried across the darkened pool area. Cleopatra held up a hand, signaling the others to pause. Through the gate, she could make out Betty and several other white trainees, their pale forms ghostly in the dim lighting.

"The sign says closed," one of them pointed out, gesturing to the familiar notice.

Betty's voice dripped with smug superiority. "It's closed to them. Not us."

"Last one in is Hitler's girlfriend!" Another white trainee's laugh pierced the night air.

Cleopatra's jaw clenched as she watched them strip down to their swimsuits, their casual entitlement burning in her chest like acid. Then she spotted something that made her blood run cold - Sadie Lewis, alone in the shadows by the pool's edge.

The white women noticed her too, their laughter cutting off abruptly. Betty's voice took on that particular tone reserved for putting "uppity" Blacks in their place.

"What are you doing here?"

Sadie's quiet "Nothing" barely carried to where Cleopatra stood watching.

"The pool is closed to you," Betty continued, her words precise and cutting. "You people think that you can do whatever you want, don't you? I've seen you in the mess hall. You're the one that none of the other Negroes sit with. You must be real nasty if even they won't be your friend. Just because some NAACP moron thought you deserved to be a WAC, does not make you our equal."

As Sadie tried to leave, one of Betty's friends shoved her into the pool. The splash was followed by cruel laughter, though Betty's irritated voice cut through it: "Why did you do that? Now we can't get in the pool."

Something snapped inside Cleopatra. All the careful restraint, all the practiced smiles and strategic submission - gone in an instant. She strode through the gate, her voice ringing out clear and strong.

"I told you it wasn't closed."

Betty's head whipped around, her face twisting with disdain. "It's closed to you."

Cleopatra's eyes found Sadie in the pool, clothes soaked and dignity wounded. A lifetime of stage training helped her keep her voice steady, infused with just the right amount of casual defiance.

"Looks open to us to me."

Without waiting for a response, Cleopatra began stripping down to her suit. The other Black women followed her lead, their movements quick and decisive. Betty's protests fell on deaf ears as they jumped into the pool one by one, sending waves of water toward the white women.

Through the ensuing chaos, Cleopatra watched Sadie climb out and slip away into the darkness. Part of her wanted to call out, to offer some word of solidarity or comfort. But she recognized the need for privacy in moments of humiliation - God knew she'd experienced enough of them in her acting career.

Instead, she focused on claiming their space in the pool, her powerful strokes cutting through the water with theatrical flourish. Let Betty and her friends report them if they dared. Some things were worth whatever punishment might come.

As she executed a perfect turn at the deep end, Cleopatra's mind wandered to her last audition before enlisting. The director's dismissive words, the assistant's feigned terror, the police officer's hand on his gun - all because she'd dared to imagine herself playing a role written for a white woman.

Well, they couldn't deny her this role. She was a WAC now, same as Betty, same as any of them. Their prejudices couldn't change that fact, couldn't erase her right to be here, to use this pool, to serve her country.

The water embraced her like an old friend as she continued swimming, her movements becoming more pronounced, more performative. She could feel Betty and her friends watching from the edge of the pool, their indignation palpable in the humid night air.

"You'll regret this," Betty called out, but the threat in her voice had weakened considerably.

Cleopatra responded with her most dazzling stage smile. "Honey, the only thing I regret is not doing this sooner." She executed another flawless turn, making sure to splash water in Betty's direction.

The other Black women had found their courage now, laughing and splashing, their joy a form of defiance in itself. This moment, this claiming of space and dignity, felt more important than any role Cleopatra had ever auditioned for.

Let them report it. Let them try to justify why the pool was simultaneously open and closed. Let them explain how patriotism and service to country somehow depended on skin color. Cleopatra would play her part perfectly - the dignified Negro servicewoman, respectful but unwavering in her rights.

As she floated on her back, staring up at the stars, Cleopatra allowed herself a small smile. Maybe this was her greatest role yet - not playing at equality, but demanding it, claiming it, one closed pool at a time.

The night stretched on, the water growing cooler as they continued their aquatic protest. Eventually, Betty and her friends retreated, their threats and protests fading into the darkness. But Cleopatra kept swimming, each stroke a declaration, each breath a quiet revolution.

As they finally climbed out of the pool, wrapping themselves in towels, Cleopatra caught sight of her reflection in the still water.

She looked different somehow - stronger, more defiant, more herself than she'd ever been on any stage.

Back in the barracks, Cleopatra lay awake long into the night, replaying the events in her mind. She thought of Sadie, wondered if she was alright.

As sleep finally claimed her, Cleopatra's last thought was of the stage. She'd spent years trying to break through barriers, to claim roles denied to her because of her race. Maybe this was where she belonged all along - not playing at life on a stage, but living it fully, fighting real battles, making real change.

A pounding on the barracks door jolted Cleopatra awake. A stern-faced MP stood in the doorway, ordering her to report to Company Headquarters immediately.

The fluorescent lights of the headquarters building buzzed overhead as Cleopatra stood at attention, her still-damp hair tucked hastily under her cap. Betty and her group occupied one side of the room, while Cleopatra and her fellow Company 8 women stood on the other. Colonel Davis's face was thunderous as he surveyed them all, Sergeant Carter a stoic presence at his shoulder. In the corner, a white female clerk seemed to be trying to make herself invisible.

"I was dragged away from my bed for this nonsense," Colonel Davis growled. "Explain yourselves."

Betty stepped forward, her voice dripping with sanctimonious indignation. "These Negroes broke into the pool. The pool needs to be drained and cleaned and they should never be allowed in it again."

The casual racism of the statement made Cleopatra's blood boil, but she kept her voice steady and professional as she responded. "There was already a Company 8 WAC in the pool when we got there." She wouldn't name Sadie, wouldn't drag her further into this mess. "Every other time we've tried to use the pool during 'our' pool hours, it's always closed. Yet they can go in whenever they want."

Colonel Davis's attention shifted to the clerk cowering in the corner. "Is it true they haven't been able to use the pool?"

The woman's voice quavered. "There has been some confusion with the pool cleaning schedule."

Confusion, Cleopatra thought bitterly. That's what they're calling it now.

"Fix it," Colonel Davis barked. "Get out of my sight. All of you."

"What about--" Betty started to protest, but the Colonel cut her off.

"I said dismissed."

As they filed out, Cleopatra caught the Colonel's words to Sergeant Carter: "Keep your women in line, Sergeant."

"Yes, sir," Carter responded, her face unreadable.

Behind them all, Cleopatra heard the Colonel's final order to the clerk: "Make sure that pool is drained and cleaned immediately."

The implied insult stung, but Cleopatra held her head high as they left the building. They'd made their point, even if it came with the bitter reminder of how deep prejudice ran. Let them drain the pool - they couldn't drain away the fact that Company 8 had stood their ground.

CHAPTER 16:
SADIE

Another sleepless night drove Sadie from her narrow bunk, the walls of the barracks pressing in like a tomb. She moved silently through the darkness, years of practice making her footsteps ghostlike. Behind her, Wanda's eyes tracked her movement, though Sadie pretended not to notice.

The night air wrapped around her like a familiar friend as she settled on the barracks steps. Her cards came next, the familiar weight offering cold comfort. The Lovers card appeared in her spread, and suddenly she was transported back to another night, another life.

Their wedding night. The memory was so vivid she could smell the soap Andrew had used, could feel the warmth radiating from his bare chest as he emerged from their bathroom. She'd sat on their bed in her new negligee, consulting the cards while waiting for him.

His kiss had been passionate, playful. "Is this really how you want to make use of our bed on our wedding night?"

"I was waiting on you." Her voice had held none of the shadows that haunted it now.

He'd picked up one of her cards, curiosity overtaking his initial teasing. "What's this one?"

"You're just going to say it's silly." She'd started to put them away, but he stopped her.

"No, I won't. Come on, tell me."

The memory of her explanation echoed in her mind. "It's the lover's card. See the man and woman are protected and blessed by the angel above. They are happy in their home. The lovers have trust and unity."

"Mmmm, I like that. Unity." His lips had found her neck, sending shivers down her spine.

But then he'd picked up another card randomly, and her blood had turned to ice. The death card. She could still see his face when she told him, the way he'd brushed off the omen.

"Ain't nobody thinking about death tonight. I want to focus on life. Matter of fact, I think we should make us a baby right now."

He'd swept the cards aside then, and she'd let herself be caught up in his enthusiasm, in his love. The warning had seemed distant, unimportant in the face of such happiness.

Now, sitting alone on the barracks steps, Sadie pressed the Lovers card to her heart. "I should have never let you enlist," she whispered into the darkness.

Her hands moved automatically, drawing another card. The death card stared up at her, its meaning no longer a distant warning but a brutal reality.

Dawn found her sneaking back into the barracks, her mind heavy with memories and regret. But something was wrong. Her uniform, carefully laid out the night before, had vanished. Panic rose in her throat as she searched frantically, aware of the other women beginning to stir.

Wanda's smirk told her everything she needed to know, but there was no time to confront her. Morning inspection loomed, and Sadie had nothing to wear.

The Georgia sun beat down mercilessly as she stood in line, conspicuously out of uniform. Sergeant Carter's inspection came to a halt before her, disapproval radiating from every pore.

"Where is your uniform?"

"I don't know Sergeant."

"You don't know?"

"Yes, Sergeant. I mean no Sergeant. No, I don't know. I couldn't find it this morning."

The Sergeant's voice dripped with sarcasm. "Everyone else seemed able to find their uniforms this morning. But you couldn't find yours?"

"No, Sergeant."

"Get out of my line. Go clean your barracks for Saturday inspection. Those floors better be white. Snow white."

"Yes, Sergeant."

She felt Wanda's satisfaction and Paige's guilt as she walked away, but neither emotion touched her. Physical discomfort seemed distant, unimportant compared to the spiritual isolation that surrounded her.

Hours later, on her hands and knees scrubbing the barracks floor, Sadie caught a glimpse of familiar fabric peeking from the trash. Her uniform lay crumpled among the refuse, a final indignity in a long line of them.

As she retrieved the soiled garment, Sadie felt something shift inside her. The cards had warned her about death, but they'd never warned her about this kind of living death - this isolation, this constant reminder that she didn't belong.

Yet as she clutched her recovered uniform, a strange calm settled over her. They could hide her clothes, could whisper about devils and conjuring, could isolate her at meals and in the barracks. But they couldn't take away what really mattered - her gift, her memories of Andrew, her determination to serve despite it all.

Andrew had understood. He'd listened to her warnings, had respected her gift even when he didn't fully believe. But he'd enlisted anyway, driven by the same sense of duty that had brought her here. Now she carried that duty for both of them, would endure whatever came her way to honor his sacrifice.

Let them whisper. Let them hide her things. Let them fear what they couldn't understand. Sadie Lewis had seen death coming and couldn't stop it. Nothing they could do would hurt more than that.

As she finally finished the floors, Sadie allowed herself a moment of quiet pride. The surface gleamed like new snow, reflecting the morning light. Whatever else they might say about her, they couldn't deny she did her duty thoroughly.

She gathered her soiled uniform, planning how to clean it without missing any duties. One day at a time, one task at a time, she would prove herself worthy of the sacrifice that had brought her here. The cards might have shown her death, but they had also shown her love. She would hold onto that, no matter what came next.

CHAPTER 17:
PAIGE

Paige picked absently at her lunch, her appetite diminished by the guilt gnawing at her conscience. Scripture readings from that morning's devotional kept running through her mind, particularly those about bearing false witness and treating others with Christian charity.

Movement caught her eye as Sadie walked past their table, back in her recovered uniform. Before Paige could stop her, Wanda's sharp voice cut through the mess hall.

"Looks like someone's been digging in the trash."

Paige's stomach clenched as Sadie stopped, her back straightening. "I don't want any trouble."

"Trouble?" Wanda's mock innocence dripped with malice. "I don't know what you mean."

"Don't start nothing, won't be nothing." Sadie's quiet voice carried a note of warning that made Paige's skin prickle.

Wanda shot to her feet, getting in Sadie's face. "Is that a threat?"

"That's up to you."

As Wanda moved closer, Paige found herself rising, stepping between them. "Come on, let's finish eating." Her voice shook slightly as she tried to defuse the situation.

But Sadie wasn't finished. "Touch my stuff again, and we're going to have a problem."

The mess hall fell silent as other women turned to watch the confrontation. Paige's heart hammered in her chest. This was exactly what she'd feared - their attempt to cleanse the barracks of evil influence had only created more strife.

"You need to drop out," Wanda snapped.

"You're the one with the issue," Sadie responded coolly. "Sounds like you should be the one leaving."

As Wanda moved forward again, Paige tried once more to intervene. "Come on."

"You three. In my office. Now."

Sergeant Carter's voice cut through the tension like a knife. Paige's heart sank as she followed the others to Company Headquarters, her mind racing with prayers for guidance.

The Squad Leader's presence in Sergeant Carter's office only heightened Paige's anxiety. They stood at attention as the Sergeant surveyed them with clear disappointment.

"What was that in the mess hall?"

None of them spoke. Paige's palms grew sweaty as the silence stretched.

"I see you located your uniform," Sergeant Carter said to Sadie.

"Yes, Sergeant."

"Where was it?"

"I must have just overlooked it this morning."

"Overlooked it?"

"Yes, Sergeant."

Paige held her breath as Sergeant Carter's gaze swept over them. "You two are bunkmates."

"Yes, Sergeant," Sadie and Wanda responded in unison.

"What is your involvement in this?"

Paige struggled to keep her voice steady. "No involvement in this or anything, Sergeant."

"We have no time for foolishness here. If there is one more incident, I will see to it that the three of you are discharged and brought up on charges. Understood?"

"I had nothing to do with--" Paige started to protest.

"Understood?"

"Yes, Sergeant," they chorused.

"I'll be assigning you to overnight duty tonight. Get out of my office."

As they filed out, Paige's mind whirled with conflicting emotions. She'd stayed silent about Wanda's actions with the uniform, had even helped anoint the room against Sadie's supposed evil influence. But now that silence felt less like protecting her friend and more like complicity in something shameful.

What would Joe think if he knew his mama was involved in such meanness? She'd raised him to be better than that, to treat everyone with respect regardless of their differences. The hypocrisy of her recent actions sat heavy in her stomach. Yet she couldn't shake her fear of Sadie's practices either.

As they walked back to the barracks, Paige found herself caught between two fears - the fear of evil influences and the fear of becoming someone her son wouldn't recognize. She needed guidance, needed to find a way to protect her faith without compromising her integrity.

The overnight duty assignment loomed ahead, promising hours of shared discomfort with both Wanda and Sadie. Paige sent up a silent prayer for strength. She would need divine help to navigate this minefield of conflicting loyalties and beliefs.

Perhaps, she thought, this was her real test - not the physical challenges of training or the academic rigors of their classes, but this spiritual struggle between fear and compassion, between judgment and understanding. The Lord worked in mysterious ways, after all.

Tonight's duty would show her what kind of soldier - and what kind of Christian - she truly was.

CHAPTER 18:
CLEOPATRA

Cleopatra crossed the base, her stride purposeful despite the oppressive heat. Movement caught her eye - a cluster of white WACs posing for photographs, their uniforms pristine and faces carefully arranged in patriotic enthusiasm. But it was the photographer who held her attention.

Lieutenant William McDonald moved with an artist's grace as he directed his subjects, his strong hands adjusting the camera with practiced ease. Cleopatra found herself slowing, watching the interplay of light and shadow through his viewfinder. Betty Clarke stood front and center, of course, preening like a peacock in mating season.

Betty's pose faltered as she noticed Cleopatra's presence. "Are you lost?"

Cleopatra glanced around, making a show of looking for who Betty might be addressing. "Are you talking to me?"

"You're the only one standing there gawking." Betty's voice dripped with disdain.

A lifetime of stage training helped Cleopatra maintain her composure as she arched an elegant eyebrow. "I'm just wondering what is so interesting about you that someone would want to take your picture."

Before Betty could respond, the photographer stepped forward, and Cleopatra got her first clear look at his face. Handsome didn't quite cover it - there was an intelligence in his eyes that spoke of seeing beyond surface appearances.

"Lt. William McDonald," he introduced himself. "Photographer, Army press corp."

"Enchanté." Cleopatra allowed a hint of her theatrical training to color the word.

Betty's face twisted with indignation. "You're supposed to salute. Haven't they taught y'all anything?"

"My apologies." Cleopatra kept her voice smooth as honey, refusing to let Betty's barbs draw blood.

"And you are?" William's genuine interest was a balm against Betty's hostility.

"Cleopatra Laurier."

"That cannot be your real name." Betty's sneer couldn't quite mask her envy.

William continued as if Betty hadn't spoken. "I'm here documenting what life looks like as a WAC. The public is very anxious to see what it's like to be a woman in the Army Corp."

Cleopatra saw her opening and took it with the precision of a master performer. "If you find yourself needing some better models, come and find me. Company 8."

"They want to see what it's like for us WACs," Betty cut in sharply. "Not you. No one wants to look at pictures of women who are not even wanted in this war."

Something dangerous flashed in Cleopatra's eyes. "You'd do well to mind your mouth."

She threw William a jaunty salute, infusing her departure with all the grace and dignity of a curtain call. She could feel his eyes following her as she walked away, even as Betty's throat-clearing demanded his attention return to her photo session.

Betty and her kind could pose all they wanted, but they'd never understand that real beauty came from something deeper than carefully arranged features and properly pressed uniforms. It came from the kind of strength that let you face daily indignities with grace, that kept you standing tall when others tried to diminish you.

That was the story Cleopatra wanted William to capture - not just hers, but all of Company 8's. The world needed to see that they weren't just tolerated additions to the WAC, but proud soldiers serving their country despite every obstacle thrown in their path.

The encounter had not lasted more than a few minutes, but Cleopatra knew a pivotal scene when she played one. Whatever happened next, she had claimed her spotlight, if only briefly. Now it was up to William to decide what kind of story he really wanted to tell.

CHAPTER 19:
MARY MCLEOD BETHUNE

The late afternoon sun slanted through the White House windows as Mary McLeod Bethune gathered her papers, her movements measured and deliberate. Another day of battles fought in these marble halls, some won, some lost, but all part of the longer war for equality.

Howard's sudden appearance made her spine stiffen, though she kept her face carefully neutral. The Chief of Staff had a way of materializing when least welcome, like a shadow at sunset.

"I don't want you to take what I'm about to say the wrong way." His attempt at diplomacy couldn't mask the condescension in his tone.

Mary met his gaze steadily. "I'm sure I will take it in the spirit it's intended."

"The President may think that you and this 'Negro Cabinet' are making some sort of contribution to minority affairs." The way he emphasized "Negro Cabinet" made the words sound like something distasteful. "Minority affairs are not America's affairs. I am the Chief of Staff. Not you. You'd do well to remember that."

The threat beneath his words was clear, but Mary had faced down worse than Howard's bureaucratic bullying. "Minorities are also Americans," she replied, her voice carrying the weight of decades of struggle. "You'd do well to remember that. Step aside."

Later that evening, in the warmth of her brownstone apartment, Mary hosted a very different kind of meeting. The members of her "Negro Cabinet" gathered in her living room, surrounded by carefully curated Black artwork that spoke to their shared heritage and aspirations. The atmosphere was intimate but purposeful - these were warriors gathering to plan their next campaigns.

Thurgood Marshall's passionate voice filled the room as he detailed the Port Chicago situation. "First, it's segregated. Only our men, half of them barely eighteen, out there loading munitions with no training, no safety equipment. We're the only ones out there doing this back-breaking work, not the white guys. And the Whites that are supposed to be the officers in charge are taking bets against each other, pushing the men to go faster."

"It's a damn shame," one of the Cabinet members interjected, shaking his head.

"I'm not going to lie to you," Thurgood continued, his frustration evident. "It's going to be an uphill battle. I can only get so close to it because of all the military red tape."

Mary watched him with understanding in her eyes. "We know they are in capable hands." The others nodded their agreement - Thurgood's reputation for tenacity and legal brilliance was well-earned.

"Where are we with the women going overseas?" another Cabinet member asked, steering the conversation toward their newest initiative.

"Exactly where we need to be," Mary replied, allowing herself a small smile of satisfaction. She'd spent weeks vetting potential leaders for the battalion, knowing how crucial this first step would be.

"All eyes will be on this," someone pointed out. "Negro press, white press, Congress. This has to succeed."

"We will be successful," Mary assured them with quiet confidence. "I have found the perfect woman to lead the way."

As she looked around at these dedicated faces, Mary felt the weight of history pressing down on them all. They were attempting something unprecedented - not just integrating women into the military but proving beyond doubt that Negro women could serve with distinction in roles previously denied them.

The Port Chicago disaster had shown the tragic consequences of segregation and discrimination in the military. But perhaps through the 6888th Battalion, they could demonstrate a better way forward. These women would carry not just mail but the hopes and dreams of their entire race.

Mary rose to refill drinks, her mind already planning next steps. Howard might see them as a threat to his power, but she saw something far greater - the slow but inevitable march toward true equality. Every small victory, every barrier broken, brought them closer to that goal.

She had chosen Major Dixon carefully, seeing in her the same fire and determination that had driven Mary's own accomplishments. The women of the 6888th would face challenges, certainly, but they would face them under leadership that understood both the military mission and the larger struggle it represented.

She had found her perfect leader. Now it was time to ensure she had every possible support in her mission. The eyes of the nation would indeed be watching - and Mary intended to show them something remarkable.

CHAPTER 20:
MAJOR DIXON

Major Dixon watched the Georgia countryside roll past her car window, the manila folder in her lap containing both her mission and her legacy. "6888th Central Postal Battalion," the label read - simple words that carried the weight of history. Her fingers traced the edges of the folder as she reviewed its contents for the hundredth time, though she had already committed every detail to memory.

Seven million pieces of mail. Two years of backlog. Six months to complete what teams of white servicemen couldn't accomplish. The challenge would have been daunting enough without the added pressure of being the first all-Black, all-female battalion to serve overseas.

Her early arrival at Fort Oglethorpe had been carefully calculated. She believed in seeing things as they truly were, not as people prepared them to be seen. The young private at the desk - Lewis, according to her nameplate - had provided her first unvarnished glimpse of the task ahead.

"Major Dixon, checking in."

The private had consulted her list with growing confusion, clearly unprepared for this moment. When Major Dixon repeated herself, Lewis had snapped to attention with almost comical speed.

"At ease," Dixon had said, studying the woman's face. There was something in those eyes.

"I'm sorry Major. I've never seen those stripes before. I didn't even know that--" Lewis had caught herself, but Dixon understood.

"You didn't know what? What's your name?

"Sadie. Sadie Lewis. Private Lewis"

" Speak freely. "

"I didn't know that we could be Majors."

The words had struck Dixon like a physical blow, though she maintained her composure. "Well, we can be. And I am."

Now, touring the base with Sergeant Carter the next morning, Dixon's mind kept returning to that moment. How many other Black women had never seen someone who looked like them in a position of authority? How many didn't know what was possible?

"It's obvious that you and your staff care greatly about making sure our women have the skills needed to make strong contributions to the Women's Army Corp," she observed.

"Yes, Major," Carter replied crisply.

"How is it working with the Commander?"

Their shared look spoke volumes about the challenges of serving under white male leadership that viewed them as an experiment at best, a mistake at worst.

"Yes, I gathered as much from our meeting with him," Dixon said dryly.

Carter shifted uncomfortably. "Again, I apologize that we were caught unprepared for your arrival last night. I would have been there to welcome you had I known."

"It was my decision to travel early." Dixon paused, then asked the question that had been nagging at her. "The private working CQ last night, Lewis? What's her story? We only spoke briefly, but I wasn't quite sure what to make of her."

"That seems to be the sentiment all around where she is concerned."

Before Dixon could probe further, the squad leader approached with news of a visitor waiting in Sergeant Carter's office - with Colonel Davis, no less. Dixon's instincts prickled. Unscheduled meetings with a colonel rarely brought good news.

Major Greer's presence in the office confirmed her suspicions. The white WAC officer radiated the particular brand of condescension Dixon had encountered throughout her short career - the kind that masked itself as concerned mentorship while revealing deep-seated prejudice.

After the Colonel's departure, Greer wasted no time establishing her perceived superiority. "I hope you don't mind if I speak freely."

"Please do." Dixon kept her voice neutral, though she already knew what was coming.

"Do you honestly believe that Negro women will agree to travel overseas for this battalion?"

"Why wouldn't they?"

"I would think that Negro women would be afraid to travel that far, overseas and all."

Dixon met her gaze steadily. "Why would a Negro WAC find the prospect of Europe less appealing than any other WAC?"

"I imagine that for most of them, this is their first time leaving home. That's daunting enough, and now you want them to cross an ocean?"

The conversation deteriorated from there, with Greer laying out every doubt, every prejudice, every assumption about their capabilities.

Something fierce and defiant rose in Dixon's chest. She thought about the six-month deadline given to her. "We'll do it in three."

Greer's laughter grated against her ears. "Three? I assume you mean three years."

"No. Three months. We'll do it in three months."

Dixon had learned long ago that sometimes you had to meet condescension with audacity. As she watched Greer depart, her mind was already calculating logistics, strategies, ways to prove every doubt wrong.

"I see I have my work cut out for me," she said to Carter. "Sergeant Carter, have you ever thought about Europe?"

Carter's smile told her everything she needed to know. They would face whatever challenges came their way together, would prove their worth not just as individuals but as a unit.

Later that night, alone in her quarters, Dixon pulled out the folder again. Seven million pieces of mail. Three months. Impossible, Greer had said. But Dixon had built her career on accomplishing the impossible, on being not just good but exceptional, on proving that excellence knew no color barrier.

She thought of Private Lewis, of that moment of revelation when the woman realized what was possible. That alone made every struggle worthwhile. They weren't just sorting mail - they were sorting history, delivering hope not just to soldiers waiting for letters but to every young Black girl who needed to see what was possible.

Three months. Dixon smiled as she closed the folder. They would do it in three months, and they would do it so well that even Greer wouldn't be able to deny their success. Because that's what this was really about - not just completing a mission, but changing minds, opening doors, creating possibilities.

The Six Triple Eight would be more than a battalion. They would be proof of what Negro women could accomplish when given the chance. And Major Dixon intended to give them every chance to shine.

CHAPTER 21:
CLEOPATRA

The evening air held the last remnants of Georgia heat as Cleopatra walked across the Fort Oglethorpe grounds. Her feet moved with practiced grace, each step measured and deliberate despite her racing heart. When she spotted William standing alone in the gathering dusk, she knew it wasn't a coincidence.

Their eyes met across the distance, his smile confirming her suspicions. She sauntered over, adding just enough swing to her hips to make it interesting while staying within military propriety. Her salute managed to be both regulation-perfect and subtly flirtatious.

"Good evening," William said, his voice warm with something more than simple courtesy.

Cleopatra allowed herself a knowing smile. "If I didn't know any better, I'd say you were out here waiting on me."

"I'm just out here enjoying this beautiful night." The way his eyes lingered on her face made it clear he wasn't talking about the weather.

She took a half step back, maintaining her professional demeanor. "Well, you enjoy the rest of it, Lieutenant."

"I was thinking about what you said," he called as she started to turn away. "I agree it would be a good idea to get some pictures of the women in Company 8 as well. Maybe I could start with you? Sunday?"

Her heart skipped, but years of stage training kept her voice steady as she nodded her agreement. She walked away with the same measured grace, though every nerve ending tingled with awareness of his gaze following her retreat.

Sunday arrived with agonizing slowness. Cleopatra stood atop the concrete steps, the morning sun warming her precisely pressed uniform as William adjusted his camera settings below. She had performed on stages across the country, but something about being the focus of his lens made her more nervous than any audience.

"Perfect," he said after several shots.

"I know." The quip came automatically, drawing a laugh from him that made her stomach flutter.

When he offered his hand to help her down the steps, she took it without hesitation. The moment their fingers touched, electricity arced between them. His hand was warm and steady, the contact lasting a fraction longer than necessary.

Cleopatra's theatrical training helped her maintain composure as she offered a regulation salute and walked away. But inside, her mind raced with the dangerous possibilities of what had just passed between them.

She had played enough romantic leads to recognize chemistry when she felt it. But this wasn't a stage production where the curtain would fall and everyone would go their separate ways. This was real life, with real consequences.

A white officer and a Negro WAC. Even thinking it felt like playing with fire. Yet as she made her way back to her barracks, she couldn't stop her mind from returning to the warmth of his hand, the intensity of his gaze through the camera lens.

She had spent her career playing roles society said she couldn't have. Now here was another forbidden part, perhaps the most dangerous one yet. The question was whether the potential cost outweighed the undeniable spark she felt whenever William was near.

As an actress, she knew the importance of timing. But she also knew that sometimes the most powerful moments happened when you went off script entirely. The trick would be figuring out which this was - a scene to play out carefully, or one to avoid altogether.

For now, she would keep her performance subtle, professional. But she couldn't deny the thrill of possibility that lingered like perfume in the air between them. Some roles, after all, chose you rather than the other way around.

CHAPTER 22:
SADIE

The morning of graduation day brought a palpable electricity to the barracks. Sadie could feel it crackling in the air as women fussed with their uniforms and checked their appearances with unusual care. She searched quietly around her bunk, trying not to draw attention to herself.

"Has anyone seen my shoes?" she finally asked, though she already knew it was futile. The other women continued their preparations as if she hadn't spoken.

"Are those your shoes over there?" Wanda's voice dripped with false innocence as she pointed toward the door. Sadie's perfectly polished shoes now sat caked in mud.

"Better hurry," Wanda added with a smirk. "We wouldn't want you to be late. Unless today's the day you decide to drop out."

Anger and determination stirred in Sadie's chest as she retrieved her shoes. She wouldn't give them the satisfaction of seeing her rattled. With quick, efficient movements, she began cleaning away the mud, putting all her focus into making them shine again.

The morning sun beat down on the parade ground as Company 8 and Company 7 stood in formation. Sadie's freshly cleaned shoes gleamed beneath her perfectly pressed uniform. Around her, the other women radiated nervous energy, but she remained still, centered. This moment felt important - not just for them as individuals, but for what they represented.

Major Dixon watched from the reviewing stand, her presence a reminder of what was possible. Colonel Davis and other dignitaries flanked her, along with members of the press eager to document this historic graduation. Sadie could feel the weight of their collective gaze.

Her heart stuttered as Sergeant Carter approached for inspection. The sergeant's eyes moved methodically over her uniform before dropping to her shoes. Sadie held her breath. After what felt like an eternity, Carter moved on without comment. Sadie exhaled slowly, allowing herself a quick glance at Wanda. Let them try to break her - she would only emerge stronger.

The inspection continued. Carter paused before Cleopatra, examining her hair with particular scrutiny, but found no fault with its perfect arrangement beneath her cap. When she reached Sammy, her voice carried clearly: "Don't let us down, Bonnet."

The Squad Leader's command rang out across the parade ground: "Attention! Forward March!"

As one unit, they began to move. Sadie felt a surge of pride as Company 8 executed each movement with flawless precision. Even Sammy, who had struggled so much during training, moved in perfect harmony with the group. They were proving themselves with every step, showing what they were capable of when given the chance.

Later, as they stood at ease, the squad leader's announcement came as a surprise. "Congratulations privates. You made me proud. Be back here at 14:00 in your exercise suits. This afternoon we play. Dismissed."

The other women dispersed in excited clusters - Cleopatra and Sammy chattering animatedly, Paige and Wanda walking together. Sadie remained apart, watching them go.

"Play?" she murmured to herself, unsure what to expect.

The afternoon transformed the base into something entirely different. Squares marked off various game areas, and for the first time, the rigid segregation between Companies 7 and 8 began to blur. Sadie walked the grounds alone, observing the unexpected integration happening through play.

A tug-of-war match drew her attention. The struggle was brief but decisive - Company 8 pulled together with such unity that the white women of Company 7 tumbled forward.

"Moore, Thomas, and Lewis. Over to the softball ring. Now." The squad leader's voice cut through the celebrations.

Sadie hesitated as Paige and Wanda moved to comply.

"Now, Lewis!"

She fell in behind them, maintaining her distance. The softball field had drawn a crowd - even Colonel Davis had come to watch. Company 8 was down by one run when Sammy stepped up to bat, facing Betty on the pitcher's mound.

"Come on Sammy! Tie it up!" Cleopatra called out.

"Don't let us down, Bonnet!" the drill instructor added her voice to the chorus of encouragement.

Betty's pitch came fast, but Sammy connected solidly on her first swing. The crack of bat meeting ball seemed to surprise everyone, including Sammy herself. She took off running as the white women scrambled after the ball. First base, second, third - Sammy's farm-girl speed carried her all the way home before Betty's throw could reach the catcher.

"Safe!"

The celebration that erupted from Company 8 felt like more than just a reaction to a game. They were celebrating every barrier broken, every expectation exceeded.

Major Dixon moved to whisper something to the Squad Leader, whose next words dropped like stones into suddenly still water: "Lewis, you're up."

"I don't think I should--" Sadie started to protest.

"We have a chance to win this," Wanda interrupted. "Let me go in."

The squad leader's voice brooked no argument. "Moore, if I wanted your opinion I would give it to you. You're up Lewis."

Silence fell as Sadie approached the plate. Her first swing missed completely.

"Strike one!"

The second pitch met the same fate. She could hear the collective groan from her company, could feel Paige and Wanda's glares boring into her back.

But when she turned, she met Major Dixon's steady gaze. The Major gave her a small nod of encouragement - not pity or frustration, but genuine belief. Something shifted inside Sadie as she took a deep breath.

Betty's third pitch came toward her, and suddenly time seemed to slow. Sadie saw it with the same clarity that sometimes accompanied her visions - not the future this time, but the perfect present moment. Her swing connected solidly, sending the ball soaring over the outfielders' heads.

She stood frozen until the squad leader's voice shook her into motion: "Run fool! Run!"

The bases blurred past as she ran - first, second, third, home. Company 8's celebration exploded around her, but she remained separate, watching from the edges as they hugged and jumped and screamed.

"Good job, Lewis." The squad leader's praise was gruff but sincere.

Sammy appeared before her, beaming. "That was amazing."

The genuine enthusiasm in her voice caught Sadie off guard. "Thank you."

As Sammy trotted off to rejoin the celebration, Sadie found Major Dixon watching her. The Major gave her another nod, this one carrying a different message: I see you.

Sadie allowed herself a small smile in return. For the first time since arriving at Fort Oglethorpe, she felt something shift in her isolation. The walls weren't gone, but perhaps they had developed the tiniest of cracks.

The afternoon light slanted across the base as the games wound down. Sadie's hands still tingled from the impact of the bat, a physical reminder that she was more than her gift, more than her grief. She was a soldier who had completed her training, a woman who could contribute to victory in ways that had nothing to do with cards or visions.

The sun sank toward the horizon, painting the Georgia sky in shades of purple and gold. Tomorrow would bring new challenges, new opportunities to prove themselves. But today, Sadie Lewis had helped win more than just a softball game. She had won a small victory in the larger battle for acceptance, for belonging.

It wasn't everything, but it was something. And sometimes, something was enough to build on.

The next morning, Sadie stood silently on the dusty parade ground. All around her, women of both companies chattered excitedly as they tore open the envelopes containing their assignment orders.

Sadie watched detachedly as Betty sauntered by with the rest of her white entourage. "I got Administrative Specialist school," Betty crowed, waving her orders triumphantly. "I get to handle all the secret info."

"Radio school," boasted another white woman next to her. Their giddy laughter trailed behind them as they continued on.

Turning her attention to the women in her own company, Sadie observed Sammy crowding close to Cleopatra, both of them eagerly scanning their orders.

"Bakers and Cooks school?" Sammy exclaimed in dismay. "I don't want to be cooking for nobody."

Cleopatra scoffed derisively as she read her own assignment. "Motor Transport School? What was all of that testing for? Surely, my talents can be put to better use."

A burst of elated shrieks drew Sadie's gaze over to Paige and Wanda, who were practically jumping for joy.

"Medical Technician school!" Paige shouted gleefully. "Thank you, Jesus. Joe's going to be so proud."

"Me too!" Wanda squealed. "I'm so happy!" Then casting a vicious glare at Sadie, she added snidely, "Even happier to get away from here. Ft. Devens, here we come."

With slumped shoulders and downcast eyes, most of the Black women began drifting away, their hopes dashed by lackluster assignments that fell far short of what they had dreamed of. Steeling herself, Sadie finally slid a trembling finger beneath the flap of her own envelope and tugged out the single sheet of paper inside.

"Supply clerk," she read hollowly. Without a word, Sadie refolded the orders, tucked them back in the envelope, and walked away alone. Her footsteps scuffed listlessly through the dust.

CHAPTER 23:
MAJOR DIXON

Major Clarissa Dixon paced the narrow confines of Sergeant Carter's office, her polished boots clicking crisply against the scuffed hardwood with each tightly controlled step. Though her face remained an impassive mask, inside, her mind churned with a relentless barrage of doubts and questions.

"I've got to recruit enough women," she muttered, almost to herself. "And the right kind of women."

Sergeant Carter glanced up from the hefty stack of personnel files spread out on the desk before her. "According to this," she said, tapping a meticulously manicured finger on the topmost folder, "you are to pull the women you need. No need to worry about recruiting."

Clarissa shook her head, unwilling to concede the point so easily. "True. And I will as needed," she acknowledged. "But in order to be successful, these women need to want to go overseas and need to be excited about being a part of the 6888th battalion. They have got to be physically and psychologically fit."

She placed heavy emphasis on those final words, allowing them to linger poignantly in the cramped space between them. Clarissa knew all too well the monumental task that lay ahead - and the razor-thin margin for error. One weak link, one unstable mind or faltering spirit, could bring the entire endeavor crashing down around them. There could be no room for doubt, no tolerance for less than total commitment.

Sergeant Carter leaned back in her chair, regarding Clarissa with a penetrating gaze that seemed to peer directly into her racing thoughts. "We have a lot of women here that fit the bill," she assured her. "Most of whom are very unhappy about what they just received as their next assignment."

A wry smile tugged at the corner of Clarissa's mouth. Of course. The assignment orders. She had seen the crestfallen faces, heard the barely muffled curses and groans of disappointment as the women had torn open those innocuous white envelopes a mere hour ago. How many crushed dreams lay crumpled in the dust of that sunbaked parade ground?

But where some might have seen only disillusionment and despair, Clarissa saw opportunity. Those disillusioned women, with their thwarted hopes and seething resentment, could be just the catalyst she needed. Properly motivated, properly led, their frustrated energy could be harnessed into something powerful. Something unstoppable.

"Gather them up," Clarissa commanded, a new note of resolve hardening her voice. "Let's see what they think."

Thirty minutes later, Clarissa strode to the front of the crowded mess hall, her ramrod-straight posture and purposeful steps commanding instant attention from the assembled women of Company 8. A sea of deep brown faces stared back at her, some openly curious, some guardedly skeptical, all of them waiting to hear what this unfamiliar officer had to say.

Clarissa took her time surveying the room, making eye contact with as many individuals as she could. She wanted each and every one of them to feel the weight of her next words, to understand the enormity of what she was about to propose.

"For those of you I haven't yet met," she began, pitching her voice to carry to the farthest corners, "my name is Major Dixon. I am here because I wanted to make a real difference. I believe that we can win this war."

She paused, allowing the bold declaration to sink in. "But I am also here," Clarissa continued, "because I want the world to see that Negro women can do anything."

A ripple of surprise, and then a burgeoning murmur of agreement, passed through the crowd at this. Clarissa could see the women exchanging glances, sitting up a bit straighter, a new light kindling behind their eyes.

"One of you told me the other night upon meeting me that you didn't know a Negro woman could be a Major," she went on. "Well, I'm living proof that we can be anything that we put our minds to."

Clarissa felt her heart swelling with fierce, defiant pride as she spoke the words, infusing them with every ounce of hard-won conviction in her being. Lord knew, it had been a long, unforgiving road to reach this moment - the scorn, the slights, the doors slammed in her face by those who said a colored woman would never wear the gold oak leaves of a Major. Yet here she stood, her very presence a living rebuke to those small-minded cynics.

"We now have an opportunity to do something no Negro woman has done before," Clarissa declared, her voice ringing out like a clarion call. "I will be leading the first and only all-Negro, all-female battalion. We will be the first and only all-female battalion to be deployed overseas."

A collective gasp rolled through the mess hall at this revelation, electrifying the air with a sudden, vibrant tension. Clarissa could feel the women's anticipation building, their latent hunger for purpose and meaning and glory stirring to life.

"This is our opportunity," she pressed on fervently, "to disprove the notion that the Negro woman is inferior. Many in this country doubt we are capable. Let's be honest, some of our own people doubt that we are capable. But I know that we are more than capable."

Clarissa almost had to shout to be heard over the rising tide of cheers and applause now. The women were on their feet, clapping and stomping, their faces alight with awakened hope and determination. She had them now, utterly in her thrall, ready to follow her lead into the crucible of history.

"Our mission," she called out over the joyous din, "will be to distribute the mail in the European Theater. We have servicemen that have not received mail in almost two years. I appeal to you to consider joining me and the 6888th postal battalion that will be stationed in Birmingham, England."

Clarissa thrust a hand toward the back of the hall, where Sergeant Carter was already laying out the sign-up sheets on a long folding table. "If you are interested in this assignment," she urged, "write your name on the sheets at the back of the room. Thank you."

With that, Major Dixon pivoted crisply on her heel and strode down the center aisle, Sergeant Carter falling into step just behind her. She could feel the electricity crackling in her wake, the women's eager chatter swelling to a rising roar as they surged toward the sign-up table in a great wave.

Bursting out into the blessedly cool evening air, Clarissa finally allowed herself a small, triumphant smile. It was a start. There were still innumerable obstacles to overcome, daunting logistics to be orchestrated, before her vision could become reality. But she had planted the seed. What happened next would be up to them.

"Sergeant Carter - " Clarissa began, about to issue a string of rapid-fire orders. But before she could complete the sentence, a lone figure emerging from the shadows caught her eye - a familiar face, pinched and haunted, moving with weighted steps.

"Private Lewis," Clarissa called out, halting the woman in her tracks.

Sergeant Carter, astute as ever, snapped off a brisk salute and departed without a word, leaving Clarissa alone with the wary-eyed private.

"Did you sign up?" Clarissa asked, studying the woman's shuttered expression closely.

Sadie shifted her frame almost imperceptibly, as if trying to disappear into herself. "No, Major," she mumbled, her voice scarcely more than a whisper.

Clarissa felt a twinge of disappointment at this, but she kept her face carefully neutral. There was something about this Lewis woman, something undefined yet undeniably compelling, that made Clarissa want to reach out to her. To draw her into the fold.

"What assignment did you receive?" she inquired, genuinely curious.

"Supply clerk." The words dripped with leaden resignation.

Clarissa nodded slowly, thoughtfully. "Hmmm. Well, I hope you'll reconsider the 6888th. What do you have to lose?"

She hadn't meant it as anything more than gentle encouragement, but as soon as the question left her lips, Clarissa saw something flicker across Sadie's face - a flash of raw, unguarded anguish that vanished as quickly as it had appeared. In that fleeting instant, Clarissa glimpsed the well of loss and sorrow that lay beneath the surface of this woman's stoic facade.

Sadie said nothing, merely standing there in brooding silence. After a long moment, Clarissa dipped her head in acknowledgement and turned to depart, deciding it best not to press the matter further. She had made her case. The choice to act on it remained the private's alone.

But then, just as Clarissa began to walk away, she heard the private's voice waft out of the shadows behind her, so soft she almost missed it: "I have nothing left to lose, Major."

Clarissa paused mid-stride, a sudden swell of empathy rising in her chest. She was about to turn back, to offer some word of comfort or encouragement. But as she watched, Sadie squared her narrow shoulders, straightened her spine, and marched wordlessly back into the mess hall with a newfound purpose. And through the window, Clarissa saw the young woman stride directly to the sign-up table and resolutely add her name to the list.

Pride, bright and fierce, surged through Clarissa's veins at the sight. That was her girl. A fighter.

This battalion, Clarissa knew, would be built on such small moments of resilience and resolve. One by one, woman by woman, they would forge an unbreakable bond of sisterhood, strong enough to withstand whatever trials lay ahead. Together, they would show the world what Negro women were truly made of.

And God help anyone who dared to stand in their way.

CHAPTER 24:
PAIGE

As the rickety Army truck lurched to a stop at Fort Devens, Paige Thomas felt a pang of guilt twisting in her gut. She couldn't shake the image of Sadie's haunted eyes boring into her as she'd climbed aboard, Wanda hurling one last withering glare over her shoulder. Lord, the venom in that gaze! You'd think they were fleeing the gates of Hell itself.

But Paige pushed the unsettling memory aside, determined to focus on the opportunity that lay ahead. This was her chance, she told herself firmly - her chance to build a better future for herself and for Joe. She wouldn't squander it by dwelling on what she'd left behind.

"Just look at this place!" Wanda exclaimed as they clambered down from the truck, her voice pitched high with excitement. "Have you ever seen anything so grand?"

Paige had to admit, the sprawling redbrick hospital complex was quite a sight, its pristine white-trimmed windows gleaming in the crisp New England sunlight. Everywhere she looked, churning knots of olive-drab and army-brown uniforms swarmed across the manicured lawns, a hive of urgent activity. It was a far cry from the rough-hewn shacks and sweltering drill fields of Fort Oglethorpe, that was certain.

But as she and Wanda fell into step behind the brusque white sergeant leading their orientation tour, Paige felt her initial rush of eagerness beginning to falter. With each new corridor they traversed, each ward they peeked into, the giddy light in Wanda's eyes seemed to dim a little more. And Paige could see why.

At every turn, it was Negro WACs they saw toiling away at the most menial of tasks - scrubbing floors on calloused knees, emptying bedpans with pinched noses, hauling overflowing laundry sacks and garbage bins. Not one of them wore the crisp white uniform of a nurse or medical technician they had been promised.

"This is not what we signed up for," Wanda hissed under her breath, her earlier enthusiasm curdling into bitter disbelief. "We thought we were getting medical training."

"Something that would help us become nurses," Paige added, trying and failing to keep the dismayed tremor from her voice.

The sergeant scarcely even broke stride, his stony expression betraying not a flicker of concern. "You'll do what Uncle Sam tells you to do," he barked over his shoulder. "Like we all do."

With that, he quick-marched away, leaving Paige and Wanda standing slack-jawed and crestfallen in his wake. For a long moment, neither of them spoke, the weight of crushed hopes hanging heavy in the sterile air.

"That's it then," Wanda said finally, her tone listless with defeat. "All that big talk about serving our country, making something of ourselves, and this is what it comes to. Scrubbing toilets and changing sheets, same as if we never left home at all."

She kicked savagely at an invisible pebble, a muscle working in her jaw. "Guess I should've known better than to get my hopes up. Colored folks always get the shit end of the stick, don't we?"

But some stubborn spark within Paige refused to be so easily snuffed out. She thought of her son, Joe. She couldn't let him down, not like this, not without a fight. There had to be another way, another path to the purpose she craved. And suddenly, she knew exactly what it was.

"What about the 6888th?" Paige asked urgently, grasping Wanda's elbow. "There's talk they're still looking for women to go overseas."

Wanda yanked her arm away, eyeing Paige like she'd just suggested they sprout wings and fly. "Are you out of your mind? I am not going back to Georgia just to get on some damn boat to Europe. My negro ass is staying right here, thank you very much."

She spun on her heel and started to stalk off, but Paige lunged after her, desperate to make her see reason. "Wanda, please! Just think about it for a minute. This might be our last chance to do something that matters, something we can be proud of."

"Nope." Her voice softened a fraction, almost apologetic. "Sorry, I guess this is it for me".

Before Paige could muster a response, Wanda shouldered past her and disappeared into the milling crowd, her figure soon swallowed up by the sea of uniforms. Paige stood rooted to the spot, frustration and abandonment rising like bile in her throat. Left alone with her spinning thoughts, Paige knew she had no choice but to find a way to transfer back to Georgia and join the 6888th.

CHAPTER 25:
NATHAN

Nathan sat across the scratched wooden table from Thurgood Marshall, hardly daring to believe what he'd just heard. After all these long, excruciating months of waiting, of pacing his cell until his legs ached and his mind felt scraped raw, could it really be this simple? Just a few words from this sharp-eyed young lawyer, and suddenly freedom was within reach?

"Now that your testimony is over," Thurgood said, his voice calm and measured, "we should be able to get you released."

Nathan gripped the edge of the table, his heart hammering against his ribs. "Thank you," he managed, the words sticking in his throat. "When?"

Thurgood's gaze flicked to the barred window, gauging the angle of the wan sunlight. "Should be a few days at most."

A few days. After an eternity behind bars, the promise of liberation seemed dizzying, almost too much to comprehend. Nathan's head spun as he tried to wrap his mind around the sudden shift in his fortunes. What would he do first, when he finally stepped outside the prison gates?

Nathan's fingers tightened on the rumpled letter in his lap, the paper gone soft and thin from countless readings. Sadie. He had to find Sadie. Had to put this precious, fragile piece of Andrew's soul into her hands and watch the light of recognition dawn in her eyes. It was the very least he owed the man who should have been sitting here in his place.

Thurgood's gaze sharpened, drawn by the small movement. "Do you want me to mail that?" he asked gently.

Nathan shook his head, a faint smile tugging at the corners of his mouth. "I think I'll deliver it myself now," he said. "Thank you."

He meant it with every fiber of his being. Thank you for taking on a case the whole white world had already written off as a lost cause. Thank you for standing up in that courtroom day after day, facing down those hate-filled glares and poisonous whispers, and still delivering the best damn defense any man could ask for. Thank you for giving a damn about justice for colored folks, when it seemed like no one else did.

But there was one more question burning in Nathan's gut, one he couldn't leave unasked. He leaned forward, searching Thurgood's face for any flicker of doubt.

"What about the other men?"

Thurgood sighed, his shoulders slumping almost imperceptibly. "The trial continues," he said. "We'll see."

It wasn't the ringing endorsement Nathan had hoped for, but he understood why Thurgood couldn't make any promises. The Port Chicago 50 had been dragged through hell by the Navy, humiliated and demonized at every turn. Even with Thurgood and the NAACP in their corner, the outcome was far from certain.

Nathan felt a sudden surge of guilt, as if his own impending freedom was a betrayal of his brothers still languishing in the stockade. How could he walk out into the sunlight while they remained caged in the dark? What right did he have to smile, to laugh, to start rebuilding his life, when their futures lay in ruin?

But even as the bleak thoughts threatened to drag him under, Nathan forced himself to push them aside. Feeling guilty wasn't going to help anybody, least of all the other men. The best thing he could do, the only thing, was to keep fighting the good fight on the outside.

And if that meant tracking Sadie down to the ends of the earth, just to fulfill one man's dying wish? Well, that was a burden Nathan would gladly shoulder. He owed Andrew that much and more.

The sound of approaching footsteps echoed down the cellblock, jarring Nathan from his reverie. He and Thurgood exchanged a quick glance, an unspoken understanding passing between them. Their time was up.

Thurgood's smile was brief but genuine, a flash of warmth in his solemn features. Then he was gone, his lean form disappearing into the gloom of the corridor.

He stood slowly, every muscle aching with disuse. The letter felt heavy in his hand, freighted with unspoken grief and longing. But it was more than just a letter, Nathan realized. It was a lifeline. A slender thread of hope connecting him to a future beyond these walls, beyond the shadow of Port Chicago.

And Sadie... she was the key to it all. The living embodiment of everything Andrew had fought and died for. Finding her, putting that letter in her hands... it felt like more than just a promise to a fallen friend. It felt like destiny.

Come hell or high water, he would find Sadie Lewis. He would look into those brown eyes and tell her how her face had been the last thing Andrew saw in this world. How her love had given him courage in his final moments. How even in death, his soul had reached out to her, desperate for one last touch.

And maybe, just maybe, in the telling, they could both find some measure of peace. Some whisper of closure in a world that so often felt like nothing but a gaping wound. It was a fool's hope, perhaps. But it was all Nathan had left to cling to.

He had no idea if he was going to find Sadie, or what he would say to her when he did. Didn't know how to even begin untangling the complicated knot of emotions that welled up in him whenever he thought of her face.

But he knew he had to try.

CHAPTER 26:
SADIE

Sadie had stood apart from the other members of the 6888th, watching with a strange mix of detachment and envy as they said their goodbyes. All around her, women embraced, trading tearful promises to write and whispering fervent prayers for each other's safety. But no one approached Sadie, no one pulled her into a fierce hug or pressed a treasured keepsake into her hand. She was, as always, an island unto herself.

Sadie told herself it didn't matter, that she was used to being alone. And really, wasn't it better this way? Easier to focus on her training, on preparing herself for whatever challenges lay ahead, without the distraction of meaningless chatter and forced camaraderie. She had learned that attachments only led to heartache in the end.

Still, as she watched Paige and Wanda climb into the truck bound for Fort Devens, their faces bright with barely contained excitement, Sadie felt a pang of something uncomfortably close to longing. What would it be like, she wondered, to have someone to share her hopes and fears with? Someone who understood the weight she carried, the secret pain that gnawed at her heart?

But then Wanda turned, catching Sadie's eye over the tailgate. Her lip curled in a sneer of pure disgust, as if the very sight of Sadie made her stomach turn. Sadie met her gaze steadily, refusing to look away, until the truck rumbled to life and carried Wanda out of sight.

Good riddance, Sadie thought bitterly. Let Wanda go play nurse with Paige at Fort Devens. She was better off without their judgment and scorn. She had a higher calling now, a chance to make a real difference in this war. And she wouldn't let anything, or anyone, stand in her way.

As the days turned into weeks, Sadie threw herself into her training with a single-minded intensity that bordered on obsession. She ran harder, pushed herself further, than any of the other recruits, ignoring the burning in her lungs and the trembling in her legs. She volunteered for every extra duty, every unpleasant task, determined to prove her worth, her dedication.

While the other women grumbled about the endless drills and the grueling physical regimen, Sadie reveled in the ache of her muscles, the sweat stinging her eyes. The pain was a reminder that she was alive, that she still had a purpose. And if sometimes, in the darkest hours of the night, her mind strayed to Andrew, to the gaping hole his loss had left in her life... well, she just ran harder the next day, until her body screamed for mercy and her thoughts were too exhausted to wander.

All that mattered was the nod of approval from Major Dixon, the glimmer of respect in Captain Carter's eyes as they watched her progress.

Even so, the loneliness gnawed at Sadie, an ever-present ache that no amount of training could completely dull. It was almost a relief when the orders finally came through for the company's first town pass. Sadie hadn't set foot off the base since arriving at Fort Oglethorpe, and the thought of escaping, even for a few short hours, was intoxicating.

But as she walked the streets of the small Georgia town, Sadie felt her initial spark of excitement quickly fade. Ahead of her, Sadie spotted a flash of familiar figures - Cleopatra and Sammy, their heads bent together in conversation as they stood outside a dress shop. Sammy glanced over her shoulder and met Sadie's eye. For a moment, her face lit up in a smile, and she raised her hand in an eager wave.

"Hey! Hey! Over here!" she called out, her voice bright and inviting.

Sadie's heart leaped at the friendly overture. She hadn't realized how starved she was for simple human connection until that moment. Her feet started to carry her forward almost of their own volition, drawn by the warmth in Sammy's eyes.

But then, like a bucket of cold water to the face, she felt her pain creep back in. So Sadie simply raised a hand in a half-hearted wave, pasted on a thin smile, and kept walking. She felt Sammy's puzzled gaze boring into her back, sensed her hurt and confusion at the abrupt dismissal. But it was kinder this way, in the long run. A clean break, before the bond between them could grow any deeper or more tangled.

Sadie walked until the shops and houses began to thin out, until the road narrowed to little more than a dusty track winding into the piney woods. She had no particular destination in mind, just a bone-deep need to escape the suffocating press of other people's expectations and judgments.

So she was almost startled when she glanced up to find herself standing outside a ramshackle storefront, its weathered sign proclaiming "Sister Erzulie's Spiritual Emporium" in faded gilt letters. Bundles of dried herbs and strange, twisted roots hung in the grimy window, alongside crude wood carvings of naked figures in provocative poses. A crudely painted eye stared out from the center of the display, seeming to follow Sadie's every movement.

For a long moment, Sadie hesitated outside the door, torn between revulsion and a strange, morbid curiosity. Places like this, with their air of cheap mysticism and tawdry exoticism, had always filled her with a vague sense of unease. The charlatans who ran them preyed on the desperate and vulnerable, offering false hope in exchange for hard-earned cash.

Before she could think better of it, Sadie pushed through the door, a bell jangling harshly above her head. The shop was dim and cluttered inside, smelling strongly of incense and some heavier, muskier odor that Sadie couldn't quite place. Shelves groaned under the weight of dusty books and strange, arcane artifacts - animal bones and dried snake skins, bundles of feathers and vials of murky liquid.

Behind a small table sat a woman, her features hidden beneath a voluminous purple turban and an air of almost palpable disdain. Sadie got the distinct impression that she was being sized up, measured against some private yardstick and found wanting.

"What can Sister Erzulie do for you today, child?" the woman asked, her voice a throaty purr. "You got man trouble? Money worries? Maybe a hex you need lifted?"

Sadie fought the urge to turn around and walk right back out the way she'd come. This was a mistake, a foolish whim born of loneliness and desperation. What could this fraud possibly tell her that she didn't already know? That death and grief were her constant companions, that true happiness would always dance just beyond her grasp?

But something held her fast, some flicker of intuition that refused to be ignored. So she swallowed hard and took a seat across from the fortune teller, the chair creaking under her weight.

"I keep seeing the death card," Sadie heard herself say, surprised at the steadiness in her voice. "In my readings, over and over again. I don't know what it means."

Sister Erzulie arched one penciled eyebrow, her expression unreadable. "Death got more than one meaning, you know," she said cryptically. "Don't always have to be literal."

Sadie's heart hammered against her ribs, her throat suddenly dry as dust. "But what if... what if it is? Literal, I mean." She swallowed convulsively, forcing the next words out through numb lips. "Do you think that's the only way I'll ever see my Andrew again? If I die too?"

The fortune teller leaned back in her chair, studying Sadie with eyes that seemed to strip her bare, to peel away all her careful layers of protection and leave her utterly exposed. For a long, excruciating moment, she said nothing, just gazed at Sadie with that unsettling mixture of pity and understanding.

"I don't think that's what it means," she said at last. "Death can be a kind of transformation too. A shedding of the old, a rebirth into something new."

Sadie felt a sob rising in her throat, hot and choked with bitter disappointment. That was it? Some useless words about transformation and rebirth? She had come seeking true insight, a glimpse beyond the veil, and instead she got empty platitudes.

The rage boiled up in her like a living thing, scalding the back of her throat. She surged to her feet, knocking over her chair with a clatter. "Why won't he come to me?" she demanded, her voice raw and ragged. "I've seen things I didn't want to see, folks I didn't want to be visited by. I want to see him. I *need* to see him. Why won't he come? Why?"

The words poured out of her in a torrent, half prayer and half accusation. All the pent-up anguish of the past months, the gnawing emptiness of a life cut brutally short, seemed to swell inside her, too vast to be contained. She could feel herself shaking, could hear the high, thin note of hysteria creeping into her voice.

Sister Erzulie stood abruptly, her face a mask of alarm. She grasped Sadie firmly by the shoulders and marched her towards the door, her grip surprisingly strong for one so slight.

"You need to leave," she said brusquely. "Now."

And just like that, Sadie found herself stumbling out into the harsh sunlight, blinking back tears of rage and humiliation. She felt hollowed out inside, scoured raw by the intensity of her own emotions. What was wrong with her? Why couldn't she just accept Andrew's loss, honor his memory and move on? Why did she have to keep prodding at the wound, worrying it like a dog with a bone?

But even as the bleak thoughts chased themselves around her mind, Sadie knew the answer. She couldn't let go because letting go meant forgetting. It meant consigning Andrew to the past, to a rapidly receding history that had no place in her present or future. And that felt like the greatest betrayal of all.

As she walked, the anger slowly drained out of Sadie, leaving behind a numb weariness that settled into her bones like damp.

CHAPTER 27:
CLEOPATRA

Cleopatra and Sammy stood outside the dress shop. Sammy's normally sunny face was drawn into a petulant frown. "Well, she could at least wave back," she grumbled. "It's only polite."

Before Cleopatra could formulate a response that wouldn't involve cussing or smacking some sense into the girl, a flash of color in the shop window caught her eye. She grasped Sammy's elbow and steered her towards it, determined to distract her from her Sadie-shaped woes.

"Now would you look at that," she purred appreciatively as they drew closer. "I haven't seen a frock that pretty since my last curtain call."

And it was a gorgeous dress, all shimmering emerald silk and daring décolletage. It probably cost more than a month of Cleopatra's Army salary, but oh, how it would feel against her skin, clinging to every curve like a lover's caress.

Sammy, bless her heart, looked more perplexed than impressed. "It's awful low-cut, ain't it?" she asked doubtfully. "I don't know if I'm bold enough to wear something like that."

Cleopatra laughed, throwing an arm around the younger woman's shoulders. "Well, I am definitely bold enough for the both of us," she declared. "Come on, let's go try it on. I bet it'll look even better on a real live body."

She practically dragged Sammy into the shop, ignoring the startled look on the salesgirl's face as two Negro WACs came sashaying through the door. Cleopatra knew that look all too well - the wary mixture of disdain and trepidation that clouded white folks' eyes whenever they saw a colored person step out of line, even just a little bit.

She simply breezed past the girl without so much as a glance, making a beeline for the dress that had caught her eye. Up close, it was even more stunning - the rich, jewel-toned fabric seemed to glow under the lights, throwing off emerald sparks with every ripple and fold.

Cleopatra reached out to stroke one sleeve, marveling at the liquid softness of the silk. She could practically feel it against her skin already, cool and sensuous and utterly decadent. It was the kind of dress that demanded to be worn by a woman who knew her own power, who could walk into a room and bring every man to his knees with a single smoldering glance.

"If you are not going to buy anything, you need to leave."

The salesgirl's nasal voice shattered Cleopatra's reverie like a brick through a stained-glass window. She spun around, one hand still possessively clutching the dress, and fixed the girl with a glare that could have melted steel.

"I beg your pardon?" she asked coldly, drawing herself up to her full height.

The girl didn't even have the grace to look abashed. "You are welcome to buy, not to browse," she said primly, as if explaining something to a particularly slow child.

Cleopatra felt her temper flare, hot and bright as a lit match. It was one thing to endure this kind of treatment from her white commanders, who at least had the authority of rank to bolster their bigotry. But to be spoken down to by some snot-nosed little woman? No way.

She opened her mouth to deliver a blistering retort, but Sammy beat her to the punch.

"How are we supposed to know what we want to buy if we can't look first?" she demanded, her voice trembling with indignation.

The sales responded swiftly, "You two need to leave".

Sammy tried desperately to hold back her tears. "You can't treat us like this. We're soldiers!"

The salesgirl's lip curled in an ugly sneer. "In here," she said slowly, as if savoring the words, "you're just niggers."

The slur landed like a physical blow, knocking the breath from Cleopatra's lungs. She had been called worse in her time, of course - much worse. But there was something about hearing that hateful word here, in this pretty little shop with its gleaming mirrors and soft jazz playing on the radio, that made it cut all the deeper.

For a moment, Cleopatra could only stand there, her whole body vibrating with the force of her rage. She wanted to lunge across the counter and shake the girl until her teeth rattled. Wanted to snatch up that beautiful green dress and tear it to shreds right in front of her smug little face. Wanted to scream and curse and break things until the whole world knew the depth of her fury, her pain, her bottomless disgust at the way things were and always would be.

But she didn't do any of those things. Because she was a soldier now, and soldiers had to be better than that. They had to rise above the pettiness and ignorance of small-minded people, no matter how much it hurt. They had to keep marching forward, even when every step felt like wading through quicksand.

So Cleopatra simply turned on her heel and stalked towards the door, her head held high. "Come on, Sammy," she said, her voice as cold and flat as a frozen lake. "Let's go, before I wind up in jail for knocking somebody out."

Tears flowed down Sammy's cheeks. It broke Cleopatra's heart to see it. She wanted to gather Sammy into her arms and shield her from all the cruelty and ignorance that lay ahead. Wanted to tell her that it would get easier, that the insults and indignities would someday bounce off her like rubber arrows off a steel breastplate.

But she knew it would be a lie. The truth was, it never got easier. You just got harder, more callused, until you could take the blows without flinching. Until you learned to wear your scars like armor, like a badge of bitter pride.

So instead of comforting Sammy, Cleopatra simply grabbed her hand and tugged her towards the exit. "We don't need this," she said firmly. "We don't need anything from folks like her."

And as the shop door swung shut behind them with a mocking tinkle of bells, Cleopatra told herself that it was true. That she didn't need the approval or acceptance of small-minded bigots, didn't need their pretty dresses or their poisoned smiles.

CHAPTER 28:
MARY MCLEOD BETHUNE

Mary McLeod Bethune settled into the plush armchair, carefully arranging her skirts as she poured tea for her distinguished guest. Major Clarissa Dixon sat across from her, back ramrod straight and dark eyes gleaming with a fierce intelligence that belied her youth. Mary had known the moment she first laid eyes on the girl that she was destined for great things - had felt the tug of divine providence, as sure and insistent as a hand on her elbow.

"Thank you for agreeing to come to D.C.," Mary said warmly, passing a delicate china cup across the low table. "The doctors don't want me traveling so far right now."

Major Dixon accepted the tea with a gracious nod, her grip on the saucer steady and sure. "It's my pleasure, Dr. Bethune."

Mary waved a hand, dismissing the formality. "Please, call me Mary. We're going to be working closely together, you and me. No need to stand on ceremony."

She punctuated the words with a conspiratorial wink and was gratified to see a small smile tug at the corners of Major Dixon's mouth. The girl had a serious manner, but Mary sensed a warmth beneath the surface, a deep well of compassion and humor that the Army had not yet managed to train out of her.

"Mary, then," Major Dixon conceded, inclining her head. "I must admit, I was surprised to receive your invitation. I know how valuable your time is, especially now..."

She trailed off delicately, but Mary could hear the unspoken question in her voice. It was no secret that her health had been failing in recent months, her once-boundless energy sapped by the advancing years and the endless battles, both political and personal. There were some who whispered that it was time for her to step down, to make way for a new generation of leaders.

But Mary had never been one to go gentle into that good night. She had fought tooth and nail for every inch of ground she'd gained, every victory she'd won for her people. And she would keep fighting until her last breath, keep pushing and prodding and agitating until the world looked a little more like the one she knew was possible.

And that was why she had called Major Dixon here, to this quiet sanctuary in the heart of the capital. Because she knew, with the same bone-deep certainty that had guided her all her life, that this young woman was the key to unlocking the next great chapter in their struggle.

"I wanted to tell you in person," Mary said quietly, holding the Major's gaze with her own, "before you leave for Europe. That you have my full support. If you need anything, if you run into any obstacles, do not hesitate to reach out."

Major Dixon's eyes widened fractionally, the only outward sign of her surprise. "I... Thank you," she managed after a moment. "That means more than you know."

Mary smiled, reaching across the table to lay a hand over the Major's own. "I know exactly what it means," she said gently. "Because I've been where you are, Clarissa. I've stared down the doubters and the naysayers, the ones who said a colored woman had no business dreaming big or aiming high. I've felt the weight of all those hopes and expectations, the fear of letting down the people who are counting on you."

Major Dixon's hand trembled slightly under her own, but her voice was steady when she spoke. "Why did you choose me to lead this battalion?" she asked softly. "You barely know me."

Mary leaned back in her chair, considering the question. It was a fair one, and she knew the Major deserved an honest answer.

"Because I know you will be successful," she said simply. "All my life, I've been guided by something I call divine providence. God connecting me to the right person at the right time. To be in the right place at the right time. People seeing something in me that I didn't see in myself."

She paused, lost in memory for a moment. She thought of Lucy Craft Laney, the fierce and brilliant educator who had taken a scrappy young Mary under her wing, nurturing her talents and stoking the fires of her ambition. Of Booker T. Washington, the visionary leader who had recognized her potential and given her a platform to speak truth to power. Of Eleanor Roosevelt, the indomitable First Lady who had become her dearest friend and staunchest ally, opening doors that Mary had once thought forever sealed.

"They took an interest in me," Mary continued softly. "Helped me get a scholarship for college. Helped me raise money to start my own college. Because they saw something special in me. Something I didn't always see in myself."

Her eyes found Major Dixon's once more, holding them fast. "And now, I see that same spark in you. That same fire, that same unshakable conviction. I hand-picked you for the first officer's class. I hand-picked you to lead this battalion. Because I know, in my bones, that you are the woman for this moment. The one who will carry our people forward, even when the way seems dark and the obstacles insurmountable."

Major Dixon drew in a sharp breath, her eyes shining with emotion. For a moment, she seemed at a loss for words, her usual composure ruffled by the force of Mary's conviction.

"I... I don't know what to say," she managed at last, her voice thick. "Except thank you. Thank you for believing in me, for giving me this chance. I won't let you down."

"No," Mary agreed, squeezing her hand. "You won't. Because letting me down would mean letting yourself down, and I know you're not the kind of woman who does that. You're the kind who plants her feet and lifts her chin and keeps marching forward, no matter how rocky the road or how fierce the winds of resistance."

She sat back, a hint of mischief sparking in her eyes. "And besides," she added wryly, "can you imagine how insufferable the men would be if they thought we couldn't handle our business? We'd never hear the end of it."

That startled a laugh out of Major Dixon, bright and sudden as a bird taking wing. "You're right about that," she chuckled, shaking her head. "I've already had a few sideways looks from the brass, like they're just waiting for me to fall on my face."

Mary tutted disapprovingly. "Well, they are fools," she declared. "Because you're not going to fall, Clarissa. You're going to fly. Higher and farther than any of those small-minded men ever dreamed."

She meant it with every fiber of her being. Looking at Major Dixon now, with her straight-backed pride and her clear, steadfast gaze, Mary felt the weight of history settling on the younger woman's shoulders like a mantle. Felt the currents of destiny swirling around her, propelling her forward into the unknown.

It was a heady feeling, and a humbling one. To know that she had played some small part in shaping this moment, in nurturing the seeds of greatness in yet another gifted young mind. It was the work of a lifetime, and one that Mary knew she would never tire of.

But she also knew that her own role in this particular story was drawing to a close. Major Dixon's journey was just beginning, and it was one that she would have to walk largely on her own. Mary could offer guidance and support from afar, but in the end, it would be up to Clarissa to chart her own course, to weather the storms and navigate the shoals ahead.

It was a daunting prospect, but one that Mary knew the Major was more than equal to. She had seen the steel in her spine, the fire in her eyes. Had felt the force of her conviction, as bright and unwavering as a North Star.

And so, as their tea cooled and the shadows lengthened across the parlor floor, Mary found herself imparting a few last words of wisdom. A benediction, of sorts, for the long road ahead.

"Remember this, Clarissa," she said softly, holding the younger woman's gaze. "You are not alone in this fight. You carry with you the hopes and dreams of every colored woman who ever dared to imagine a better world. Every mother who ever prayed for her child's future, every sister who ever lifted her voice in song or defiance. They are with you, always. And so am I."

She reached out, clasping Major Dixon's hands in her own gnarled, age-spotted ones. "And when the way seems dark and the burden too heavy to bear, remember too that you are a daughter of the Most High. That you walk in the footsteps of queens and warriors, of pioneers and prophets. That you are part of a lineage that stretches back to the very dawn of time, and forward into an eternity of possibility."

Major Dixon's hands tightened around her own, the calluses on her palms testament to the hard work and harder choices that had brought her to this moment. "I will remember," she whispered, her voice thick with emotion. "I will carry your words with me, always. And I will make you proud, I swear it."

"You already have," Mary assured her, blinking back the sudden sting of tears. "More than you can possibly know."

And it was true. In this brave, brilliant young woman, Mary saw the fulfillment of all her deepest hopes, all her most cherished dreams. Saw the future taking shape, bright and bold and so achingly beautiful that it stole the very breath from her lungs.

And so Mary McLeod Bethune sat back in her armchair, sipped her cooling tea, and smiled a small, secret smile. The smile of a woman who had seen the promised land, and who knew, beyond all shadow of doubt, that her people would one day reach it.

CHAPTER 29:
SADIE

Sadie stood in formation, the morning sun already burning the back of her neck as she waited for the day to begin. As more women joined the group, a flash of recognition jolted through Sadie like a bolt of lightning. That lanky, long-limbed frame, that wary set to the shoulders...

Paige.

Their eyes met across the dusty expanse, and for a moment, the rest of the world seemed to fall away. Sadie saw her own shock mirrored back at her, undercut by something darker, more complicated. Anger, perhaps. Or fear. Or maybe just the bone-deep weariness of a woman who had thought she'd left her demons behind, only to find them waiting for her on the other side.

Sadie tore her gaze away first, fixing it straight ahead as the drill sergeant barked out the day's orders. But she could feel Paige's presence like a physical weight, pressing down on her from a few scant feet away. It made her skin prickle, her breath come short and shallow in her chest.

She tried to push the thoughts away, to lose herself in the mindless repetition of drills and marches. But every time she turned her head, every time the formation shifted and realigned, there was Paige. Stalking through the exercises with a tightly coiled fury, her jaw clenched and her eyes blazing.

It all came to a head at the rope climb, one of the final challenges in the long, grueling gauntlet of their training. Sadie watched as Paige attacked the thick hemp with a savage determination, hauling herself up hand over hand, her muscles straining against the sweat-soaked fabric of her fatigues.

But determination could only take her so far. Halfway up the rope, Paige's grip faltered, her fingers scrabbling uselessly against the fibers. For a single, suspended moment, she hung there, teetering on the brink. And then, with a strangled cry, she fell.

Sadie didn't stop to think. Didn't pause to consider the consequences, or the cost. She simply lunged forward, thrusting out a hand to catch Paige before she could hit the ground.

Their fingers met and tangled, Paige's skin hot and slick against her own. For a moment, they were frozen there, locked in a strange, silent struggle. Sadie could feel the other woman's pulse hammering against her palm, could see the play of emotions warring in her dark, narrowed eyes.

And then, as quickly as it had begun, it was over. Paige snatched her hand away as if burned, her lip curling in a snarl of disgust. She scrambled to her feet on her own, pointedly ignoring Sadie's outstretched arm, and stalked back to her place in line without a backward glance.

Sadie let her own hand fall to her side, feeling oddly bereft. She hadn't expected gratitude, exactly. But the sheer, searing force of Paige's hostility still took her breath away.

What had she done, really, to earn such loathing? Was her very existence so offensive, her strange and unsettling gifts so repugnant, that even a simple act of human kindness was unacceptable?

The questions chased themselves around her mind as the day wore on, as the sun climbed high and hot in the cloudless sky. She went through the motions of the final drills in a daze, her body performing the necessary tasks while her thoughts spun and whirled like leaves in a gale.

And then, all at once, it was over. The squad leader was calling them to attention, her voice ringing out over the assembled ranks with a note of fierce, unfettered pride.

"You did it," she barked, pacing up and down the line. "You are off to Europe. Congratulations, troops. Get your things together tonight. You depart for Camp Shanks, New York, last stop in the U.S.A., in the morning. Dismissed!"

All around her, the women of the 6888th erupted into whoops and cheers, their faces bright with triumph and relief. They clustered together in knots of two and three, hugging and laughing and making breathless plans for their last night on American soil.

But Sadie hung back, watching from the fringes as she always did. Her heart felt leaden in her chest, weighed down by a strange, nameless grief.

This was supposed to be a moment of celebration, of hard-won achievement. A chance to savor the sweet, giddy rush of accomplishment before plunging headlong into the unknown. But all she felt was a hollow ache, a sense of something vital and irretrievable slipping through her fingers.

Standing on the cusp of her greatest adventure yet, Sadie felt more alone than ever. More keenly aware of the invisible walls that separated her from the rest of the world, the unbridgeable distances that yawned like chasms at her feet.

And what waited for her on the other side of the ocean? More of the same, most likely. More sidelong glances and whispered speculation, more cold shoulders and closed ranks. An endless, exhausting battle to carve out a space for herself in a world that seemed determined to deny her one.

The thought made her want to scream. Made her want to turn tail and run, to find some quiet corner of the earth where she could lick her wounds in peace, free from the weight of other people's expectations and judgments.

But even as the urge rose up in her throat, bitter as bile, Sadie knew she could never go through with it.

She shuffled the worn, familiar deck with trembling fingers, breathing in the musty scent of old paper and faded ink. And then, with a whispered prayer to whatever gods might be listening, she drew.

The Death card stared back at her, its grinning skull seeming to mock her from the center of the spread. Sadie felt her stomach lurch, her breath catching in her throat.

It was always the Death card. No matter how many times she shuffled, how many different spreads she laid out, that skeletal figure kept dancing through her dreams, dogging her waking steps. As if it were trying to tell her something, some cryptic message she was still too blind, too stubborn to decipher.

But what could it mean? What message could be so urgent, so vital, that it would follow her halfway around the world, haunting her even in this moment of triumph and possibility?

Was it a warning? A prophecy of some fresh hell waiting to claim her, some new and terrible grief lurking just beyond the horizon?

Or could it be... could it be something else entirely? A sign of transformation, perhaps. A herald of change, of old patterns breaking and new paths emerging from the rubble.

Sadie didn't know.

She didn't know if she had the strength, the courage. But as Sadie packed her few, meager possessions that night, as she folded her uniform with shaking hands and laid her cards to rest into her treasured battered box, she made herself a promise.

She would try.

CHAPTER 30:
NATHAN

Nathan stood on the cracked sidewalk, squinting up at the weathered brick facade of the apartment building. His heart hammered against his ribs, his palms slick with sweat where they clutched the letter in his pocket. He had come so far, crossed so many miles and months, to reach this moment. But now that he was here, standing on the threshold of his best friend's old life, he found himself hesitating.

What would he say to her, this woman he had never met but felt he knew as intimately as his own breath? How could he even begin to explain who he was, what he meant to Andrew? What Andrew had meant to him?

He pictured her face, traced its delicate contours in his mind's eye. He had spent hours staring at that faded photograph, committing every detail to memory. The soft curl of her lips, the graceful arch of her brow. The way her eyes seemed to dance with some secret mischief, some hidden fire that even the black and white of the image couldn't quite conceal.

Sadie. Her name was a prayer on his lips, a talisman against the doubts and fears that clawed at his gut.

Taking a deep breath, Nathan mounted the stairs to the second floor, his footsteps echoing hollowly in the narrow stairwell. He counted the doors until he reached the one he sought, the brass numbers tarnished but still legible.

For a long moment, he simply stood there, his hand raised to knock. The words he had rehearsed so carefully seemed to stick in his throat, tangling on his tongue like thorns.

But before he could summon the courage to let his knuckles fall, a voice rasped out from behind him, making him jump.

"You lookin' for somebody?"

Nathan spun around to see an old woman leaning out of the downstairs window, her face a map of deep, suspicious lines. She squinted at him through the dusty screen, her eyes narrowed to slits.

"I'm looking for Mrs. Andrew Lewis," Nathan said, fighting to keep his voice steady. "Sadie."

The woman's frown deepened, her mouth puckering like she had bitten into something sour. "She ain't there no more," she said flatly. "Joined the WAC. Nothin' but loose women join, if you ask me."

Nathan felt his stomach drop, a cold, sinking feeling settling in his chest. Joined the WAC? Sadie? He couldn't picture it, couldn't reconcile the vibrant, laughing girl from the photograph with the image of her beauty hidden beneath drab olive drab.

"Do you know how to get in touch with her?" he asked, hating the tremor that crept into his voice.

The old woman shrugged, her thin shoulders sharp beneath her faded housecoat. "Accordin' to the postman, her mail's bein' forwarded to Georgia. Fort Oglethorpe, I think he said."

"Georgia?" Nathan repeated dumbly. The word seemed to echo in his ears, as distant and unreal as a dream.

Georgia. Miles from here. It might as well have been the moon, for all the hope he had of reaching her there.

But even as despair welled up in him, bitter as bile, Nathan felt a spark of something else kindling in his chest. Something small and fierce and stubborn, glowing like an ember in the ashes of his disappointment.

He had come this far, hadn't he? Had clawed his way back from the brink of death and despair, dragged himself hand over hand out of the pit of grief and loss. And all for her. All for the chance to look into those fathomless eyes, to press Andrew's letter into her hand and watch the dawning light of understanding bloom across her face.

He couldn't give up now. Couldn't let a few hundred miles of road, a few flimsy barriers of distance and circumstance, stand between him and his purpose.

And Sadie was the key. The last living link to the man Nathan had loved like a brother, the compass that would guide him out of the wilderness of his own shattered heart.

He had to find her. Had to look into those haunted, hungry eyes and tell her that her husband's last thoughts, his last breath, had been for her.

It was a slim chance, he knew. A fool's hope, born of equal parts grief and desperation. But it was all he had left, the only thread still tying him to the world of the living.

And so, with a final nod of thanks to the old woman, Nathan turned and began to descend the stairs, his steps heavy but purposeful. He would go to Georgia. He would scour every inch of Fort Oglethorpe, turn over every rock and stone until he found her.

And when he did... when he finally stood before her, Sadie's face swimming into focus through a haze of tears and disbelief...he would give her Andrew's letter. Would watch the crumpled pages smooth beneath her trembling fingers, the faded ink blooming to new life in the heat of her gaze.

And then, perhaps, they could begin to heal. Could start to pick up the shattered pieces of their lives, to fashion them into something new and whole and strong. Something that honored Andrew's memory, that carried his spirit forward into a brighter, more hopeful future.

It was a beautiful dream, fragile as a soap bubble. But as Nathan stepped out into the chilly Illinois wind, he felt it take root in his chest, spreading its tendrils through the cracks in his battered soul.

Sadie. He whispered her name like a prayer, a promise all the way to Fort Oglethorpe.

New York?

The soldier's words hit Nathan like a physical blow, driving the air from his lungs in a sharp, painful burst. For a moment, he simply stood there, reeling, as the world seemed to tilt and spin around him.

New York. She was gone. Again.

It felt like some cosmic joke, a cruel twist of fate designed to punish him for daring to hope. But even as the bitter disappointment welled up in his throat, Nathan fought to push it back down. He couldn't let himself succumb to despair, not now. Not when he was so close, the ghost of her presence still lingering in the air like perfume.

He squared his shoulders, lifted his chin. Forced himself to meet the soldier's impassive gaze, to keep his voice steady and strong.

"Please," he said quietly. "It's important. I have something I need to give her, a message from... from someone she loved very much."

He let his hand drift to his pocket, to the precious cargo hidden within. For a moment, the soldier simply stared at him, his expression unreadable. Nathan held his breath, bracing himself for another rejection, another door slammed in his face.

But then, miraculously, something flickered in those icy blue eyes. Something that might have been sympathy, or perhaps just a weary sort of resignation.

"Look," the soldier said gruffly. "I can tell you this much. The 6888th is shipping out from Camp Shanks on Tuesday morning. If you hurry, you might be able to catch her before they leave."

Nathan's eyes widened, a sudden, dizzying rush of hope surging through his veins. Tuesday. Three days from now. It wasn't much, but it was something. A chance, however slim, to see her one last time before she disappeared into the chaos of war.

"Thank you," he breathed, his voice raw with gratitude. "Thank you so much. You have no idea what this means to me."

The soldier just shrugged, his gaze already sliding away, back to the list of names and numbers that consumed his days.

With a final, fervent nod of thanks, he turned and began to run, his feet pounding against the dusty Georgia road as he raced towards the distant horizon. Towards New York, towards Sadie. Praying with every fiber of his being that he would not be too late.

That somehow, against all odds and reason, he would find her in time.

CHAPTER 31:
SADIE

Sadie stood alone on the bow of the ship, a solitary figure amidst the bustle of WACs, soldiers and all manner of military personnel headed to Europe. As the whistle blew and the vessel began to pull away, she watched as a tall, broad-shouldered man with a chiseled jaw and a military bearing came running down the dock, his eyes fixed on the departing ship with a mix of determination and desperation. Sweat beads glistened on the man's chestnut face as he breathlessly shouted for the ship to wait. Something about him caught Sadie's eye, though she couldn't say why. As he watched in distress while they sailed off, she wondered who he was and what had driven him to such a hopeless, futile gesture. But Sadie was too lost in her own despondency to give it more than a passing thought.

Sadie leaned against the railing of the SS Île de France, watching the last sliver of American coastline disappear into the gathering dusk. The sea breeze whipped at her hair, tugging strands loose from their pins to dance around her face like restless spirits. She closed her eyes, let the salt spray sting her cheeks and lips, savoring the sharp, clean bite of it on her tongue.

This was it. The moment she had been dreading and yearning for in equal measure, ever since that fateful day when she had signed her name in the 6888th recruitment ledger. The point of no return, the threshold between the life she had known and the great, yawning unknown that awaited her on the other side of the Atlantic.

She should have felt something, she supposed. Excitement, or fear, or the stirrings of some greater purpose taking root in her bones. But all she felt was numb. Hollowed out, like a dead tree still standing by sheer stubborn inertia.

She stood there for hours as around her, the deck of the ship swarmed with bodies, their faces bright with anticipation and nervous energy. They chattered and laughed and called out to friends old and new, their voices blurring into a cacophonous hum that made Sadie's head ache.

She didn't belong here. Didn't belong anywhere, really, not since Andrew died. Slowly, as if in a dream, Sadie felt her hand drift inside her bag. Felt the worn edges of her wooden box press against her fingertips.

Andrew's box. The one he had carved for her during those long, honeyed summer days before the war, when their future had stretched out before them like a road paved with gold. He had spent hours hunched over the fragrant cedar, his brow furrowed in concentration as he worked the wood with loving, patient hands.

And when he had finished, when the last curl of oak leaf and heart-pierced arrow had been etched into the gleaming surface, he had presented it to her with a flourish and a grin that could have lit up the world.

"For your cards," he had said, his eyes dancing with mischief and something deeper, something that made her breath catch in her throat. "So you'll always have a piece of me with you, wherever you go."

Sadie had laughed then, had swatted him playfully on the arm and told him he was being foolish. That she would never be parted from him, not truly, not in any way that mattered.

Oh, what a naive little fool she had been.

And now, here she was. Alone on a ship of strangers, a vagrant wind tossed on the storm-wracked sea of war. Andrew's box a leaden weight in her hands, his absence a howling void at the center of her being.

The world had ended, and yet somehow life went on. The sun still rose and set, the seasons still turned in their inexorable dance. And Sadie... Sadie was still here. A ghost among the living, drifting through the motions of existence without purpose or plan.

She had thought, in some distant corner of her mind, that joining the 6888th would change that. That by throwing herself into the great crusade of the war, by losing herself in the larger rhythms of duty and sacrifice, she could somehow outpace the grief that dogged her every step.

But now, standing here on the cusp of her great adventure, she felt more adrift than ever. More keenly aware of the emptiness at her core, the yawning chasm where her heart had once beat in time with Andrew's.

She placed the box back in her bag. Slowly, unconsciously, Sadie's hand curled around the railing. The metal was cold beneath her fingers, the chill of it seeping into her bones like the first frost of winter. She stared down at the churning water below, watching the foamy swells rise and fall like the chest of some great, slumbering beast.

It would be so easy, she thought distantly. So simple, to just let go. To vault over the railing and let the icy embrace of the sea swallow her whole. To sink down into the dark and the silence, to let the currents carry her far away from the pain and the longing and the endless, aching emptiness.

Slowly, dreamlike, Sadie lifted one foot. Felt the worn sole of her boot scrape against the rough planking of the deck. One step, and then she would be free. One step, and the nightmare would be over at last.

But before she could take that final, fateful stride, a sound pierced the haze of her despair. A small, broken sound, like a wounded animal crying out in the night.

Sadie froze, her heart stuttering in her chest. For a moment, she wasn't sure if she had imagined it, if the sound had been nothing more than a trick of the wind and the waves. But then it came again, louder this time, and she realized with a start that it was coming from somewhere nearby.

Turning, she scanned the deck, squinting into the shadows that pooled in the corners and crevices. At first, she saw nothing but the endless stretch of sea and sky, the dim shapes of artillery and lifeboats looming like specters in the gloom.

But then, there. Huddled against the wall of the deckhouse, a small, shivering figure curled in on itself like a frightened child.

Sammy.

Sadie hesitated, torn between the pull of the abyss and the tug of something she couldn't quite name. Sympathy, perhaps. Or maybe just the simple human instinct to reach out, to offer comfort to a fellow soul in pain.

Before she quite knew what she was doing, she found herself moving towards the younger woman. Found herself crouching down beside her, one hand hovering awkwardly in the air between them.

"What are you doing out here?" she asked, her voice rough and rust from disuse.

Sammy lifted her head, her eyes red-rimmed and swollen in the faint light. She looked at Sadie for a long moment.

"I could ask you the same thing," she said at last, her voice thin and thready as a line of smoke.

Sadie shrugged, the movement feeling stiff and unnatural. "I couldn't sleep," she said, the lie tripping off her tongue with practiced ease. "I just come up here to...to think."

It sounded foolish, even to her own ears. But what else could she say? That she had been teetering on the brink of oblivion, ready to fling herself into the dark and never look back? That the only thing that had stayed her hand, the only thing that had dragged her back from the precipice, was the sound of Sammy's sobs echoing in the night?

No. So she simply sat there, awkward and still, as Sammy's tears began to flow anew. As great, shuddering sobs wracked her narrow frame, the force of them seeming to shake her very bones.

"Your turn," Sadie said quietly, when the worst of the storm seemed to have passed.

"I'm not going to make it," Sammy whispered, her voice raw and ragged. "I've never been so sick in my life. And I miss my Daddy. I even miss my brothers. This was a mistake. I want to go home."

Sadie felt something twist in her chest, a sharp, aching pang that had nothing to do with the chill of the wind or the sting of the salt spray. She knew that feeling all too well, that desperate, clawing homesickness that could turn even the most mundane of tasks into a Herculean effort.

But she also knew that there was no going back. No undoing the choices that had brought them here, to this moment, to this lonely stretch of ocean with nothing but the stars and the ghosts of their pasts for company.

"Well, it's too late for that now," she said, the words coming out harsher than she had intended.

Sammy flinched as if struck, her eyes welling up with fresh tears. For a moment, Sadie thought she would bolt, would scramble to her feet and flee back into the bowels of the ship, back to the dubious comfort of her bunk and her sorrow.

But she didn't. She just sat there, hugging her knees to her chest, her thin shoulders shaking with the force of her sobs. And Sadie... Sadie felt something break open inside her, some hidden reservoir of compassion that she had thought long since dried up.

"You should get back now," she said gruffly, fighting to keep the sudden, treacherous swell of emotion from her voice. "It's cold out here."

Sammy shook her head, her hair a wild tangle around her tear-streaked face. "I can't let folks see me like this," she hiccupped, scrubbing at her cheeks with the back of her hand. "They already call me country bumpkin. What are they going to call me if they see me crying like this?"

Despite herself, Sadie felt a small, wry smile tug at the corner of her mouth. "I've been called worse," she said dryly. "Trust me. This feeling will pass."

She hesitated, the next words sticking in her throat like shards of glass. But she forced them out anyway, a quiet, tentative offering in the dark.

"You are going to love Europe," she said softly, the lie tasting bitter on her tongue.

Sammy looked up at her, her eyes wide and wondering. "You think so?" she whispered, something like hope kindling in the depths of her gaze.

Sadie swallowed hard, fought back the sudden, irrational urge to laugh. Or maybe to cry, she wasn't quite sure.

"I know so," she said instead, the words ringing hollow in her own ears.

"How do you know?" Sammy asked, a tiny furrow appearing between her brows.

Sadie just shrugged, a strange, reckless feeling unfurling in her chest. "I just do," she said simply.

And then, on impulse, she reached into her pocket. Slowly, deliberately, she withdrew her hand. Held it out to Sammy, the little foil-wrapped square glinting dully in the moonlight.

"Eat this," she said gruffly, pressing the ginger candy into the younger woman's palm. "It will settle your stomach. And you should get back inside now. Catching a cold is only going to make you feel worse."

For a moment, Sammy simply stared at the candy, her expression unreadable. Sadie felt a sudden, irrational flutter of panic, a conviction that she had overstepped some unspoken boundary, violated some sacred code of conduct.

But then, Sammy's fingers closed around the sweet. She looked up at Sadie, something like wonder dawning in her eyes.

"You're right," she said softly, a watery smile tugging at the corners of her mouth. "Thank you, Sadie."

Sadie just nodded, a strange tightness constricting her throat. She watched as Sammy clambered to her feet, watched as she brushed the worst of the dirt and grime from her uniform.

For a moment, she thought the younger woman would simply leave, would vanish back into the belly of the ship without another word. But then, she paused. Turned back to look at Sadie, her head cocked slightly to the side.

"You coming?" she asked, a note of hesitation creeping into her voice.

Sadie felt something lurch in her chest, a sudden, dizzying rush of vertigo. For a moment, she was tempted. Tempted to follow Sammy back into the light and the warmth, to let herself be buoyed by the younger woman's tentative overture of friendship.

But then, the moment passed. The old, familiar darkness settled over her once more, heavy and implacable as a shroud.

Slowly, deliberately, Sadie turned away. Fixed her gaze on the vast, empty expanse of the ocean, the endless stretch of black that seemed to call to her, to whisper her name in the voice of the wind and the waves.

"No," she said softly, the word barely audible over the rush of the sea. "You go on. I'll be along in a minute."

And then, Sadie was alone once more. Alone with the night and the sea and the ghosts that crowded close around her, their spectral fingers plucking at the ragged edges of her soul.

And then, she turned away. Away from the abyss, away from the temptation of surrender and release. Back towards the light, towards the warmth and the noise and the messy, glorious cacophony of life.

One step. And then another. And another, until the door to the lower decks loomed before her, a rectangle of warm, golden light in the darkness.

One step at a time. One day, one hour, one breath.

CHAPTER 32:
MAJOR DIXON

Clarissa leaned over the battered desk in the makeshift headquarters, her brow furrowed as she studied the list of tasks before her. The muted light of the single bare bulb overhead cast deep shadows across the room, but she hardly noticed. Her mind was awhirl with a thousand details, a thousand potential pitfalls and problems that needed to be addressed before her troops arrived.

Beside her, Captain Carter shifted uneasily, her own face a mask of tightly controlled anxiety. Clarissa could feel the tension radiating off the other woman in waves, a palpable force that set her own nerves jangling like live wires.

But she couldn't afford to indulge in fear or uncertainty. Not now, not with so much riding on the success of this mission. Her women were counting on her to lead them through whatever challenges lay ahead. To be the steady hand on the rudder, the unwavering voice of command in the midst of chaos and confusion.

And so, with a deep breath and a final, decisive nod, Clarissa straightened up. Fixed Captain Carter with a look of steely resolve, her voice ringing out crisp and clear in the close confines of the room.

"Our priorities," she said firmly, "are finalizing the work on the quarters and making sure the units are ready. We need to get the job assignments finalized and the mess hall and laundry up and running."

Captain Carter nodded, her shoulders straightening almost imperceptibly at the note of authority in Clarissa's voice. "Yes, Major," she said crisply, her own gaze sharpening with renewed focus.

Clarissa allowed herself a small, fleeting smile. Carter was a good officer, steady and dependable and fiercely loyal to the women under her command. With her by her side, Clarissa knew that they could face whatever obstacles the war threw their way.

But even as the thought formed, a flicker of doubt crept in at the edges. A nagging whisper of uncertainty that she couldn't quite shake, no matter how hard she tried.

"Lord knows what mental and physical condition the women will be in when they arrive in Scotland," she said quietly, almost to herself. "We have to get Special Services immediately focused on morale."

It was a daunting prospect, and one that weighed heavily on Clarissa's mind. These women had already sacrificed so much, had endured hardships and indignities that most people couldn't even begin to imagine. And now, they were being asked to give even more. To march headlong into the teeth of the greatest conflict the world had ever seen, to put their lives on the line for a country that had never truly valued them as equals.

The least Clarissa could do was to make sure that they had every possible support, every small comfort and convenience that could be scrounged or improvised in this bleak and war-torn landscape. And that started with the basics - a warm bed, a hot meal, and a chance to feel human again after the long, grueling journey across the Atlantic.

Captain Carter cleared her throat, breaking the silence that had settled over the room like a shroud. "It would have been nice to have the beauty parlor up and going," she said wistfully, "but I'm being told there are no provisions for the equipment."

Clarissa felt a flare of irritation at that, a hot, prickling sensation that crawled up the back of her neck like a rash. It was just like the WAC, to nickel-and-dime them on even the smallest of creature comforts. As if a few curling irons and straightening combs were too much to ask, too frivolous a request for women who were risking their lives in service to their country.

But she tamped down on the anger, forced it back down into the pit of her stomach where it could simmer and stew without boiling over. There would be time enough later to rage against the machine, to fight for every scrap of dignity and respect that her women deserved. For now, she had to focus on the task at hand. On getting her troops settled and squared away, ready to take on whatever challenges the war threw their way.

"Make it happen," she said firmly, her gaze boring into Captain Carter's with unwavering intensity. "Even if we have to source it from the local market. The women need this."

Captain Carter nodded, a ghost of a smile tugging at the corners of her mouth. She reached up, patted her own carefully coiffed hair with a wry, self-deprecating chuckle.

"So do we," she said dryly, her eyes sparkling with a hint of mischief.

Despite herself, Clarissa felt an answering grin tug at her own lips. It was a small thing, a momentary flash of levity in the midst of so much grimness and uncertainty. But it was enough to remind her of why she was here. Of the bonds of sisterhood and solidarity that tied her to these women, that gave her the strength to keep pushing forward even when the way seemed dark and the road ahead impossibly steep.

But before she could savor the moment, the door to the office swung open with a bang. Major Greer strode in, her face set in a mask of cool, professional detachment that set Clarissa's teeth on edge.

"The General asked me to stop by to check-in," she said briskly, her gaze flicking over the cluttered desk and the two officers standing beside it with a hint of disdain. "My understanding is that your women are en route?"

Clarissa felt her spine stiffen, her chin lifting almost imperceptibly at the note of condescension in the other woman's voice. She had dealt with Greer's type before - the prim, proper sort who looked down their noses at the 6888th, who saw them as little more than a curiosity, a sideshow distraction from the real business of war.

But she wouldn't let it rattle her.

"That is correct," she said evenly, meeting the other woman's eyes with a steady, unflinching stare of her own. "They were delayed a bit, but now their ship is back on track."

Greer nodded, a flicker of something that might have been surprise or grudging respect ghosting across her features. "They arrive Monday," she said, glancing down at the sheaf of papers in her hand, "and the plan is for you to have them ready for inspection on Friday." She looked up, fixing Clarissa with a pointed look. "Please don't hesitate to reach out if there is anything I or my office can do to assist."

It was a polite offer, but Clarissa could hear the unspoken challenge beneath the words. The subtle implication that she and her women were in over their heads, that they would need all the help they could get just to keep from drowning in the turbulent waters of this strange and hostile land.

But Clarissa had never been one to back down from a challenge. And she certainly wasn't about to start now, with so much riding on the success of this mission.

So she simply nodded, a small, tight smile playing at the corners of her mouth. "We'll have them ready on Wednesday," she said firmly, her voice ringing out with quiet conviction.

Major Greer blinked, a flicker of surprise crossing her face before she could quite master it. "Wednesday?" she repeated, her brow furrowing in confusion.

Clarissa felt a thrill of satisfaction at the other woman's reaction, a small, fierce surge of pride in her own audacity. "Yes, Major," she said calmly, holding Greer's gaze with unwavering intensity. "Wednesday."

For a moment, the two women simply stared at each other, a silent battle of wills playing out in the cramped, dimly lit confines of the office. But then, almost imperceptibly, something in Major Greer's expression shifted. A flicker of grudging respect, perhaps, or maybe just a hint of wariness at the steel in Clarissa's voice.

"I'll make arrangements," she said at last, her tone carefully neutral. And with a final, curt nod, she turned on her heel and strode out of the room, the door swinging shut behind her with a decisive click.

For a moment, silence reigned in the office, broken only by the faint, distant sounds of activity filtering in from the streets outside. And then, almost hesitantly, Captain Carter spoke.

"Wednesday?" she asked, her voice tinged with a hint of trepidation.

Clarissa turned to face her second-in-command, her jaw set with grim determination. "Let's make it happen," she said firmly, a note of challenge ringing out in her voice.

Because really, what choice did they have? The eyes of the world were on them now, watching and waiting to see if this bold experiment in racial and gender equality would succeed or fail. And Clarissa knew, with a bone-deep certainty, that failure was not an option.

They would show them all what the women of the 6888th were made of. They would prove, beyond a shadow of a doubt, that they were every bit as capable, every bit as competent and courageous, as any man who had ever worn the uniform.

And they would do it on their own terms. Not Friday, not when some white general deigned to give them his seal of approval. But Wednesday, on the schedule that they had set for themselves. The schedule that they would move heaven and earth to meet, no matter what obstacles or setbacks stood in their way.

It was a tall order, Clarissa knew. A challenge that would test them all to the very limits of their strength and endurance.

But they would rise to meet it. They had to. For themselves, for each other, and for all the women who would come after them. The ones who would look back on this moment, on this ragtag band of sisters who had dared to dream of a different world and know that anything was possible.

Clarissa felt a fierce, unshakable pride swell up in her chest at the thought. A sense of purpose and destiny that burned like a flame, bright and hot and unstoppable.

They were the 6888th. And they would show the world what they were made of. One way or another, come hell or high water.

They would make it happen.

CHAPTER 33:
SAMMY

Sammy practically bounced on her toes as she entered the barracks, her eyes wide with excitement. A new place, new friends, new adventures - it was almost too much for her country girl heart to take. She had never been this far from home before, had never even dreamed of setting foot on foreign soil. But now, here she was, a real-life WAC in the middle of England. It was like something out of a storybook.

She glanced around the cramped, dingy room, taking in the rows of narrow cots and battered footlockers. It wasn't exactly the Ritz, that was for sure. But to Sammy, it might as well have been a palace. Because it was hers, a space that belonged to her and her alone, a place where she could be more than just little Sammy Love Bonnet from Alabammy.

Her eyes lit up as she spotted a familiar face – Cleopatra. She hugged her with excitement. "Yay, we get to bunk together."

Before Cleopatra could respond, another woman entered the barracks, her green duffel bag slung over one shoulder. She was pretty, Sammy noted, with smooth brown skin and intelligent eyes that seemed to take in everything at once.

"I remember you from Ft. Oglethorpe. Do you remember me?"

Paige laughed. "No one could forget you Sammy."

Sammy watched, curious, as Paige began to unpack her things. She didn't have much - a few changes of clothes, a small stack of books, a handful of toiletries. But what caught Sammy's eye was the framed photograph that emerged from the depths of the bag, the glass gleaming in the dim light.

"Who is that?" she asked, unable to contain her curiosity.

Paige glanced down at the picture, a soft smile playing at the corners of her mouth. "That's my son, Joseph," she said, her voice warm with affection. "We call him Joe."

Sammy leaned in for a closer look, her eyes widening in appreciation. The boy in the photo was handsome, no doubt about that. Smooth skin, bright eyes, a jaw that looked like it could cut glass. He was the kind of boy that would have had all the girls back home giggling behind their hands and batting their eyelashes.

"He sure is handsome," she said aloud, a note of wistfulness creeping into her voice. "We didn't have any men like that in my hometown."

Cleopatra snorted, shooting her a wry look. "Did you have any men at all?" she teased. "Didn't you say the population was ten?"

Sammy rolled her eyes, swatting at the other girl playfully. "Of course we had men," she said, a hint of defensiveness creeping into her tone. "Well, there were my brothers, Danny and Rammy. They don't count though. They are my brothers after all. And then there was--"

"Your brother's name is Rammy?" Paige interrupted, a hint of disbelief in her voice.

Sammy grinned, unabashed. "Well actually it's Raymond," she explained, "but everybody likes to call him Rammy because it kinda rhymes with Sammy and Danny."

Cleopatra shook her head, a smile tugging at the corners of her mouth. "Little Sammy from Alabammy," she sing-songed, her voice rich with amusement. "You sho'll is country."

Sammy put her hands on her hips, mock-glaring at the other girl. "I know you ain't talking about somebody's name, Cleopatra," she shot back, trying and failing to keep a straight face.

Cleopatra just laughed, tossing her head with a playful flourish. "My mother must have known that I was going to be an artist," she declared dramatically. "That's why she gave me a fancy name."

Paige looked up from her unpacking, curiosity flickering in her eyes. "What kind of artist are you?" she asked.

"I'm an actress," Cleopatra replied, as if it were the most obvious thing in the world. "Of course."

Paige raised an eyebrow, a hint of skepticism in her voice. "What was your real job?"

Cleopatra drew herself up to her full height, a look of affronted dignity on her face. "Being an actress is a real job," she sniffed, her tone as prim as a schoolmarm's.

Paige held up her hands in a placating gesture, a smile tugging at the corners of her mouth. "Alright," she conceded. "I was a seamstress."

"Why'd you sign up?" Sammy asked, plopping down on the edge of her cot.

Paige was quiet for a moment, her gaze drifting back to the photograph of her son. "I wanted to make a better life for myself and my son," she said at last, her voice soft but determined.

Sammy glanced down at the picture again, noting the strong, sure set of Joe's shoulders, the hint of a man peeking out from behind the boyish features. "Your son looks pretty grown already in this picture," she observed.

"He's seventeen," Paige replied, a note of pride in her voice.

Sammy's eyes widened, a look of surprise flashing across her face. "And you just left him?" she blurted out, before she could stop herself.

Paige's expression tightened, a flicker of pain dancing behind her eyes. "He wasn't too happy about it," she admitted quietly. "But I want to be able to do better for him. Send him to college."

Sammy nodded slowly, a thoughtful look on her face. "I might go to college too when I get out," she mused. "They say the G.I. Bill will pay for it."

"That is what they say," Paige agreed, a hint of wistfulness in her voice. "When I saw they were recruiting, I went to sign up and the man told me they weren't taking any Negroes. I told him, it says right here you are. He sent me away. I had to go two towns over just to sign up."

Sammy felt a flare of indignation at that, a hot, prickling sensation crawling up the back of her neck. It wasn't right, the way they treated colored folks. Like they were something less, something not quite human. But before she could give voice to her anger, something else caught her eye.

Cleopatra was unpacking her gear, and amidst the standard-issue uniforms and sensible shoes, Sammy spotted a flash of something bright and colorful. Wigs, she realized with a start. A whole slew of them, in every shade and style imaginable.

"You have more wigs than I thought," she said slowly, unable to keep the note of curiosity from her voice. "That's... curious."

Paige glanced over, a hint of amusement dancing in her eyes. "You know what they say about curiosity," she remarked dryly.

Sammy blinked, momentarily nonplussed. "What do they say?" she asked, a furrow appearing between her brows.

Paige and Cleopatra exchanged a look, their expressions caught somewhere between exasperation and affection. But Cleopatra just shrugged, a smile tugging at the corners of her mouth.

"I brought these wigs because I like to change up my look," she explained, running a hand over the glossy strands.

"I hear they are going to have a beauty parlor here," Sammy piped up, her eyes bright with excitement. "Major Dixon insisted."

Cleopatra nodded, a look of satisfaction on her face. "I like to switch my looks up," she said, "and I can't be fighting with 800 other women for a time to get my hair done."

Paige snorted, shaking her head. "I don't think you need to worry too much about looking good in a mail room full of women," she remarked dryly.

But Cleopatra just grinned, a mischievous glint in her eye. "You never know," she said breezily. "I might meet a handsome soldier or a nice Englishman. I need to be able to look gorgeous at a moment's notice."

Sammy's eyes widened, a look of surprise flashing across her face. "You would date an Englishman?" she asked, her voice hushed with something like awe.

"Of course I would," Cleopatra replied, as if it were the most natural thing in the world.

Sammy shook her head, a bemused expression on her face. "But aren't Englishmen white?" she asked, her brow furrowing in confusion.

Cleopatra just laughed, tossing her head back with a playful flourish. "Why yes," she drawled, her voice rich with amusement. "I believe they are."

Sammy was quiet for a moment, chewing on her bottom lip as she mulled that over. "I don't think I ever thought about dating a white man," she said at last, her voice thoughtful. "I'm looking for one strong, strapping Negro man."

Paige smiled, reaching over to pat Sammy's hand. "You have plenty of time for that," she said kindly.

But Cleopatra just grinned, a wicked gleam in her eye. "Stick with me, Sammy," she said, slinging an arm around the younger girl's shoulders. "I'll find you somebody. I should have plenty of opportunities to scope out the scenery in town as part of Special Services."

Paige raised an eyebrow, a hint of skepticism in her voice. "In other words," she remarked dryly, "you won't have to work very hard."

Sammy nodded, a look of excitement on her face. "I'm mail room," she said brightly.

"Me too," Paige added, with a small smile.

But Cleopatra just shook her head, a look of mock indignation on her face. "That could not be further from the truth," she declared. "Special Services is responsible for making sure that you all are happy while you are here. We have to organize social events, sports clubs, and artistic outlets. We are here to make sure you have something to do other than sorting mail."

Sammy nodded slowly, a thoughtful look on her face. "I guess I better start unpacking," she said at last, heaving herself up off the cot. "And find the showers."

Paige glanced up from her own unpacking, a hint of amusement dancing in her eyes. "Showers are outside in the courtyard from what I hear," she remarked.

Sammy's eyes widened, a look of dismay flashing across her face. "Outside?" she squeaked, her voice rising an octave. "I have to take a shower outside? It's freezing!"

Cleopatra just laughed, shaking her head. "You are in the WAC," she said, as if explaining something to a particularly slow child. "It's wartime, and you are a Negro. What did you think, they were going to put us up at the Ritz London?"

Before Sammy could formulate a response, the door to the barracks swung open. She glanced up, a welcoming smile already forming on her lips - only to freeze in place, her eyes widening in shock.

It was Sadie. Sammy had caught glimpses of her on the journey over, had seen the way she still kept to herself, never joining in with the other women's chatter and laughter.

But now, seeing her up close, Sammy felt a strange flutter in her chest. A sense of kinship, almost, despite the wary set to Sadie's shoulders and the guarded look in her eyes.

Beside her, Paige had gone still as well, a look of stunned recognition on her face. For a long, tense moment, the two women simply stared at each other, the air between them crackling with some unspoken history.

But Sammy, oblivious to the sudden tension in the room, simply bounded over to Sadie with a grin, throwing her arms around the startled woman in an exuberant hug.

"You're our fourth bunkmate?" she exclaimed, practically vibrating with excitement. "I was wondering who it was gonna be. I'm so happy it's you!"

Sadie stiffened in her embrace, her body rigid with surprise. But Sammy just hugged her tighter, undeterred by the other woman's obvious discomfort.

Sammy grinned, gesturing behind her at the other two women. "You know Cleopatra and Paige," she said. "I hope that bunk is alright. Since you weren't here, we went ahead and chose."

Sadie just nodded, her expression unreadable. "It's fine," she said shortly.

Undeterred by her brusque tone, Sammy forged ahead. "I'm assigned to the mailroom," she said. "So is Paige. Cleopatra is Special Services. Where are you?"

"Mailroom," Sadie replied, her gaze darting around the room as if searching for an escape route. "I need to find the toilets."

And with that, she set her bag down on the empty bunk and slipped out of the room, as quietly as she had come.

For a moment, the three women simply stared after her, a heavy silence settling over the barracks. Then Paige spoke, her voice tight with some unspoken emotion.

"I can't bunk with her," she said flatly, her gaze fixed on the door.

Cleopatra sighed, shaking her head. "I don't think you have much choice," she remarked, not unkindly.

Paige shot her a sharp look, her eyes narrowing. "You must have heard about her," she said, a note of accusation in her voice. "She's the one who's always looking at those devil worship cards."

Sammy frowned, a flicker of unease dancing in her stomach. She had heard the whispers about Sadie, the rumors that followed her like a dark cloud. Hoodoo woman, they called her. Witch.

But something in her rebelled at the thought, some stubborn, contrary part of her that refused to believe the worst of anyone. Especially not someone as sad and alone as Sadie seemed to be.

"I heard those cards can tell the future," she said slowly, a hint of wonder creeping into her voice.

Paige shot her a sharp look, her expression tight with disapproval. "I don't believe in that," she said firmly. "You best be advised to stay away from that, and from her. That's the devil's work."

Sammy bit her lip, a furrow appearing between her brows. "You really believe that?" she asked, a note of uncertainty in her voice.

Paige nodded, her expression grim. "My mama was Methodist and daddy was Baptist," she said, as if that explained everything. "So we went to both churches, every Sunday. I know what the Bible says."

But Cleopatra just shrugged, a hint of amusement dancing in her eyes. "Ain't nothing wrong with fortune tellers," she remarked, leaning back against her pillow. "We had one down the street from us who my mama used to visit from time to time. She was a healer too. She could tell you all kinds of herbs to use. It goes all the way back to Africa."

Paige shot her a sharp look, her expression tight with disapproval. "She can put a root on you too," she said darkly. "That ain't nothing but witchcraft - hoodoo, voodoo, whatever you want to call it. I've got to get out of this room."

As if on cue, the door swung open and Sadie slipped back inside, catching the tail end of the conversation. For a moment, she simply stood there, her expression unreadable as she took in the tension crackling in the air.

Then she spoke, her voice soft but unflinching. "I'm sure your oils will protect you," she said evenly, holding Paige's gaze with her own.

Paige stiffened, her eyes flashing with something like fear. But before she could respond, Sammy piped up, unable to contain her curiosity any longer.

"Is it true that you are the hoodoo woman?" she blurted out, her eyes wide with a mix of apprehension and fascination.

"Sammy!" Cleopatra chided, shooting her a disapproving look.

But Sammy was undeterred. "Well, is it?" she pressed, leaning forward eagerly.

Paige shook her head, her expression tight with disgust. "I'm going to find the showers," she announced, gathering up her toiletries.

"I'll come with you," Cleopatra said quickly, shooting Sammy a warning glance as she followed Paige out of the room.

Left alone with Sadie, Sammy suddenly felt a flicker of uncertainty. Maybe she had overstepped, pried into things that were none of her business. But before she could apologize, her gaze fell on the wooden box sitting on Sadie's bunk.

Unable to help herself, she reached out to pick it up - only to have Sadie snatch it away, her eyes flashing with something like panic.

"Don't touch this," she said sharply, her voice tight with emotion.

Sammy blinked, taken aback by the other woman's vehemence. "I was just wondering what was inside of it," she said slowly, a hint of apology in her tone.

Sadie's jaw clenched, her knuckles white where they gripped the box. "I don't like people touching my things," she said, her voice low and measured. "Especially this."

Sammy bit her lip, a furrow appearing between her brows. "What's in it?" she asked, unable to contain her curiosity. "Some hoodoo or conjure spell stuff?"

Sadie's eyes flashed, a hint of anger sparking in their depths. "It's personal," she said shortly, setting the box back down on her bunk with a definitive thud.

Sammy held up her hands, a placating gesture. "Alright," she said softly, taking a step back. "I'm sorry. I didn't mean to pry."

For a moment, Sadie simply stared at her, her expression unreadable. Then, almost imperceptibly, her shoulders relaxed. "It's alright," she said quietly.

Sammy nodded, a small smile tugging at the corners of her mouth. "You really saved me on the boat with that ginger," she said, changing the subject. "I didn't get to thank you."

Something flickered in Sadie's eyes at that, a hint of warmth behind the wariness. "In a way, you saved me too," she said softly, almost to herself.

Sammy blinked, unsure what to make of that. But before she could ask, Sadie's gaze fell on the framed photograph sitting on Paige's bunk.

"Who is this?" she asked, picking it up to study the handsome young man in the image.

"That's Paige's boy," Sammy replied, moving to stand beside her. "Isn't he handsome? I hope I find me a man as cute as he is one day."

Sadie glanced over at her, a hint of amusement playing around the corners of her mouth. "I'm sure you will," she said, something like fondness creeping into her voice.

Sammy's eyes widened, a spark of excitement kindling in her chest. "Really?" she exclaimed. "Do you see him in my future? What's he look like?"

But before Sadie could answer, a deafening noise began outside. Sammy yelped, her heart leaping into her throat as she instinctively ducked down, covering her head with her arms.

Around them, the walls shook and the windows rattled in their frames. Through the thin glass, Sammy could see the other women of the 6888th running for cover, their faces tight with fear.

Beside her, Sadie was perfectly still, her expression calm and unruffled as she watched Sammy scramble for her helmet with shaking hands. Another explosion boomed in the distance, closer this time, and Sammy let out a whimper of terror.

"What in the world was that?" she gasped, her voice thin and reedy with panic.

Sadie glanced over at her, her dark eyes unreadable. "That was a buzz bomb," she said evenly, as if discussing the weather. "No need to be scared. Unless one lands on us."

Sammy gaped at her, incredulous. How could she be so calm, so utterly unfazed in the face of such danger? But before she could ask, Sadie was standing up, gathering her toiletries.

"I'm going to take my shower," she announced, heading for the door.

Sammy stared after her, her mouth opening and closing like a fish out of water. "Is one going to land on us?" she called out, hating the tremor of fear in her voice.

But Sadie was already gone, disappeared into the chaos outside. Leaving Sammy alone in the barracks, trembling and wide-eyed, with nothing but the echoes of the explosions and the hammering of her own heart for company.

She huddled there on her bunk, knees drawn up to her chest, trying desperately to slow her breathing. She thought of her daddy and her brothers back home in Alabama, of the way they used to tease her for being such a scaredy-cat. If they could see her now, shaking like a leaf at the first sign of trouble...

But then, unbidden, Sadie's face swam before her eyes. That calm, steady gaze, the quiet strength that seemed to radiate from every pore. If Sadie could face this with such unflinching courage, then surely Sammy could too. Surely she could find that same well of bravery within herself, that same unshakeable core.

Slowly, tentatively, she uncurled from her protective ball. Drew in a deep, shuddering breath, letting it out in a long, slow exhale. The explosions had stopped, she realized dimly. The world outside had gone quiet once more, as if holding its breath in the aftermath of the attack.

Sammy stood up, her legs shaky but holding. Took one step towards the door, then another. Out there, she knew, lay a whole new world of danger and uncertainty. A world where buzz bombs fell from the sky and the very ground beneath her feet could shatter at any moment.

She could do this. She would do this. And if that meant facing her fears head-on, staring down the barrel of her own terror until it blinked first?

Then that's exactly what Private Sammy Love Bonnet would do. With a little help from her friends, and a whole lot of stubborn, bullheaded courage.

Watch out, Hitler, she thought fiercely, squaring her shoulders as she marched towards the showers. The women of the Six Triple Eight had arrived.

And they weren't going anywhere until the job was done.

CHAPTER 34:
PAIGE

P aige stood ramrod straight in formation, her heart swelling with a fierce, defiant pride as she marched through the streets of Birmingham, England. All around her, the women of the 6888th moved in perfect unison, their faces set with grim determination beneath their smartly cocked caps.

To her left, Sadie marched as if in a trance, eyes fixed straight ahead, a muscle working in her jaw. And just past her, Sammy was practically vibrating with barely contained glee, a huge grin splitting her face as she drank in the cheering crowds and fluttering flags.

Paige couldn't blame her. There was something intoxicating about this moment, something that made the blood sing in her veins and her shoulders straighten with purpose. Here they were, 855 strong, the first all-Black, all-female battalion to serve overseas. Marching tall and proud beneath the pale English sun, claiming their place in history with every crisp, unified step.

It was a heady feeling, almost dizzying in its intensity. For so long, Paige had fought and scraped and struggled just to be seen, to be acknowledged as a full and equal human being.

But now, striding through the heart of Birmingham with her sisters-in-arms, Paige felt a surge of something like triumph burning in her chest. A sense that maybe, just maybe, all those years of quiet, stubborn persistence had been worth it. That the seeds she had planted in the rocky soil of a world that had never wanted her might finally be starting to take root and grow.

She risked a glance over at Major Dixon. The Major's face was a mask of steely composure, but Paige could see the glimmer of fierce, unfettered joy in her eyes. The knowledge that she had done something remarkable here, something that would echo through the ages long after they were all dust and memory.

Beside the Major, General Leach and his entourage looked on with expressions of grudging respect, their stiff-backed postures and crisply pressed uniforms a stark contrast to the jubilant chaos of the crowd. Paige felt a flicker of satisfaction at the sight of the white WAC Major standing just behind them, her face pinched and sour as she watched Major Dixon accept the general's enthusiastic handshake.

Good, Paige thought fiercely. Let her see what colored women could do when given half a chance. Let her choke on the bile of her own prejudice and small-mindedness.

The parade seemed to last both an eternity and no time at all, a blur of waving hands and beaming faces and the steady, rhythmic pounding of 855 pairs of feet against the cobblestones. And then, almost before Paige could blink, it was over.

But the glow of pride and purpose lingered, a warm, steady flame in Paige's chest as she fell out of formation and followed her fellow WACs back to the converted school that served as their barracks and headquarters.

There was still work to be done, she knew. Miles to go before they could rest on their laurels and call their mission accomplished. Even now, as they traded their dress uniforms for the drab, functional skirts and blouses of the mailroom, Paige could feel the weight of all those waiting letters settling back onto her shoulders like a tangible thing.

But there was a new spring in her step as she took her place at the sorting table, a new determination thrumming in her blood. They had shown the world what they were made of today, had carved out a space for themselves in the annals of history. Now it was time to prove that they could live up to that legacy, could shoulder the burdens and responsibilities of their post with grace and grit and unwavering resolve.

Beside her, Sadie and Sammy fell into their seats, reviewing the stacks of envelopes and parcels. But even as they worked, Paige could feel the tension crackling between her and Sadie like a living thing, the weight of all their tangled history and unspoken hurts hanging heavy in the air.

It had been like this ever since that first day in the barracks, when Sadie had walked in and set Paige's whole world tilting on its axis. The simmering knot of suspicion and distrust, the bone-deep conviction that there was something not quite right about the strangeness coiled beneath Sadie's skin.

Paige was startled out of her thoughts by the sound of Sammy's voice, bright and irrepressible as always. "Three months!" she exclaimed, shaking her head in wonder. "She must be out of her mind."

Paige glanced up sharply, a frown tugging at the corners of her mouth. "Shh," she admonished, shooting a warning glance at the other women hunched over their own sorting tables. "You can't say things like that out loud about Major Dixon, you'll get in trouble."

Sammy rolled her eyes but lowered her voice to a conspiratorial whisper. "Alright," she conceded. "I won't say things like that out loud, I'll just think them in my head."

She held up a hand, waggling her fingers in Paige's face. "I've got paper cuts on top of paper cuts. I could go the rest of my life without seeing another letter."

Despite herself, Paige felt a smile tugging at the corners of her mouth. Trust Sammy to find the humor in even the most tedious of tasks, the most trying of circumstances. It was one of the things she loved most about the younger girl, that irrepressible spark of joy and mischief that seemed to light her up from within.

But the smile faded as her thoughts turned back to the towering stacks of mail still waiting to be sorted, the endless procession of names and addresses that blurred before her tired eyes. "I'd like to see a letter from Joe," she said quietly, a wistful note creeping into her voice.

Beside her, Sammy's face softened with sympathy. "You think he's still mad about you signing up?" she asked gently.

Paige sighed, her shoulders slumping minutely. "I hope one day he'll understand," she said, more to herself than to Sammy. "I hope he'll see that I did this for him, for us. That I wanted to be the kind of mother he could be proud of, the kind who fought for something bigger than herself."

Sammy was quiet for a moment, her brow furrowed in thought. Then she turned to Sadie, a hint of mischief sparking in her eyes. "What about you, Sadie?" she asked brightly. "You waiting on anybody to write you?"

Paige tensed, her fingers stilling on the envelope in her hand. She darted a glance at Sadie, saw the way the other woman's shoulders had gone rigid, her jaw clenching tight.

"No," Sadie said shortly, her voice flat and expressionless.

Sammy blinked, taken aback by the brusque response. "You ain't got nobody back home?" she pressed, a note of disbelief in her voice.

But Sadie just shook her head, her gaze never leaving the letter in her hand. And Paige felt a sudden, unexpected pang of sympathy, a sense of the yawning loneliness that seemed to emanate from every pore of Sadie's being.

What must it be like, she wondered, to have no one waiting for you on the other side of the ocean? No warm thoughts or loving prayers to buoy you up in the long, cold nights, no promise of reunion and reconciliation to light your way through the darkness?

But before she could pursue the thought further, Sammy changed the subject, her voice bright and chipper once more. "Why is it so cold in here?" she asked, rubbing her arms theatrically. "Can't we get some more heat? Now I've got goosebumps on top of my paper cuts."

She squinted down at the letter in her hand, holding it up to the dim light. "And it's so dim in here, I can hardly see. I'll be blind by the time I get home."

Paige shot her a quelling look, trying to ignore the answering shivers that raced down her own spine. "Stop complaining," she said firmly, more to herself than to Sammy.

But Sammy just shook her head, a hint of genuine frustration creeping into her voice. "How in the world are we supposed to get all this mail to the right place?" she asked, brandishing a handful of envelopes. "Look at this one. All it says is 'Sam, U.S. Army.' Sam who?"

She rifled through the stack, her frown deepening. "And look at this. I've come across a boatload of Robert Smiths. Robert A. Smith, Robert W. Smith, Robert B. Smith..."

"Alright," Paige cut her off, a hint of exasperation creeping into her tone. "We get it."

But even as the words left her mouth, the bell signaling the end of their shift rang out, loud and jarring in the cavernous space of the mailroom. All around them, women began to push back from their tables, stretching out cramped muscles and chattering eagerly as they prepared to head back to the barracks.

Sammy let out a whoop of relief, practically launching herself out of her chair. "Finally," she exclaimed, a grin splitting her face. "I didn't think this shift would ever end."

Paige followed more slowly, her movements stiff and deliberate as she gathered up her own stack of sorted letters. She glanced over at Sadie, saw that the other woman was making no move to leave, her head still bent over her work.

"Let's go," Paige said quietly, jerking her chin towards the door.

But Sammy, oblivious as always, turned back to Sadie with a hopeful smile. "You coming?" she asked brightly.

Paige felt a flare of irritation, a sudden, irrational urge to grab Sammy by the arm and drag her bodily from the room. "Let's go, Sammy," she said shortly, cutting off her friend's invitation with a pointed look.

For a moment, Sammy looked torn, her gaze darting uncertainly between Paige and Sadie. But then she shrugged, falling into step beside Paige as they made their way out of the mailroom and into the weak, watery sunlight outside.

Paige didn't look back, didn't allow herself to wonder what thoughts might be swirling behind Sadie's dark, inscrutable eyes as she watched them walk away. She just kept her head high and her shoulders straight, marching forward into the unknown future with all the stubborn, defiant determination she could muster.

CHAPTER 35:
SAMMY

Sammy practically skipped across the King Edward School campus, her cheeks flushed with excitement and the crisp English air. Beside her, Paige walked at a more sedate pace, her brow furrowed as if deep in thought. But Sammy barely noticed, her mind awhirl with a thousand thrilling possibilities.

She had done it. She had really, truly done it. Little Sammy Love Bonnet from Alabammy, marching in a parade in front of generals and dignitaries, sorting mail for the brave boys fighting for freedom overseas. It was like something out of a dream, a fairy tale come to life.

And now, as she drank in the bustle and energy of the base around her, Sammy felt a swell of pride and purpose rising up in her chest. She was a part of something bigger now, something important and meaningful and real. And nothing, not even the ache of homesickness or the bone-deep weariness of long shifts in the mailroom, could dim the glow of that feeling.

Lost in her reverie, Sammy almost didn't notice Cleopatra walking towards them, a tall, handsome soldier by her side. But as they drew closer, she felt her steps falter, her breath catching in her throat.

It was him. The man from her dreams, the one she had been waiting for all her life. She knew it with a certainty that defied reason or explanation, a bone-deep recognition that sent tingles racing down her spine.

"My future," she breathed, grabbing Paige's arm in a vise-like grip.

Paige glanced over at her, confusion wrinkling her brow. "What?"

Sammy nodded towards the approaching pair, her eyes wide and shining. "That man with Cleo," she whispered, her voice trembling with excitement. "I think he's my future. I gotta ask Sadie if he's my future."

Paige snorted, shaking her head. "Stop talking crazy," she said firmly. "Hush that mess."

But Sammy barely heard her, too caught up in the wild, giddy rush of her own emotions. As Cleopatra and the soldier reached them, she felt her heart kick into overdrive, hammering against her ribs like a caged bird.

"I've been looking for you," Cleopatra said, a mischievous glint in her eye. "Ladies, I would like to introduce you to Private Otis Louis McGhee."

The soldier smiled, a slow, easy grin that made Sammy's knees go weak. "You can just call me Otis," he said, his voice rich and warm as honey.

Sammy swallowed hard, trying to find her voice. "Nice to meet you, Otis," she managed, sticking out her hand. "I'm Sammy. Sammy Love Bonnet. Miss Sammy Love Bonnet."

Otis took her hand, his calluses rough and warm against her skin. "Pleasure to meet you," he said, his eyes crinkling at the corners.

Sammy felt a blush rising up her neck, threatening to engulf her face in flames. She dropped Otis's hand like a hot coal, turning to gesture towards Paige. "Oh, and this is Paige," she said quickly, trying to cover her fluster.

Paige just nodded in greeting, her expression unreadable. But Otis barely seemed to notice, his gaze still fixed on Sammy.

"Yes, Cleopatra was telling me about you all on the walk over here," he said, a hint of amusement in his voice.

Sammy shot a glance at Cleopatra, her brow furrowing. The other woman just grinned, slinging an arm around Otis's shoulders.

"Otis here is going to be bringing over the mail addressed to us," she said breezily. "We got to talking and his people are related to my people, which means we're practically cousins."

Sammy's heart sank at that, a leaden weight dropping into the pit of her stomach. She leaned in close to Cleopatra, her voice a hoarse whisper. "So that means you ain't trying to date him?" she asked, a pleading note creeping into her tone.

Cleopatra just laughed, shaking her head. "Anywho," she said, waving a dismissive hand. "He has a problem and I told him that we could talk to my friends in the mailroom to see if y'all could help him."

Paige sighed, rubbing her arms against the chill. "Cleopatra, it's freezing out here," she said, a hint of impatience in her voice.

But Cleopatra just waved her off, turning to Otis with an encouraging smile. "This will only take a second," she said. "Otis darling, tell them your problem."

Otis shuffled his feet, looking suddenly uncertain. "Well, I'm from Laurel, Mississippi," he began, his voice hesitant.

Sammy perked up at that, a grin splitting her face. "I'm from Alabama!" she exclaimed, bouncing on her toes.

Otis shot her a quick smile before continuing. "Well, I wrote my girl back in Laurel a letter asking her to be my wife," he said, his brow furrowing.

Sammy felt her heart plummet, a cold, sinking feeling washing over her. "Oh," she said softly, her voice barely above a whisper. "You're engaged."

But Otis just shook his head, a rueful smile tugging at his lips. "Well see, that's my problem," he said. "I don't know if I'm engaged or not. I wrote the letter ages ago and ain't got no response yet. Her letters are probably sitting somewhere in those piles."

He sighed, running a hand over his close-cropped hair. "I just can't think straight not knowing if I'm engaged or not," he admitted. "Heck, I don't even know if she's still waiting on me. She might have a new fella for all I know."

Paige frowned, her brow creasing in thought. "Why don't you just write her again?" she asked, as if it were the most obvious thing in the world.

But Otis just shook his head, a hint of frustration creeping into his voice. "I wrote to her three times asking her," he said. "I ain't got a response. A man can only ask so many times."

Cleopatra nodded, a look of sympathy on her face. "So I told Otis that y'all would be on the lookout for mail addressed to him," she said, turning to Sammy and Paige. "And that you would get it to him right away if you run across it."

Paige's eyes widened, a look of disbelief flashing across her face. "Do you know how much mail is waiting to be sorted?" she asked incredulously. "What are the odds one of us will find it?"

But Cleopatra just shrugged, a hint of mischief dancing in her eyes. "I know the odds are small," she admitted. "But here, I had him write down his information."

She held out a slip of paper, waving it enticingly in front of Sammy's face. Sammy snatched it up eagerly, clutching it to her chest like a precious treasure.

"You can count on me to be on the lookout," she said fervently, her voice ringing with conviction.

Otis's face softened, a look of gratitude shining in his eyes. "You don't know how much this means to me," he said quietly. "I'm much obliged."

He glanced around at the shivering women, a hint of concern creasing his brow. "Well, I'll let you get out of the cold," he said, taking a step back.

But before he could leave, Paige spoke up, a look of curiosity on her face. "So we have mail here now for us?" she asked, turning to Cleopatra.

Cleopatra grinned, a sparkle of excitement in her eyes. "It's being sorted as we speak," she said. "And just you wait, Special Services is also working on another surprise."

Sammy's eyes widened, her heart leaping in her chest. "Is it the beauty parlor?" she asked breathlessly. "Has all the equipment come in? I hate not looking my best."

Otis glanced over at her, a shy smile playing around the corners of his mouth. "If you don't mind me saying so," he said softly, "I think you look mighty nice."

Sammy felt a blush rising up her neck, a warm, fluttery feeling spreading through her chest. "No," she said, ducking her head. "I don't mind you saying so."

Cleopatra just laughed, shaking her head. "No, it's not the beauty parlor," she said. "We're working on it. I'll tell you later. Ta-ta!"

And with that, she looped her arm through Otis's and started off across the campus, leaving Sammy and Paige staring after them.

For a long moment, Sammy just stood there, her gaze fixed on Otis's retreating back. She felt like she was floating, like her feet might lift right off the ground at any moment and carry her up into the pale English sky.

Because even though she had only just met him, even though she knew next to nothing about him beyond his name and his hometown, Sammy was certain of one thing.

Otis Louis McGhee was her future. Her destiny. The man she had been waiting for all her life, even if she hadn't known it until that very moment.

And as Paige tugged on her arm, leading her back towards the barracks with a look of fond exasperation on her face, Sammy couldn't keep the grin from spreading across her cheeks.

She had a mission now. A purpose that went beyond sorting mail and marching in parades, beyond proving herself worthy of her uniform and her country.

She was going to find that letter. The one that held the key to Otis's heart, the answer to the question that had been haunting him for so long.

And when she did, when she placed that precious piece of paper into his waiting hands and watched the joy and relief bloom across his face...

Well. Sammy had a feeling that would be a moment worth waiting for. Worth fighting for, with every ounce of stubborn, bullheaded determination she possessed.

Because if there was one thing Sammy Love Bonnet knew how to do, it was fight for what she wanted. And right now, more than anything in the world, she wanted Otis Louis McGhee.

CHAPTER 36:
NATHAN

Nathan sat across from Thurgood Marshall, the weight of the verdict hanging heavy in the air between them. Fifteen years hard labor. The words echoed in his mind, a grim, inescapable refrain. It was a sentence that would break lesser men, that would grind them down to dust and ashes beneath the pitiless heel of military justice.

But Nathan knew the men of Port Chicago. Knew the strength and resilience that had carried them through the long, dark days of waiting, the endless hours of uncertainty and dread. They would endure this, too. Would come out the other side battered and scarred, but with their heads held high and their spirits unbroken.

Still, the thought of them suffering, of wasting away in some godforsaken labor camp while the world moved on without them...it was almost more than Nathan could bear. He clenched his fists beneath the table, feeling the familiar surge of anger and helplessness rising up in his throat.

But Thurgood just leaned back in his chair, his eyes glinting with a fierce, determined light. "We're not going to let that happen to them," he said firmly, his voice ringing with conviction. "We're still fighting. How can I help you?"

Nathan blinked, taken aback by the question. He had come here seeking answers, seeking some way to make sense of the senseless tragedy that had upended his life and the lives of so many others. But he hadn't expected Thurgood to turn the tables on him, to offer his own aid and support.

For a moment, he simply sat there, his mind racing as he tried to formulate a response. What did he want? What could possibly ease the ache in his chest, the gnawing sense of loss and longing that had dogged his every step since that fateful night on the pier?

And then, in a flash of sudden clarity, he knew. Knew with a bone-deep certainty that there was only one thing that could bring him peace, one way to honor the memory of the man who had been closer to him than a brother.

"I need you to help me get assigned overseas," he said, the words tumbling out in a rush.

Thurgood's eyebrows shot up, surprise and confusion warring on his face. "Overseas?" he repeated, as if unsure he had heard correctly. "Why?"

Nathan took a deep breath, steeling himself against the pain that always came with speaking Andrew's name aloud. "I have something I need to deliver," he said quietly, his hand drifting unconsciously to the breast pocket of his uniform. "A letter. From my friend Andrew, to his wife Sadie."

Understanding dawned in Thurgood's eyes, followed quickly by a flash of sympathy. He leaned forward, his expression softening. "I see," he said gently. "And you feel like you need to do this in person?"

Nathan nodded, a lump rising in his throat. "I do," he said hoarsely, blinking back the sudden sting of tears. "I can't explain it, but...it feels important. Like it's the last thing I can do for him, the only way to make things right."

He looked up at Thurgood, his gaze pleading. "I know it's a lot to ask," he said, his voice cracking slightly. "But I'm begging you. Help me find a way to get to her. To look her in the eye and tell her how much he loved her, how he never stopped fighting to get back to her."

For a long moment, Thurgood simply studied him, his gaze thoughtful and assessing. Then, slowly, he nodded. "Alright," he said quietly, a note of respect creeping into his voice. "I can't make any promises. But I'll do what I can to get you assigned to a unit heading to Europe."

Relief crashed over Nathan like a wave, so strong it nearly knocked him backwards in his chair. He closed his eyes, feeling the hot prickle of tears gathering behind his lids. "Thank you," he whispered, his voice choked with emotion. "Thank you."

Thurgood just waved a dismissive hand, his face creasing into a small, knowing smile. "Don't thank me yet," he said wryly. "The Army has a way of throwing a wrench into even the best-laid plans. But I'll pull what strings I can, call in what favors I'm owed. We'll get you there, one way or another."

Nathan nodded, a fierce, determined light kindling in his chest. He would get there. Would move heaven and earth and every stubborn, bureaucratic obstacle in his path to make it happen. For Andrew. For Sadie. For the chance to bring some small measure of peace to the two people who had meant more to him than anyone else in the world.

And as he rose to leave, his hand clasped tight in Thurgood's firm, reassuring grip, Nathan felt a flicker of something like hope stirring in his chest. A sense that maybe, just maybe, there was still some good left in the world. Still some shred of justice and humanity that even the darkest of times couldn't snuff out completely.

He would hold onto that hope, he vowed silently. Would cling to it with every ounce of strength and resolve he possessed, through whatever trials and travails lay ahead.

Because he owed it to Andrew. To the brave, beautiful soul who had taught him the meaning of brotherhood, of sacrifice and unwavering loyalty.

And he owed it to himself. To the man he wanted to be, the man he knew he could become, if only he had the courage to take that first, faltering step.

Towards healing. Towards wholeness. Towards a future that held more than just pain and loss and the endless, aching absence of what might have been.

It was a long road, he knew. A hard and lonely one, fraught with uncertainty and doubt.

But as Nathan squared his shoulders and stepped out into the bright, beckoning sunlight, he felt a surge of something like peace washing over him. A quiet, unshakable conviction that he was exactly where he was meant to be, doing exactly what he was meant to do.

For Andrew. For Sadie. And for the small, stubborn spark of hope that refused to be extinguished, no matter how dark the night or how fierce the storm.

He would carry that hope with him, wherever the winds of fate might blow. A talisman against despair, a reminder of all that he had lost and all that he still had left to fight for.

And in the end, maybe that would be enough. Enough to see him through, to guide him home to the ones he loved and the peace he so desperately craved.

It was a slim chance. A fragile dream, as delicate and insubstantial as a wisp of smoke on the breeze.

But it was his. And for now, that was all that mattered.

CHAPTER 37:
MAJOR DIXON

Clarissa stood in the shadows of the mail room, watching with quiet satisfaction as her troops worked diligently into the night. The cavernous space was a hive of activity, a sea of bent heads and flying fingers illuminated by the harsh glare of overhead lamps. The air hummed with a palpable sense of purpose, of dedication to the vital task at hand.

Beside her, Captain Carter observed the scene with a similar air of contentment, her face softening with a rare smile. "They're really hitting their stride now, aren't they?" she murmured, her voice low and warm with pride.

Clarissa nodded, feeling a swell of emotion rising in her chest. These women, her women...they never ceased to amaze her. Day after day, they threw themselves into their work with a fervor and commitment that took her breath away. No matter how daunting the backlog or how grueling the hours, they met every challenge with grit and grace, their spirits indomitable.

"They certainly are," she agreed, letting a note of quiet wonder creep into her voice. "I knew they had it in them, but seeing it in action...it's something else entirely."

Captain Carter hummed in agreement, her gaze drifting over the sea of bent backs and flying fingers. For a moment, they simply stood there, drinking in the sight of their troops in full flow, marveling at the sheer scope of what they had accomplished in such a short time.

"Get some rest Captain Carter. I'll see you in the morning."

"Good night".

As Clarissa headed towards the exit, her eyes drifted to a movement in the small, forgotten hallway tucked away at the very back of the mail room, a narrow space that she had never even noticed before.

She crept closer, her footsteps echoing loudly in the stillness. And there, hunched over a small folding table, was Sadie. She was working by the light of a single flickering lantern, her face a mask of concentration as she sorted through a towering stack of envelopes.

For a moment, Clarissa simply stood there, drinking in the sight of her. The proud set of her shoulders, the graceful curve of her neck as she bent over her task. There was something almost reverent about the way she handled each letter, as if she could feel the weight of the words and emotions contained within.

But then, as if sensing her presence, Sadie's head snapped up. She leapt to her feet, snapping off a smart salute as she came to rigid attention.

"At ease," Clarissa said softly, fighting back a smile at the woman's obvious discomfort.

Sadie relaxed fractionally, but the wariness didn't quite leave her eyes. Clarissa took a step closer, her gaze sweeping over the clutter of envelopes and papers scattered across the table.

"What are you doing out here?" she asked, genuinely curious. "Didn't I see you working the day shift?"

Sadie ducked her head, a hint of color rising in her cheeks. "I don't sleep well, Major," she admitted, her voice barely above a whisper. "So I thought I would just keep working."

Clarissa felt a pang of sympathy at that, a flash of understanding. She knew all too well the demons that could haunt a soldier's dreams, the ghosts that crept in the moment the lights went out and the world grew still.

"Is there a problem with your bunk?" she asked gently, half-expecting Sadie to clam up or brush off the question.

But to her surprise, the private shook her head. "No, Major," she said simply, meeting Clarissa's gaze with a frankness that was almost unnerving.

Clarissa studied her for a long moment, taking in the shadows beneath her eyes and the taut line of her jaw. There was a story there, she knew. A history of pain and loss that went far beyond the simple rigors of military life.

But she also knew that it wasn't her place to pry. Not here, not now, with the weight of command heavy on her shoulders and the eyes of the world watching their every move.

So instead, she simply nodded, letting her gaze drift back to the stack of letters on the table. "Why are you out here alone?" she asked, genuinely curious.

Sadie hesitated for a moment, as if weighing her words carefully. Then, with a small, tentative shrug, she spoke. "I am taking the letters marked 'return to sender - deceased' and writing something more personal," she said quietly, her voice thick with some unspoken emotion.

Clarissa blinked, taken aback by the unexpected answer. In all of her service, she had never heard of anyone going to such lengths, taking on such a heartbreaking task of their own volition.

"Did someone instruct you to do that?" she asked, half-expecting to hear that some misguided superior had put Sadie up to it as a cruel joke or punishment.

But Sadie just shook her head, a flicker of defiance sparking in her dark eyes. "No, Major," she said firmly, her voice ringing with quiet conviction. "I just don't think that it should be returned marked 'return to sender - deceased'. Even if the person who gets the letter back knows their loved one has died, it's still a little cold to receive mail back with just that big black mark across it."

Clarissa felt something catch in her throat at that, a sudden, sharp ache blooming beneath her breastbone. She had seen those letters herself, had felt the weight of all that grief and loss like a physical thing. But never once had she considered the impact they might have on the ones left behind, the families and sweethearts waiting desperately for word from the front.

"That is a good observation," she managed at last, her voice rough with emotion. "As you were, Private."

And with that, she turned on her heel and strode away, her eyes burning and her heart thrumming a wild beat in her chest. She could feel Sadie's gaze on her back as she went, could sense the unspoken questions that hung in the air between them.

But she didn't look back. Couldn't bring herself to meet those dark, knowing eyes, to face the quiet strength and compassion that shone out of them like a beacon in the night.

Because in that moment, Clarissa knew that Sadie had seen right through her. Had glimpsed the chink in her armor, the tiny crack in the facade of cool, unflappable competence that she had worked so hard to cultivate.

And that knowledge terrified her more than any buzzbomb or artillery shell ever could. Because it meant that she was vulnerable. That beneath the starch and brass of her uniform, beneath the mantle of command that she wore like a second skin...she was just as human, just as fallible and fragile, as any of the women under her command.

It was a truth that she had always known, deep down. But one that she had never dared to acknowledge, even to herself.

Until now. Until a quiet, watchful private with a heart too big for her own good had shone a light into the darkest corners of her soul.

As she walked away from Sadie and back out into the clamor and chaos of the mail room, she couldn't shake the feeling that something had shifted between them. That some invisible line had been crossed, some unspoken understanding reached.

And though it terrified her, though it went against every instinct and training that had been drilled into her over the years...

Somehow, deep down, she knew that she would never be quite the same again.

CHAPTER 38:
SAMMY

Sammy practically skipped across the base, her heart fluttering in her chest like a caged bird. She couldn't keep the grin off her face as she spotted Otis climbing out of his army truck, his tall frame unfolding with the easy grace of a born soldier.

"Hey," she called out, bounding up to him with a wave.

Otis turned, his eyes crinkling at the corners as he smiled down at her. "Hey, Sammy."

Sammy felt a blush rising in her cheeks at the warmth in his voice, the way her name sounded like honey on his tongue. She ducked her head, suddenly shy.

"I just thought I'd check with you to see if you got your letter from Vera yet," she said, scuffing the toe of her boot against the ground.

Otis's smile faltered, a shadow passing over his face. "No, not yet," he said quietly.

Sammy's heart clenched at the disappointment in his voice, the wistful longing that he couldn't quite hide. She reached out impulsively, laying a hand on his arm.

"I promise to keep looking for it," she said earnestly, willing him to see the sincerity in her eyes.

Otis's gaze softened, his hand coming up to cover hers briefly. "Thank you," he murmured, his voice low and warm.

Sammy felt a tingle run down her spine at the contact, a shiver of something that wasn't quite excitement and wasn't quite fear. She swallowed hard, gathering her courage.

"I haven't had a chance to walk around town much yet," she said, aiming for a casual tone. "I was thinking if you're free tomorrow, maybe we could walk around together?"

Otis hesitated, a flicker of uncertainty crossing his face. Sammy's heart sank, sure she had overstepped. But then he smiled, slow and sweet, and nodded.

"Alright," he said, his eyes crinkling at the corners. "That sounds good. Meet you here around this time tomorrow?"

Sammy beamed, unable to contain her joy. "It's a date," she blurted out, before quickly correcting herself. "I mean, see you then."

Otis chuckled, shaking his head fondly. "I better get to it," he said, jerking his chin towards the waiting truck.

"Alright," Sammy said, stepping back reluctantly. "Bye."

She watched him walk away, his broad shoulders and narrow hips disappearing around the corner. As soon as he was out of sight, she let out a squeal of delight, spinning in a giddy circle.

"I gotta find that letter," she whispered to herself, a determined glint in her eye.

Sammy burst into the barracks, her cheeks flushed and her eyes bright with excitement. She couldn't wait to tell Sadie about her upcoming date with Otis, to get her take on whether this could be the start of something real.

But as she bounded over to Sadie's bunk, she pulled up short. The other woman was sitting cross-legged on her blanket, a worn deck of cards spread out before her. As soon as she caught sight of Sammy, she hastily swept the cards back into their box, a wary look stealing over her face.

Sammy felt a pang of hurt at the gesture, at the way Sadie seemed to close herself off whenever anyone got too close. She knew the other women whispered about Sadie's strangeness, the eerie knowing that seemed to lurk behind her dark eyes. But Sammy had never been one to put much stock in rumors.

She opened her mouth to say something, to try and draw Sadie out of her shell. But before she could get a word out, Paige came storming into the barracks, her face like a thundercloud.

She took one look at Sadie and the box clutched in her hands, and her lip curled in distaste. Without a word, she spun on her heel and marched back out, slamming the door behind her.

Sammy gaped after her, stunned by the open hostility in the other woman's demeanor. She turned back to Sadie, a question forming on her lips.

But Sadie just shook her head, her eyes shadowed and distant. "Leave it be," she murmured, so softly that Sammy had to strain to hear. "Some things are best left alone."

Sammy perched on the edge of Sadie's bunk, watching the other woman stare blankly at the ceiling. She barely seemed to register Sammy's presence, lost in some dark reverie that Sammy couldn't begin to fathom.

"I need your help, Sadie," Sammy said softly, breaking the heavy silence. "I need to know if Otis is the one."

She hugged her knees to her chest, rocking slightly as she spoke. "He's so smart and handsome. He says he's going back to school after the war to be a doctor. And he says things are going to be so much better in the U.S. when we get back, that they ain't going to be able to segregate us and treat us the way they do now, now that we've been part of the war."

Sadie let out a soft snort of derision, her lips twisting in a humorless smile. Sammy frowned, taken aback by the reaction.

"What, you don't think that's true?" she asked, a note of challenge creeping into her voice.

Sadie shrugged, her eyes sliding away from Sammy's. "I think white folks plan to treat us the same way they always have," she said quietly. "War or no war."

Sammy shook her head stubbornly, unwilling to let go of her newfound hope. "But folks over here don't treat us that way," she argued.

Sadie just sighed, a bone-deep weariness settling over her features. "Well, England ain't the United States," she said, her voice heavy with resignation. "When we get back, you'll find ain't much changed."

Sammy stared at her, a flicker of unease stirring in her gut. "Did the cards tell you that?" she asked hesitantly. "Or did you just see that in the future?"

Sadie's gaze sharpened, pinning Sammy in place. "Maybe you should be open to meeting somebody else. Didn't you say he's engaged?"

Sammy shifted uncomfortably, a flush rising in her cheeks. "We don't know if he's engaged or not," she mumbled. "Or do you?"

Sadie just looked at her, something like pity in her dark eyes. "It sounds like you may be setting yourself up for disappointment," she said gently.

Sammy felt a flare of irritation at the words, the implication that she was just some silly little girl chasing after an impossible dream. "Can't you just do the cards on me?" she demanded, a note of desperation creeping into her voice.

Sadie shook her head firmly, her jaw tightening. "Stop asking me," she said, an edge of steel beneath the softness of her voice.

Sammy bit her lip, fighting back the sudden sting of tears. "Can't you just tell me whether or not that girl back home said yes or no to his proposal?" she pleaded, hating the whine in her voice but unable to stop herself.

"No," Sadie said flatly, her gaze unwavering.

Sammy's eyes widened, a spark of hope flaring in her chest. "She said no?" she asked breathlessly, leaning forward eagerly.

But Sadie just turned away, her shoulders hunching as if to ward off a blow. "Don't you have something to do?" she muttered, a note of finality in her voice.

Sammy deflated, feeling suddenly foolish and small. But then her gaze fell on the carved wooden box sitting on Sadie's bunk, the one she always kept close by her side.

"What's in the box?" she asked, unable to contain her curiosity.

Sadie's head snapped up, her eyes flashing with something like anger. "I told you," she said tightly, "that's none of your concern. Just don't mess with it."

But Sammy couldn't let it go, the mystery of it niggling at her like a loose tooth. "Please, Sadie?" she wheedled, scooting closer on the bunk. "Folks say the reason you won't let nobody see what's in the box is that you don't want nobody knowing what you use in your spells. They say you probably got herbs and chicken blood and badger teeth and cat paws in there."

Sadie's lips thinned, her nostrils flaring with barely suppressed rage. "Don't believe everything you hear," she said coldly, her hands clenching into fists at her sides.

Sammy swallowed hard, a trickle of unease running down her spine. But she couldn't seem to stop herself, the words tumbling out of her in a nervous rush.

"Some say it's hoodoo and some say it's voodoo. Paige says it's plain old witchcraft and I need to keep my distance from you. Well, what is it?"

For a long moment, Sadie simply stared at her, something ancient and unfathomable in her dark eyes. Then, slowly, she began to speak, her voice low and distant as if pulled from some deep, forgotten place.

"I was born with a veil over my eyes," she said softly, her gaze turned inward. "My great-grandfather and grandmother were born with it too. It skipped over my mother."

She paused, a shadow passing over her face. "My mother died when I was eleven," she continued, her voice thickening with grief. "And I knew she was going to die."

As she spoke, Sammy's mind conjured up an image of a younger Sadie, her face streaked with tears as she knelt by her mother's coffin. She shivered, feeling suddenly cold despite the warmth of the barracks.

"We were out in the field picking berries," Sadie went on, her eyes distant and unfocused. "And all of a sudden, I saw her clear as day, lying there in that box. She died three days later."

She fell silent, her shoulders sagging as if under a great weight. "Ever since I was a little girl," she said finally, her voice barely above a whisper, "I just knew things. Could predict things, see spirits."

Sammy stared at her, a mix of awe and terror swirling in her gut. "I don't know what you want to call it," Sadie said, her gaze snapping back to Sammy's face. "It just is."

Sammy swallowed hard, her mouth suddenly dry as dust. "I don't think I ever met somebody born with a veil," she said faintly. "You always know when someone is going to die?"

Sadie shook her head, a flicker of pain crossing her features. "No, not always."

"You see spirits?" Sammy asked, her voice hushed with a mix of fear and fascination.

Sadie's eyes shuttered, something bleak and haunted lurking in their depths. "Not the ones I want to see," she said softly, almost to herself.

A chill ran down Sammy's spine at the words, a sense of something vast and unknowable brushing against her consciousness. "What does that mean?" she asked, her voice trembling slightly. "Have you seen any here? Have you seen any in our room?"

Sadie's gaze sharpened, pinning Sammy in place. "There's nothing to be afraid of," she said firmly, a note of reassurance in her voice. "Spirits don't want to harm you."

But Sammy couldn't let it go, the question burning on the tip of her tongue. "But have you seen one in our room?" she pressed, leaning forward intently.

For a long moment, Sadie simply looked at her, something inscrutable in her dark eyes. Then, without a word, she rolled over onto her side, turning her back to Sammy in clear dismissal.

Sammy sat there for a moment, stunned by the abrupt end to the conversation. But as the silence stretched on, heavy and oppressive, she felt a flicker of understanding dawn in her chest.

Sadie didn't want to talk about it. Didn't want to be pressed or prodded or pulled out of the shadows she cloaked herself in. And maybe, Sammy realized with a pang, that was okay. Maybe some mysteries were meant to stay buried, some secrets meant to be kept.

"I guess I'll catch you later," she said softly, pushing herself up off the bunk. She paused at the door, feeling suddenly awkward and uncertain. "Thank you," she said finally, her voice barely above a whisper. "For telling me all that."

Sadie didn't answer, didn't even move from her huddled position on the bed. But as Sammy slipped out of the barracks and into the watery English sunlight, she could have sworn she heard the other woman's voice, soft and mournful as a sigh on the wind.

"Please leave me alone," Sadie whispered, her words echoing in the stillness. "I can't help you."

Sammy felt a pang of sorrow at the broken plea, a sense of some great, unfathomable weight bearing down on the other woman's shoulders. But she knew, with a sudden, fierce certainty, that she couldn't give up on Sadie. Couldn't leave her to drown in the darkness that threatened to consume her.

Maybe it was foolish, maybe it was naive. But Sammy had never been one to back down from a challenge, to turn away from a friend in need.

And so she squared her shoulders and lifted her chin, a determined glint in her eye. She would find a way to help Sadie, to drag her out of the shadows and into the light. Even if it took every ounce of stubbornness and heart she possessed.

Because that was what friends did. They stood by each other, through thick and thin, through darkness and light.

And Sammy had a feeling that Sadie needed a friend now more than ever.

CHAPTER 39:
PAIGE

Paige hesitated at the entrance to the mess hall, her stomach twisting with a now-familiar mix of dread and longing. She knew Sadie would be in there, could feel the weight of the other woman's presence like a physical thing, an itch between her shoulder blades that she couldn't quite scratch.

Taking a deep breath, Paige squared her shoulders and stepped inside, Sammy chattering brightly at her side. She scanned the room, her gaze drawn inexorably to the back corner where Sadie stood, silent and watchful as always.

For a moment their eyes met, and Paige felt a jolt of something almost like recognition pass between them. A flicker of understanding, of shared pain and loss and the bone-deep weariness of carrying on in the face of it all.

But then Sadie looked away, her gaze shuttering, and the moment was gone. Paige felt a surge of irritation, her jaw clenching as she deliberately moved to the other side of the room, putting as much distance between herself and Sadie as possible.

She knew it was foolish, this stubborn avoidance, this refusal to even acknowledge the other woman's existence. But something in her recoiled at the thought of getting too close, of letting Sadie see the cracks and fissures in her carefully constructed armor.

Because Sadie saw too much, Paige thought bitterly. Those dark, fathomless eyes seemed to strip away all pretense, all the lies and half-truths that Paige told herself just to get through each day. And Paige couldn't bear the thought of being seen like that, of being known in all her brokenness and despair.

So she kept her distance, kept her walls up high and impenetrable. Even as some small, traitorous part of her yearned to reach out, to find solace in the understanding of someone who had walked through the same valley of shadows.

A hush fell over the room, and Paige looked up to see Cleopatra standing at the front, her face alight with a fierce, almost manic energy. She began to speak, her voice ringing out clear and strong in the stillness.

"I tell you yet again, Banquo's buried; he cannot come out one's grave. To bed, to bed; there's knocking at the gate. Come, come, come, come, give me your hand. What's done cannot be undone. To bed, to bed, to bed."

Paige frowned, the words tugging at some dim memory from her schoolgirl days. Shakespeare, she thought. Macbeth. But the scene was unfamiliar, the lines delivered with a raw, haunting intensity that sent shivers down her spine.

Cleopatra finished with a flourish, her chest heaving as she looked out over the sea of dumbfounded faces. For a long, awkward moment, no one moved or spoke, the silence stretching out like a physical thing.

Then Cleopatra grinned, a fierce, almost feral thing. "This is where you applaud," she said, her voice rich with amusement.

A spattering of uncertain applause broke out, the women exchanging confused glances as they clapped. Cleopatra just shook her head, a glimmer of mischief dancing in her eyes.

"Here's the sign-up sheet," she said, brandishing a clipboard. "We meet again Thursday."

She handed the sheet to the nearest woman and then sauntered over to where Paige stood with Sammy. She pulled Sadie over with her, her hips swaying with each step.

"What was that?" Sammy asked, her voice hushed with something like awe.

Cleopatra tossed her head, a satisfied smirk playing about her lips. "It was my monologue from when I did Shakespeare's Macbeth on Broadway."

Sammy's eyes went wide, her mouth dropping open in a perfect little "o" of surprise. "You were on Broadway?"

"Of course, darling," Cleopatra said, waving a dismissive hand. "I thought you knew that. I thought everyone knew that."

She leaned in conspiratorially, her voice dropping to a stage whisper. "Picture it. 1936, directed by Orson Welles himself. An all-Negro cast, and I was Lady Macbeth. Everyone called the production Voodoo Macbeth because it was set in Haiti."

Sammy turned to Sadie, bouncing on her toes with excitement. "Ooh, Sadie, I bet you would have liked that production!"

Paige saw Sadie flinch, something like pain flashing across her features before she quickly schooled her expression back into its usual mask of careful blankness.

Cleopatra didn't seem to notice, too caught up in her own theatrical reverie. "I have finally rounded up enough women to start a 6888 theater troupe," she declared, her eyes shining with fervor. "I had to give them an example of fine theatre, of course. Are you ladies going to sign up?"

A heavy silence greeted her words, Sadie and Sammy and Paige all carefully avoiding each other's gazes. Cleopatra huffed out an exasperated sigh, rolling her eyes heavenward.

"Forget you all," she muttered, shaking her head. Then her face lit up, a sly grin spreading across her lips. "Anyway, look what I snagged for you."

She reached into her pocket and drew out a battered envelope, holding it out to Paige with a flourish. Paige felt her heart stutter in her chest, her hand trembling as she reached out to take it.

"It's from Joe," she whispered, her voice cracking on her son's name.

Cleopatra nodded, her expression softening with something almost like sympathy. "I wanted to hand-deliver it so I could see your face," she said quietly.

Paige barely heard her, her fingers already scrabbling at the envelope's seal. She drew out the letter with shaking hands, her eyes eagerly drinking in the familiar slant of her son's handwriting.

"It's dated two months ago," she murmured, almost to herself. "'Hi, Ma...'"

As she read on, the world seemed to fall away, the mess hall fading into a distant blur. In her mind's eye she could see Joe as clearly as if he were standing right in front of her, his young face earnest and determined as he put pen to paper.

"I guess you have made it over to Europe by now," he wrote, his words filled with a quiet pride that brought tears to Paige's eyes. "Your letters have made me understand how hard of a decision it was for you to enlist. I know you didn't want to leave me, but you felt it was the best choice for our future."

Paige's heart clenched at that, a wave of guilt and longing crashing over her. She had agonized over the decision to join up, had lain awake night after night weighing her duty to her son against her desperate need to do something that mattered, to be part of something greater than herself.

In the end, the call to serve had won out, the fierce, unshakable conviction that this was what God had put her on this earth to do. But the separation from Joe had been a constant ache, a wound that never quite healed no matter how much time passed.

"I've been doing a lot of thinking," Joe continued, his words taking on a new urgency, "and I've decided it's time for me to make some decisions too. I begged Grandma not to write and tell you, because I wanted to tell you myself, when everything was official."

Paige's stomach dropped, a sudden, sick sense of foreboding washing over her. She knew what was coming, could feel it in her bones even before she read the next lines.

"But I can tell you now that I'm through with basic training. I've enlisted. I've joined the Army."

The world seemed to tilt on its axis, the ground shifting treacherously beneath Paige's feet. She swayed, bile rising in her throat as the full import of Joe's words sank in.

Her son, her baby boy, was going to war. Was putting himself in harm's way, risking his precious, irreplaceable life for a country that had never seen him as fully human. The cruel irony of it, the sheer, staggering unfairness, made Paige want to scream.

Dimly, she was aware of Cleopatra and Sammy hovering anxiously at her side, their faces creased with concern. But she couldn't seem to make herself respond, couldn't force the words past the lump in her throat.

All she could do was stand there, frozen and numb, as the letter fluttered from her nerveless fingers to the floor.

From the corner of her eye, she saw Sadie take a hesitant step forward, like she wanted to say something.

Paige did the only thing she could think of, the only thing that made sense in that moment of blinding, breathless panic.

She turned on her heel and fled, her footsteps echoing loudly in the sudden, ringing silence of the mess hall.

She ran until her lungs burned and her legs trembled, until the sobs tearing at her throat finally broke free in great, heaving gasps. And then she ran some more, as if she could outpace the fear and grief and helpless rage that consumed her, as if she could somehow leave the aching, yawning void of her son's absence behind.

But even as she stumbled blindly through the base, her vision blurred with tears, Paige knew it was futile. Knew that there was no escaping the cold, hard truth that had just upended her world, no outrunning the desolate knowledge that her child, her heart, was marching into the teeth of war.

All she could do was pray. Pray with every fiber of her being, every scrap of faith and desperate, clawing love she possessed.

Pray that somehow, against all odds and reason, her beautiful boy would come back to her. That he would survive the hell of combat, the senseless brutality of a world that cared nothing for the color of his skin or the humanity of his soul.

That he would live to see a brighter tomorrow, a future where his worth was measured not by the hue of his flesh but by the content of his character.

It was a slim hope, a fragile dream as delicate and insubstantial as a soap bubble. But it was all Paige had, the only light in the sudden, yawning darkness that threatened to swallow her whole.

And so, with shaking hands and a heart that felt like it might shatter at any moment, Paige clasped her hands together and lifted her tear-streaked face to the heavens.

And she prayed like she had never prayed before, with a fierce, unshakable conviction that could move mountains and part seas.

For her son. For herself. And for a world that might one day be worthy of them both.

CHAPTER 40:
CLEOPATRA

Cleopatra stretched languorously, a satisfied smile playing about her lips as she basked in the afterglow of her lovemaking with William. The hotel sheets were rumpled and damp beneath her bare skin, the air thick with the musky scent of sex and sweat.

"Well, that was nice," William murmured, his voice husky with spent passion.

Cleopatra arched an eyebrow, pushing herself up on one elbow to look down at him. "Nice?" she purred, a teasing lilt to her voice. "Is that the best you can do?"

William grinned, his hand coming up to cup her cheek as he pulled her down for a searing kiss. "That was amazing," he breathed against her lips, his eyes dark and heavy-lidded against his pale skin.

"Is that better?"

Cleopatra hummed in approval, nipping playfully at his bottom lip. "Much better," she agreed, her own voice low and throaty with desire.

They kissed again, slow and deep, savoring the warm slide of skin on skin. But even as her body responded, a coil of heat unfurling low in her belly, Cleopatra felt a flicker of unease stirring in her chest.

This was dangerous, what they were doing. Reckless and foolhardy and utterly, delectably forbidden. If anyone found out, if word got back to the brass...

She pulled away reluctantly, swinging her legs over the side of the bed. William made a sound of protest, his hand shooting out to catch her wrist.

"Where are you going?" he asked, a petulant note creeping into his voice.

Cleopatra sighed, reaching for her slip. "I'm leaving," she said quietly, not quite meeting his gaze.

William frowned, pushing himself up on his elbows. "I thought you were on pass until tomorrow?"

"I am," Cleopatra conceded, stepping into her skirt. "But I can't stay here."

"Why not?" William wheedled, his fingers skimming up her arm, leaving goosebumps in their wake. He tugged at her gently, trying to coax her back into the tangled sheets.

Cleopatra resisted, her jaw tightening with resolve. "I would be in so much trouble if I got caught in a hotel room with a man," she said firmly, shrugging off his touch.

William's eyes sparked with mischief, a slow grin spreading across his face. "Not to mention that I'm an officer," he drawled, waggling his eyebrows suggestively.

Cleopatra threw him a quelling look, fighting back the answering smile that tugged at her lips. "You are not making this any better," she informed him primly, fastening the buttons of her blouse with quick, efficient motions.

William rolled onto his back with a dramatic sigh, flinging one arm across his face. "I would be in trouble too," he pointed out, his voice muffled. "No fraternizing between officers and enlisted personnel."

Cleopatra snorted, perching on the edge of the bed to roll her stockings up her legs. "Something tells me I would be in more trouble than you," she muttered darkly.

William's hand on her thigh pulled her out of her brooding thoughts, his touch warm and insistent through the thin fabric of her skirt. "Stay," he murmured, his voice low and cajoling. "Just a little while longer."

Cleopatra hesitated, torn between desire and duty. It would be so easy to sink back into his arms, to lose herself in the simple, primal pleasure of his body moving against hers.

But the risks were too high, the potential consequences too dire. She couldn't afford to be reckless, not when so much was riding on her success in the 6888th.

With a sigh of regret, she disentangled herself from William's embrace and stood, smoothing her hair and straightening her uniform with brisk, economical movements.

William flopped back against the pillows with a groan of disappointment. But then his eyes lit up, a sudden spark of inspiration flaring to life. He reached for the camera on the bedside table, a slow, wicked grin spreading across his face.

"You're so beautiful," he murmured, his gaze raking over her with undisguised hunger. "Let me take your picture."

Cleopatra recoiled, a hot flush staining her cheeks. "No," she protested, crossing her arms over her chest. "I'm not decent."

William chuckled, low and warm. "It's just your face," he coaxed, his eyes twinkling with mirth. "I promise."

Before she could object further, he raised the camera and snapped a quick shot, the shutter clicking loudly in the charged silence.

Cleopatra glared at him, a reluctant smile tugging at the corners of her mouth. She held out her hand imperiously, wiggling her fingers in a "gimme" gesture.

"My turn," she declared, snatching the camera from his grasp.

William shook his head, an indulgent grin playing about his lips. "You don't know what you're doing," he teased, making no move to stop her.

Cleopatra lifted her chin, a gleam of challenge in her eye. "Teach me," she demanded, her voice ringing with conviction. "I'm serious. Teach me."

And to her surprise, he did. With patient hands and gentle guidance, he showed her how to frame a shot, how to adjust the focus and aperture to capture the play of light and shadow.

Cleopatra felt a thrill of excitement as the world came alive through the lens, the drab and dingy hotel room transformed into something beautiful, something worthy of committing to film.

It was a revelation, a glimpse of a whole new way of seeing. And as she moved around the room, snapping pictures of William in various states of dishevelment and undress, Cleopatra felt a fierce, unshakable joy blooming in her chest.

This, she realized with a start. This was what she had been searching for all her life, the thing that made her feel alive and electric and utterly, incandescently free.

Not the stage, with its bright lights and clamoring crowds. Not the heady rush of applause or the sweet, intoxicating taste of fame.

But this. The power to capture a moment, to freeze it in time and space and imbue it with meaning. The chance to tell a story, to shine a light on the beauty and pain and messy, glorious complexity of the human experience.

It was a revelation, a call to arms. And as Cleopatra finally set the camera aside and slipped out into the night, her heart was full to bursting with a wild, reckless sort of hope.

She would follow this path, wherever it led her. Would chase this newfound passion with everything she had, damn the risks and the naysayers and the narrow-minded fools who would stand in her way.

Because she was Cleopatra Laurier, dammit. And she would be heard, one way or another.

The thought kept her buoyed as she made her way back to base, her steps light and her head held high. She was still riding the crest of that giddy, effervescent joy when she pushed open the door to the barracks, ready to regale her bunkmates with tales of her latest conquest.

But the scene that greeted her stopped her dead in her tracks, the smile slipping from her face like water through a sieve.

Sadie and Paige were squared off in the middle of the room, tension crackling between them like a live wire. Sammy hovered uncertainly at the edges, her eyes wide and frightened in her pale face.

"I'm not playing with you," Paige gritted out, her voice tight with barely leashed fury. "Get that out of this room before I do it for you."

Sadie said nothing, just stared back at her with those fathomless, inscrutable eyes. But Cleopatra could see the way her hands shook, the white-knuckled grip she kept on the small wooden box cradled in her lap.

"What's going on?" she asked slowly, taking a cautious step into the room.

Three heads swiveled towards her, three pairs of eyes blinking owlishly in the sudden stillness.

"Cleo!" Sammy cried, relief breaking over her face like a sunrise. "Thank goodness you're here. Paige is trying to make Sadie get rid of her...her stuff."

She flapped a hand vaguely, her gaze darting nervously to the box in Sadie's lap. Cleopatra frowned, a prickle of unease running down her spine.

She knew about Sadie's...oddities, of course. Hard not to, living in such close quarters. She had seen the other woman hunched over her strange little rituals in the dead of night, had heard the whispers and sidelong glances that followed in her wake.

But she had never paid it much mind, had never seen the need to stick her nose in business that wasn't hers. Everyone had their own way of coping with the trials and tribulations of Army life, their own little quirks and superstitions to get them through the long, lonely nights.

Who was she to judge, really? She who spent her scant free hours pursuing her own forbidden passions, chasing dreams that most folks would call impossible at best and downright scandalous at worst?

No, Cleopatra decided, straightening her shoulders with a little shake. She wouldn't be party to this...this persecution, this small-minded crusade against a woman who had done nothing to hurt anyone.

"Now listen," she began, pitching her voice to carry over the rising tension in the room. "I think we all just need to take a deep breath and..."

But Paige cut her off with a sharp shake of her head, her eyes blazing with righteous fury.

"No," she spat, jabbing a finger toward the box in Sadie's lap. "I won't have that...that *witchcraft* under the same roof as me. It's an abomination in the eyes of the Lord."

Cleopatra opened her mouth to argue, to try and inject some measure of reason into the rapidly deteriorating situation. But before she could get a word in edgewise, Sammy piped up, her voice trembling with indignation.

"It's her room too," she insisted hotly, crossing her arms over her chest. "And if she wants to keep her animal parts and herbs and...and spells in that box, well that's her business."

Paige rounded on her with a snarl, looking for all the world like she wanted to shake the younger girl until her teeth rattled.

"Hush up!" she snapped, the color high in her cheeks. "You don't know what you're talking about. The Bible says..."

But Cleopatra had heard enough. With a muttered oath, she strode forward and planted herself squarely between Paige and Sadie, her arms spread wide as if to shield the smaller woman from view.

"That's enough," she said firmly, meeting Paige's furious gaze with a level one of her own. "I won't stand by and watch you bully someone for their beliefs. Sadie isn't hurting anyone. She's entitled to her privacy, same as the rest of us."

Paige sputtered, her mouth opening and closing like a landed fish. But Cleopatra just lifted her chin, a fierce light kindling in her dark eyes.

"Now I suggest you step back and mind your own damn business," she said coldly. "Before I give you a reason to pray for forgiveness."

For a long, tense moment, no one moved. No one even seemed to breathe, the air thick with the crackle of impending violence.

But then, miracle of miracles, Paige backed down. With a final, venomous glare in Sadie's direction, she spun on her heel and stalked over to her bunk, muttering darkly under her breath.

Cleopatra let out a slow, shuddering breath, feeling the adrenaline drain out of her in a dizzying rush. She turned to Sadie, half-expecting to see gratitude or relief shining out of those bottomless eyes.

But the other woman's face was a mask, as blank and unreadable as ever. She simply clutched her box closer to her chest, hunching in on herself like a turtle retreating into its shell.

And as she watched Sadie slip silently out of the barracks, her shoulders hunched and her head bowed, Cleopatra made a silent vow.

She would do whatever she could to help the other woman find her way, to chase away the shadows that dogged her steps and let her light shine through.

Because they were all in this together, dammit. All fighting the same uphill battle against ignorance and hate.

And if they didn't have each other's backs, well...they might as well lay down and die right now.

No, Cleopatra thought fiercely, squaring her shoulders and lifting her chin. They would stand together, the women of the 6888th. Would weather every storm and surmount every obstacle, until the world sat up and took notice.

CHAPTER 41:
PAIGE

Paige walked briskly across the base, her heart fluttering with anticipation as she clutched Joe's latest letter to her chest. The crisp English air filled her lungs, invigorating her with each breath. She couldn't wait to find a quiet spot to sit and savor every word her son had written, to lose herself in his thoughts and experiences, even if only for a little while.

As she rounded the corner of a supply shed, a flash of movement caught her eye. Paige stopped short, her brow furrowing as she watched a familiar figure slip furtively into the old, abandoned horse barn at the edge of the base.

Sadie.

A prickle of unease ran down Paige's spine, her hand tightening instinctively on Joe's letter. What was that woman doing, skulking around in the shadows like some kind of criminal? Hadn't Paige made it clear that she wanted nothing to do with her hoodoo nonsense, her unnatural fascination with the occult?

Before she quite knew what she was doing, Paige found herself moving closer to the barn, her steps slow and cautious. She told herself it was just idle curiosity, a momentary diversion from the more pressing matters at hand. But deep down, she knew it was more than that.

There was something about Sadie that unsettled her, something that went beyond the usual wariness and mistrust that colored so many of her interactions on base. It was like the woman carried a darkness inside her, a yawning void that threatened to swallow anyone foolish enough to get too close.

And yet, even as the thought sent a shiver down Paige's spine, she couldn't seem to turn away. Couldn't shake the nagging sense that there was more to Sadie than met the eye, some hidden depth or complexity that she had only glimpsed in fleeting snatches.

Shaking her head, Paige crept closer to the barn, her heart pounding in her chest. She found a small, grimy window set into the weathered wood, and pressed her eye to it, peering into the gloom within.

At first, she could see nothing, just dim shapes and shadows that seemed to shift and dance in the low light. But then, as her vision adjusted, she caught a flicker of movement in the far corner.

Sadie.

The other woman was huddled in on herself, her thin frame wracked with shivers as she crouched on the dirty floor. Her lips moved soundlessly, her eyes wide and unfocused as she stared into the middle distance.

Paige's breath caught in her throat, a sudden, irrational surge of fear washing over her. Dear Lord, she thought wildly. The woman had finally cracked, driven mad by the weight of her own unholy obsessions.

But even as the thought formed, Sadie's head snapped up, her gaze zeroing in on the window with unsettling precision. Paige flinched back, her heart leaping into her throat. She held her breath, certain that she had been caught, that Sadie would come storming out of the barn at any moment to confront her.

But the seconds ticked by, and nothing happened. Slowly, hardly daring to believe her luck, Paige backed away from the window and fled, her footsteps muffled by the soft earth.

She didn't stop until she reached the safety of the barracks, her chest heaving and her mind awhirl with unanswered questions. With trembling hands, she unfolded Joe's letter, desperate for the comfort and familiarity of his words.

"I've been assigned to Camp Butner in North Carolina," he wrote, his handwriting strong and sure. Paige closed her eyes, letting the news wash over her. She pictured Joe in his uniform, his face set with determination as he marched alongside his fellow soldiers.

He was so young, she thought with a pang. So full of idealism and hope, even in the face of a world that seemed hell-bent on crushing both.

As she read on, Joe's words painted a vivid picture of life on base, of the long days of training and the even longer nights of uncertainty. Paige could almost see him hunched over a makeshift desk, his brow furrowed in concentration as he poured his heart out onto the page.

"I read in an old paper President Roosevelt's reasons for the United States joining the war," he wrote, his tone thoughtful. "He said 'The United Nations are fighting to make a world based upon freedom, equality, and justice; a world in which all persons, regardless of race, color and creed, may live in peace, honor and dignity.'"

Paige felt a lump form in her throat, her eyes stinging with sudden tears. It was a beautiful dream, she thought. A world where the color of a person's skin didn't determine their worth, where everyone had the chance to live with dignity and respect.

But even as her heart swelled with pride at her son's conviction, at the strength of his belief in a better tomorrow, she couldn't shake the nagging sense of unease that had settled in her gut.

"Once I enlisted, I realized that this world President Roosevelt described is a true contradiction of the reality of being a soldier in the United States," Joe continued, his words heavy with resignation. "We are completely segregated from the white soldiers on base. Most of us will never get the chance to go to combat."

Paige's heart clenched, a hot surge of anger and frustration boiling up inside her. It wasn't right, she thought fiercely. It wasn't fair that her son, that any of the brave, brilliant men and women of color who had stepped up to serve their country, should be treated as less than, as unworthy of the same opportunities and respect afforded their white counterparts.

But even in the face of that bitter reality, Joe's faith never wavered. "I can't say it's not discouraging," he admitted, his honesty like a balm to Paige's aching soul. "But despite the contradictions here at home, I still believe there can be a world based upon the things Roosevelt talked about. Therefore, I am still happy with my decision to enlist."

Paige drew in a shuddering breath, her vision blurring with unshed tears. That was her boy, she thought with a fierce rush of love and pride. That was the man she had raised, the soul she had nurtured and cherished and poured every ounce of her strength into.

"If it wasn't for you, I would not have had the courage," Joe wrote, his words like a benediction. "I miss you Ma, and I can't wait until this war is over and we can have that better life you've always talked about."

Paige pressed the letter to her heart, a sob welling up in her throat. She missed him too, with an ache that never lessened, a longing that gnawed at her very bones. Every day without him was a trial, a test of her fortitude and her faith.

But she would endure it, she vowed silently. She would bear the separation and the loneliness and the constant, clawing fear, because she knew that it was for a greater purpose. That by serving in this war, by fighting for the ideals that Joe held so dear, she was helping to build a better world for him, for all of them.

And when the time came, when the guns fell silent and the troops came marching home, she would be there to welcome him back with open arms and a heart full of love. They would have that better life, that brighter tomorrow that she had always dreamed of.

No matter what it took, no matter what sacrifices she had to make along the way.

With a final, tender press of her lips to the letter, Paige folded it carefully and tucked it away in her pocket. She took a deep breath, squaring her shoulders and lifting her chin. There was work to be done, duties to be fulfilled. She couldn't afford to let herself get lost in dreams and what-ifs, not when there were real, tangible battles to be fought here and now.

But even as she turned her mind to the tasks at hand, Paige couldn't shake the image of Sadie huddled in that dark, dank barn. Couldn't forget the haunted look in her eyes, the way her lips had moved in some sort of silent, desperate prayer.

What demons plagued the other woman? Paige wondered uneasily. What secrets lurked in the shadowed corners of her mind, driving her to seek solace in the cold embrace of solitude?

Paige shook her head, a shiver running down her spine. It was none of her concern, she told herself firmly. Sadie's troubles were her own, and Paige had more than enough on her plate without taking on the burdens of a woman she barely knew and deeply mistrusted.

And yet, even as she went about her duties with brisk, single-minded efficiency, Paige couldn't quite banish the nagging sense of unease that had taken root in her chest. Couldn't shake the feeling that there was something more to Sadie's strange behavior than simple eccentricity or superstition.

Something darker, more dangerous. Something that threatened to upset the delicate balance of their little world, to shatter the fragile peace they had all fought so hard to maintain.

Paige didn't know what it was, couldn't put a name to the formless dread that coiled in her gut like a snake.

CHAPTER 42:
CLEOPATRA

Cleopatra strolled down the quaint Birmingham street, drinking in the sights and sounds of the bustling town. Beside her, Sammy practically vibrated with excitement, her round face split in an irrepressible grin. "I'm so happy you came," she gushed, looping her arm through Sadie's.

Cleopatra glanced over at Sadie, her eyes distant and her shoulders hunched. "You didn't give me much choice," she said wryly, pitching her voice low so only Sammy could hear.

Sammy's smile faltered, a flicker of hurt dancing across her features. Cleopatra sighed, feeling a twinge of guilt. It wasn't Sammy's fault that Sadie was in one of her moods, all brooding silences and shuttered glances. And Lord knew the girl could use a friend, someone to pull her out of her own head and remind her that there was more to life than ghosts and shadows.

"I needed to get away from base," Sadie said abruptly, as if reading Cleopatra's thoughts. Her voice was flat, almost toneless, but there was a tension thrumming just beneath the surface, a coiled energy that set Cleopatra's nerves on edge.

"Because of Paige?" Sammy asked, her brow furrowing in concern.

Sadie didn't answer, just hunched her shoulders and quickened her pace, as if trying to outrun the question. Cleopatra exchanged a worried glance with Sammy, but before either of them could press further, the younger girl's face lit up with renewed enthusiasm.

"I need to find the perfect dress to dance with Otis," she declared, practically skipping in her excitement.

Cleopatra raised an eyebrow, a smirk tugging at the corner of her mouth. "You don't even know for sure that he's coming to the dance," she pointed out, trying and failing to suppress a chuckle at Sammy's crestfallen expression.

"Oh, he's going to come," Sammy insisted, a stubborn set to her jaw. She turned to Sadie, her eyes wide and imploring. "Right, Sadie?"

But Sadie just stared back at her, her face an inscrutable mask. Cleopatra couldn't help but laugh at the absurdity of it all, the sheer, unshakable conviction in Sammy's voice.

"Oh, honey," she said, shaking her head fondly. "You've got it bad."

They paused in front of a shop window, their reflections distorted in the wavy glass. Cleopatra's eye was immediately drawn to a dress on display, a sleek, shimmering confection of purple silk that seemed to wink and sparkle under the lights.

"What about that one?" she asked, pointing to the gown with an appreciative whistle.

But before Sammy could respond, a voice rang out behind them, crisp and authoritative. "Excuse me, Privates."

Cleopatra stiffened, her heart leaping into her throat. She turned slowly, schooling her features into a mask of polite attentiveness as she took in the group of white officers standing a few feet away.

At the front of the pack was a tall, broad-shouldered lieutenant, his face set in an expression of earnest sincerity.

Beside her, Sammy and Sadie snapped to attention, their hands flying up in crisp salutes. Cleopatra followed suit a beat later, the motion feeling stiff and unnatural.

"I just wanted to say how grateful I am, how grateful all of our men are, that the mail is finally moving again," the lieutenant said, his voice ringing with conviction. "I can't put into words how much it means to all of us to receive word from home. You women are doing a great job."

The other officers nodded in agreement, their faces solemn and sincere. All except one, Cleopatra noted with a start. One man hung back from the group, his posture rigid and his eyes fixed on the ground.

William.

Cleopatra felt a flare of anger spark in her chest, hot and bright. How dare he ignore her like this, after everything they had shared? After the long nights of passion and whispered promises, the stolen moments of tenderness amidst the chaos of war?

She lifted her chin, a challenge in her eyes as she met the lieutenant's gaze. "Thank you," she said coolly. "Do you agree we are doing a great job, Lt. McDonald?"

William's head snapped up at the sound of his name, his eyes widening in shock. For a moment, he simply stared at her, his mouth opening and closing like a fish gasping for air.

But the lieutenant just laughed, reaching out to clap William on the shoulder. "What's wrong, McDonald?" he asked jovially. "Still waiting on letters from your wife?"

Cleopatra felt the blood drain from her face, a cold, leaden weight settling in the pit of her stomach. Wife? William was married?

She searched his face for some sign of denial, some flicker of shame or apology. But he wouldn't meet her eyes, his jaw clenched tight and his gaze fixed resolutely on the ground.

"We better get going," he muttered, his voice rough and strained.

The other officers nodded, already moving off down the street. William hesitated for a moment, his eyes darting to Cleopatra's face. But she looked away, her heart twisting in her chest like a knife.

She heard his footsteps receding, the sound of his retreat like a physical blow. But she refused to watch him go, refused to give him the satisfaction of seeing her crumble.

Instead, she grabbed Sammy and Sadie by the arms and hauled them into the dress shop, her movements sharp and jerky with barely suppressed rage. She could feel the curious stares of the other patrons boring into her back, could hear the whispers and titters that followed in her wake.

But she didn't care. All she cared about was putting as much distance as possible between herself and William fucking McDonald, the lying, two-faced bastard who had played her for a fool.

Inside the shop, Cleopatra forced herself to take a deep breath, to push down the swell of hurt and humiliation that threatened to choke her. She had a job to do, dammit. She had to be strong for Sammy, had to help her find the perfect dress and salvage some small scrap of joy from this miserable excuse for a day.

So she plastered on a smile, bright and brittle as a shard of glass, and set about rummaging through the racks with a determined efficiency. She held up dresses for Sammy's inspection, offering suggestions and encouragement even as her own mind whirled with a thousand unanswered questions.

How could she have been so stupid? How could she have let herself fall for a man like William, a man who could lie to her face and then go home to his wife without so much as a backward glance?

She should have known better. Should have guarded her heart more carefully, should have remembered the hard-won lessons of a lifetime spent fighting for scraps of respect and dignity in a world that wanted her only as a curiosity or a commodity.

But even as the bitter thoughts chased themselves around her head, Cleopatra couldn't quite shake the memory of William's touch, the tenderness in his eyes as he looked at her, the passion in his kisses. It had felt real, dammit. It had felt like something true and honest and good, a connection that transcended the color of their skin or the stripes on their sleeves.

Had it all been a lie? A cruel, callous game played by a man who saw her as nothing more than a conquest, a notch on his bedpost?

Cleopatra didn't know. And in that moment, standing amidst the racks of shimmering dresses she wasn't sure she wanted to.

All she wanted was to forget. To lose herself in the simple, uncomplicated pleasure of playing dress-up with her friends, of pretending, just for a little while, that the world outside didn't exist.

But even that small reprieve was shattered when Sadie suddenly swayed on her feet, her face going pale and her eyes rolling back in her head. Cleopatra lunged forward, catching the other woman before she could hit the ground.

"Sadie?" she asked urgently, giving her a gentle shake. "Sadie, what's wrong?"

But Sadie didn't seem to hear her. She was muttering under her breath, her voice low and fevered and her eyes fixed on some distant point over Cleopatra's shoulder.

"You followed me?" she whispered, her words slurred and indistinct. "Leave me alone. I can't help you, go away."

Cleopatra exchanged a worried glance with Sammy, who hovered anxiously at her elbow. Around them, the other patrons had fallen silent, their faces a mix of concern and morbid curiosity.

"Who are you talking to?" Cleopatra asked, trying to keep her voice calm and soothing. But Sadie just shook her head, her face contorting in a grimace of pain.

"Leave me alone!" she cried, her voice rising to a hysterical pitch. "I said leave me alone!"

And then, before Cleopatra could stop her, she wrenched herself free of Cleopatra's grasp and bolted for the door, her skirts swirling around her legs as she ran.

"Sadie!" Cleopatra called after her, her heart hammering in her chest. But it was too late. Sadie was gone, disappearing into the crowded street like a ghost into the mist.

For a moment, Cleopatra simply stood there, stunned and shaken. She could feel the weight of the other patrons' stares, could hear the whispers and murmurs that rippled through the shop like a cold wind.

But she couldn't bring herself to care. All she could think about was Sadie, lost and alone and battling demons that Cleopatra couldn't even begin to fathom.

"What the hell?" she murmured, running a hand through her hair in frustration.

Beside her, Sammy looked on the verge of tears, her lower lip trembling and her eyes wide with fright. Cleopatra reached out and pulled the younger girl into a tight hug, feeling the way she shook and shuddered against her.

They would find their way through this. Together.

No matter what it took. No matter how long or hard the road ahead might be.

Because they were sisters, now and always. And sisters never left each other behind.

With a final, fierce squeeze of Sammy's shoulders, Cleopatra stepped back and squared her own. She took a deep breath, feeling the weight of her newfound purpose settle over her like armor.

"Come on," she said, her voice ringing with quiet conviction. "Let's go find our girl."

And with that, she turned and strode out of the shop, into the waiting arms of the unknown.

Later that night, Cleopatra stood behind Sammy, her fingers deftly weaving the younger woman's hair into an intricate updo. The barracks buzzed with excitement as the women prepared for the evening's big event - a dance featuring none other than Count Basie himself.

"This is taking forever," Sammy whined, fidgeting impatiently in her seat.

Cleopatra chuckled, giving Sammy's shoulder a playful squeeze. "That's why I wear wigs," she quipped, her own perfectly coiffed curls bouncing as she worked.

From her perch on a nearby bunk, Paige watched the proceedings with a mixture of amusement and exasperation. "Why are you making me be here?" she grumbled, crossing her arms over her chest. "I'm not even going to the dance."

Sammy twisted around to shoot Paige a pleading look. "This will help keep your mind off Joe," she cajoled, her eyes wide and earnest.

Cleopatra nodded sagely, her fingers never missing a beat as she continued to style Sammy's hair. "Yes, it's a good distraction from thinking about folks," she agreed, her tone carefully neutral.

Paige's eyes narrowed, a flicker of suspicion dancing across her features. "What folks are you trying not to think about?" she asked, her voice sharp.

Cleopatra felt a flicker of irritation at the question, but quickly tamped it down. "Nobody," she said breezily, waving a dismissive hand. "You need to come to help me chaperone Sammy."

At that, Sammy let out an indignant squawk. "I don't need no chaperone," she protested, crossing her arms over her chest. A sly grin spread across her face. "Otis might need one when he sees me in my dress, though."

She started to shimmy in her seat, her eyes sparkling with mischief. Cleopatra and Paige burst out laughing at the sight, the tension in the room dissipating like smoke on the wind.

"Be still now," Cleopatra chided gently, giving Sammy's hair a final, satisfied pat. "There. All done."

Sammy beamed, reaching up to gingerly touch her new 'do. "Thanks, Cleo," she said, her voice warm with affection. "You're a real artist, you know that?"

Cleopatra felt a surge of pride at the compliment, a small, secret smile tugging at the corners of her mouth. It meant more than she could say, to be recognized for her talents, her passions. To be seen as something more than just a pretty face or a sexy voice.

But before she could dwell on it too long, Paige's voice cut through her thoughts like a knife. "What would help my mind," the taller woman said sourly, "is to get another bunk assignment."

Sammy's face fell, her lower lip jutting out in a pout. "You don't want to leave us," she protested, her eyes big and pleading.

But Paige just shook her head, her jaw tight. "I want to leave her," she said flatly, jerking her chin towards Sadie's empty bunk.

Cleopatra felt a flare of protectiveness at that, a sudden, fierce urge to defend her strange, silent friend. "Sadie is harmless," she insisted, her voice brooking no argument.

Paige scoffed, her eyes flashing with something like disgust. "How can you say that after what happened in town?" she demanded, her voice rising in accusation.

Cleopatra shot Sammy a warning look, silently willing the younger woman to keep her mouth shut. But it was too late.

"Sorry," Sammy mumbled, ducking her head. "You know I can't keep a secret."

Cleopatra sighed, feeling a headache beginning to throb behind her eyes. It was going to be a long night.

The gymnasium was a sea of swirling skirts and shining brass as Count Basie and his band took the stage. Cleopatra stood off to the side, sipping a glass of punch and watching the dancers with a critical eye.

She had to admit, the man knew how to put on a show. The music was electrifying, the kind of toe-tapping, hip-swaying rhythm that made you want to jump up and join in, propriety be damned.

But Cleopatra held herself aloof, her gaze roaming the room in search of a particular face. She spotted Otis standing near the stage, his broad shoulders and easy smile drawing appreciative glances from more than a few of the women in attendance.

Cleopatra made her way over to him, weaving through the crowd with a dancer's grace. She could feel eyes on her as she moved.

"This is amazing," Otis said as she drew up beside him, his face alight with boyish enthusiasm. "I can't believe we get to see Count Basie live."

Cleopatra hummed in agreement, her eyes flicking to the stage. "I wonder if he's single," she mused, her voice deliberately casual.

Out of the corner of her eye, she saw William standing off to the side, his camera raised to his face as he snapped pictures of the band. She could feel his eyes on her, could sense the weight of his gaze like a physical thing.

But she pointedly ignored him, turning her full attention back to Otis. Let William stew in his own jealousy, she thought savagely. Let him see what he was missing out on.

Otis chuckled, shaking his head. "I've got some friends that want to meet you," he said, nodding towards a group of soldiers standing nearby.

Cleopatra followed his gaze, a slow smile spreading across her face. She reached out and ran a hand down Otis's arm, her touch lingering just a beat too long to be strictly friendly.

"I'd love to meet your friends, darling," she purred, her voice low and sultry.

"Where are your bunkmates?" Otis asked, glancing around the crowded room.

Cleopatra smirked, arching a knowing eyebrow. "You mean where's Sammy?" she teased, watching with amusement as a faint blush crept up Otis's cheeks.

"You've been spending a lot of time with her," she observed, her tone carefully neutral.

Otis ducked his head, a small, bashful smile tugging at the corners of his mouth. "I like her," he admitted softly. "I do. I'm just...confused."

He sighed, running a hand over his close-cropped hair. "It's like I've been living in limbo for so long, not knowing if Vera said yes or no. It's like I got one foot back home and one foot here with Sammy."

His face softened, a distant look stealing into his eyes. "I ain't never met nobody like her," he murmured. "She's funny, and kind, and real pretty. But you know what I like most about her?"

Cleopatra tilted her head, genuinely curious now. "What's that?"

"She's honest," Otis said simply. "She's honest about how she feels. She doesn't try to put on airs or hide her feelings. She don't play hard to get. She likes me and she makes sure I know it."

He shook his head, a wry smile tugging at his lips. "With Vera, it was always like I had to chase her. Woo her every day. It's nice to meet someone who leaves no doubt."

Cleopatra nodded slowly, something tightening in her chest. Wasn't that what they all wanted, in the end? To be seen, truly seen, for who they were underneath all the masks and pretenses?

"Yes, that's Sammy," she agreed softly. "I think you're going to have to decide what you want, letter or no letter. How long are you going to wait?"

Otis sighed, his shoulders slumping. "I don't know," he admitted, his voice heavy with resignation.

Cleopatra hesitated for a moment, torn between her loyalty to Sammy and her own hard-won wisdom. But in the end, she couldn't stay silent. Not when she saw so much of herself in the lost, yearning look on Otis's face.

"Maybe if you feel that way about Sammy," she said gently, "Vera ain't the right one for you. Even if she does say yes."

Otis looked up at that, something like hope kindling in his dark eyes. "That thought has crossed my mind," he said slowly, as if testing the shape of the words.

Cleopatra opened her mouth to respond, but before she could get a word out, her eye caught William making his way towards the exit, his camera tucked under his arm and his face set in a grim line.

Anger flared in Cleopatra's chest, hot and bright. How dare he just walk away, after everything he had done? How dare he leave her hanging, with nothing but questions and a bitter taste in her mouth?

Before she quite knew what she was doing, she was excusing herself from Otis's side and striding across the room, her heels clicking sharply against the polished floor.

She caught up with William just outside the gymnasium, the cool night air hitting her like a slap in the face. He turned at the sound of her approach, his eyes widening in surprise.

"If you're waiting for me to salute," Cleopatra said coldly, crossing her arms over her chest, "you'll be waiting a long time."

William sighed, running a hand over his face. "I was hoping to talk to you," he said quietly, his voice heavy with resignation. "I'm sorry. I should have told you."

Cleopatra scoffed, feeling a bitter laugh bubbling up in her throat. "It doesn't matter," she said, her voice dripping with disdain. "I was just a little experiment for you. A chance to try out some chocolate."

William flinched at that, something like shame flashing across his features. "It wasn't like that," he insisted, taking a step towards her.

But Cleopatra held up a hand, stopping him in his tracks. "Then what was it like?" she demanded, her voice rising in challenge.

William opened his mouth, then closed it again. He had no answer, and they both knew it.

Cleopatra shook her head, feeling a sudden, bone-deep weariness settle over her. "You should leave now," she said flatly. "I'm going back inside."

She turned to go, but William's voice stopped her. "I wanted to give this to you," he said softly, holding out a small, square object.

Cleopatra hesitated for a moment, torn between curiosity and the desire to walk away and never look back. But in the end, she reached out and took the proffered item, turning it over in her hands.

It was a photograph, she realized with a start. The one he had taken of her in the hotel room, her face soft and unguarded in the muted light.

"It's beautiful," William murmured, his voice thick with some unspoken emotion. "I wanted you to have it. I don't deserve to keep it."

Cleopatra swallowed hard, feeling a sudden, sharp ache in her chest. "No," she agreed softly. "You don't."

She stared down at the photograph for a long moment, tracing the lines of her own face with a trembling finger. It was a moment frozen in time, a snapshot of a woman she barely recognized anymore. A woman who had dared to hope, to dream of something more than the narrow confines of the life she had been given.

But that woman was gone now, lost to the harsh realities of a world that cared nothing for her hopes and dreams. In her place stood a harder, wiser creature, one who knew better than to trust in the promise of pretty words and fleeting passions.

With a final, resolute nod, Cleopatra tucked the photograph into her pocket and turned away. She could feel William's eyes on her back as she walked, could sense the weight of all the things left unsaid hanging in the air between them.

But she didn't look back. Didn't allow herself to dwell on what might have been, on the foolish, impossible dreams that had once consumed her.

She had a job to do, a mission to complete. And she would see it through to the end, no matter the cost.

Even if it meant leaving pieces of herself behind, scattered like ashes in the wind.

CHAPTER 43:
SAMMY

Sammy watched as Cleopatra and Paige left the barracks, her heart fluttering with a mix of excitement and trepidation. Cleopatra was off to the dance, ready to dazzle everyone with her wit and charm. And Paige had slipped away to the showers, no doubt seeking a moment of solitude to gather her thoughts.

Which left Sammy alone, with nothing but her nerves and the crumpled letter burning a hole in her pocket.

With trembling fingers, she reached into her skirt and pulled out the envelope, staring down at the words scrawled across the front in Otis's bold, slanting hand.

"Otis Louis McGhee," she read aloud, her voice barely above a whisper. "From Vera Williams, Laurel, Mississippi."

The name sent a pang of jealousy shooting through her chest, sharp and hot. Vera. The girl Otis had left behind, the one who still held a piece of his heart, even from thousands of miles away.

Sammy took a deep breath, trying to steady herself. She couldn't let her own insecurities get the best of her, not tonight. Not when she had finally worked up the courage to tell Otis how she really felt, to lay her own heart on the line and see if he was willing to catch it.

With a final, resolute nod, she folded the letter and tucked it back into her pocket. "Tonight," she murmured, squaring her shoulders and lifting her chin. "Tonight, everything changes."

The gymnasium was a sea of swirling skirts and shining brass when Sammy arrived, the air thick with the heady scent of perfume and pomade. She scanned the crowd eagerly, her heart leaping into her throat when she spotted Otis standing near the stage, his broad shoulders and easy smile drawing appreciative glances from more than a few of the women in attendance.

Sammy made her way over to him, weaving through the throng of dancers with a determined stride. She only had eyes for one man tonight, and damn if she was going to let anything stand in her way.

As she drew up behind Otis, Sammy felt a sudden, wicked impulse overtake her. Grinning to herself, she reached up and covered his eyes with her hands, feeling him start in surprise at the unexpected touch.

"Sammy?" he asked, a note of wonder in his voice.

Sammy let her hands drop, stepping out from behind him with a flourish. "The one and only," she said, giving a little twirl. "What do you think?"

Otis's eyes widened as he took her in, his gaze roaming over her from head to toe. Sammy felt a flush of pleasure at the open appreciation in his expression, the way his eyes seemed to drink her in like a man dying of thirst.

"You look sweeter than a biscuit covered in syrup," he murmured, his voice loud and country.

Sammy's heart stuttered in her chest, her breath catching in her throat. She had never been looked at like that before, had never felt so seen, so desired. It was heady and thrilling and terrifying all at once, like standing on the edge of a cliff and knowing that one false step could send her tumbling into the abyss.

But as she stared into Otis's dark, earnest eyes, Sammy knew that she was ready to take that leap. Ready to trust in the strength of her own feelings, in the unshakable conviction that this was where she was meant to be.

"May I have this dance?" Otis asked softly, holding out his hand.

Sammy smiled, feeling a rush of warmth in her chest. "I thought you would never ask," she said, slipping her fingers into his.

As Otis led her out onto the dance floor, Sammy felt like she was floating on air. The music wrapped around them like a cocoon, the steady thrum of the bass and the wail of the horns drowning out the rest of the world until it was just the two of them, moving together in perfect sync.

Otis's arm slid around her waist, his touch firm and sure as he guided her through the steps. Sammy leaned into him, savoring the solid warmth of his body against hers, the way his heartbeat seemed to echo her own.

"I'm sorry," Otis murmured, his breath tickling her ear. "I'm not a very good dancer."

Sammy shook her head, a soft laugh bubbling up in her throat. "You're doing alright to me," she assured him, giving his hand a gentle squeeze. "I've got something to give you before you go."

Otis's eyebrows shot up, a mischievous grin tugging at the corners of his mouth. "Oh, yeah?" he drawled, his voice dropping to a suggestive purr. "What you got to give me?"

Sammy swatted at his chest, feeling a blush rising in her cheeks. "You so silly," she chided, but she couldn't quite keep the smile from her face.

Otis chuckled, his eyes sparkling with barely contained mirth. "You keep dancing this close, you might have to give me a kiss," he teased, pulling her even tighter against him.

Sammy's heart skipped a beat, her mouth going dry. A kiss. The very thing she had been dreaming of, fantasizing about in the darkest, most secret corners of her mind. But now, with Otis's arms around her and his face so close to hers, the reality of it hit her like a punch to the gut.

"A kiss?" she repeated faintly, her voice barely above a whisper. "But I thought you said--"

Otis cut her off with a shake of his head, his expression growing serious. "I know what I said," he murmured, his gaze boring into hers with an intensity that took her breath away. "But I've been thinking. Maybe I'm wasting my time thinking about somebody thousands of miles away when I got someone beautiful right here in front of me."

Sammy's heart leapt into her throat, hope and fear warring in her chest. This was it, the moment she had been waiting for. The chance to finally lay claim to the man she loved, to stake her own place in his heart.

But even as the thought sent a thrill of excitement racing through her veins, Sammy couldn't shake the nagging sense of doubt that tugged at the back of her mind. The fear that maybe, just maybe, Otis's feelings for Vera ran deeper than he was letting on.

"What if she said yes?" she asked softly, hating the tremor in her voice. "Maybe her letter did just get lost in the mail."

Otis frowned, a flicker of confusion crossing his face. "It sounds like you trying to convince me that I should be with her," he said slowly, a note of hurt creeping into his voice.

Sammy shook her head frantically, cursing herself for her own foolishness. "I ain't trying to convince you," she insisted, reaching up to cup his face in her hands. "I just--"

But Otis cut her off with a gentle finger to her lips, his eyes softening with understanding. "You know what I want?" he murmured, his voice low and intimate. "I want just one night where I don't think about it. Who would have thought that this country boy from Mississippi would be here? I'm dancing to Count Basie, live, with the prettiest girl on the entire continent of Europe in my arms. That's alright."

He leaned in closer, his breath warm against her cheek. "And I'm about to do something I've been wanting to do for the past few weeks."

Sammy's heart stuttered to a stop, her eyes widening in anticipation. "What's that?" she breathed, hardly daring to hope.

"This," Otis whispered, and then his lips were on hers, soft and warm and achingly gentle.

Sammy melted into the kiss, her eyes fluttering closed as she savored the sweet, intoxicating taste of him. It was everything she had ever dreamed of and more, a perfect moment of connection and passion and unspoken promise.

But even as she lost herself in the feel of Otis's mouth moving against hers, Sammy couldn't shake the nagging sense of unease that tugged at the back of her mind. The letter, tucked away in her pocket like a ticking time bomb, waiting to blow her newfound happiness to smithereens.

She pulled away reluctantly, her heart aching with the knowledge of what she had to do. "Otis," she said softly, her voice trembling with emotion. "I have to tell you something."

But before she could get the words out, the band suddenly fell silent, the music cutting off abruptly as a murmur of conversation rippled through the crowd. Sammy frowned, glancing around in confusion as she saw the stricken looks on the faces of the dancers around her.

"What's going on?" she asked, a knot of dread forming in the pit of her stomach. "Why'd they stop playing?"

As if on cue, Cleopatra materialized out of the crowd, her face grim and her eyes shadowed with sorrow.

"We're ending the dance," Cleopatra said quietly, her voice heavy with unshed tears. "They're saying that President Roosevelt has died."

Sammy felt the breath leave her lungs in a rush, her knees going weak with shock. President Roosevelt, dead? It couldn't be. He was the one constant in this war-torn world, the steady hand at the helm of a nation in crisis. Without him, everything seemed suddenly uncertain, the future a yawning void of darkness and doubt.

Beside her, Otis swayed on his feet, his face draining of color. "What?" he croaked, his voice rough with disbelief. "Looks like everybody is heading back. I better go."

He started to pull away, but Sammy clung to his hand, desperate to keep him close. "Otis, wait!" she cried, reaching for the letter in her pocket with trembling fingers.

But something stopped her, some stubborn, defiant part of her that refused to let this moment be tainted by the specter of the past. She had come too far, fought too hard for this chance at happiness to let it slip away now.

"Never mind," she said softly, letting her hand drop back to her side.

Otis hesitated for a moment, his eyes searching her face. But then he nodded, leaning in to press a soft, chaste kiss to her cheek.

"I'll catch you later," he murmured, and then he was gone, swallowed up by the milling crowd as they made their way towards the exits.

Sammy stood there for a long moment, watching him go with a heavy heart. She knew that she should have told him the truth, should have given him Vera's letter and let the chips fall where they may.

But something held her back, some stubborn, selfish part of her that couldn't bear to let him go. Not yet. Not when she had just found him, had just begun to glimpse the promise of a future that could be theirs.

She would tell him tomorrow, she promised herself. She would lay all her cards on the table and trust in the strength of their connection to see them through.

But for tonight, she would hold onto this moment, this perfect, shining memory of what it felt like to be loved, to be wanted, to be seen.

And maybe, just maybe, that would be enough to sustain her through whatever storms lay ahead.

CHAPTER 44:
SADIE

Sadie lay curled on her bunk, her body wracked with tremors that had nothing to do with the chill in the air. The cards were spread out before her, their faces mocking her with their inscrutable secrets. She couldn't bear to look at them, couldn't stomach the thought of what they might reveal.

But even as she tried to block them out, to lose herself in the numb cocoon of her own misery, Sadie could feel the weight of their presence, the sickening tug of their power. It was a part of her, as much as the blood in her veins and the breath in her lungs. A curse, a burden she had never asked for and could never escape.

"Leave me alone," she whispered to the spirit, her voice cracking with desperation. "Please."

But the spirit didn't listen. They never did. He swirled around her like leaves caught in a whirlwind, his voice a cacophony of whispers and moans that filled her head to bursting.

Sadie squeezed her eyes shut, trying to block him out. But it was no use. He was next to her, a part of her, as inescapable as her own shadow.

The sound of the door creaking open barely registered through the haze of her misery. But then Sammy's voice cut through the din, high and bright with false cheer.

"You alright, Sadie? You missed your shift."

Sadie didn't answer, didn't even move. Maybe if she lay still enough, if she held her breath and willed herself to disappear, Sammy would take the hint and leave her be.

But the younger woman was not so easily deterred. Sadie heard her footsteps drawing closer, felt the dip of the mattress as Sammy perched on the edge of the bunk.

"Who were you talking to?" Sammy asked, a note of concern creeping into her voice. "I heard you talking to somebody."

"I'm not in the mood, Sammy," she gritted out, hugging her knees tighter to her chest.

Sammy sighed, and Sadie could practically feel the weight of her disappointment, her frustration. "You ain't never in the mood to talk to me," she said, a hint of petulance creeping into her voice.

And then, softer, almost to herself: "I can't take it anymore, Sadie. This guilt has me about to bust."

Sadie heard the rustle of paper, the soft rasp of an envelope being unfolded. And then Sammy's voice again, trembling with a mix of excitement and trepidation.

"I have Otis's letter. I've had it for a month."

Sadie didn't need to ask what letter Sammy was talking about. She had known about it from the moment Sammy had tucked it away in her pocket, had sensed the weight of its secrets like a physical thing.

But to hear it spoken aloud, to have the truth laid bare in all its ugly, unvarnished glory...it was almost more than Sadie could bear.

"I know," she said softly, the words like ashes on her tongue.

Sammy made a small, choked sound of surprise. "How did you know?" she asked, her voice tight with disbelief. "Never mind. What should I do? I think we have a real chance. What will I do if she said yes?"

The questions tumbled out of her in a rush, each one hitting Sadie like a tiny, stinging dart. She wanted to cover her ears, to block out the sound of Sammy's pain and confusion. But she forced herself to listen, to bear witness to the younger woman's struggle.

"Maybe I should open it myself," Sammy continued, her voice rising with a note of hysteria. "Then I'll know what to do. Or maybe I should just destroy it. But what if there is another letter coming? Or what if one already came?"

She was rambling now, her words tripping over each other in their haste to escape. Sadie could feel the panic rolling off her in waves, the desperation of a woman caught between two impossible choices.

And then, suddenly, Sammy was on top of her, her hands scrabbling at the cards that lay scattered across the blanket. Sadie jerked upright, a hot flush of anger and betrayal washing over her.

"Give me those," she snapped, making a grab for the deck.

But Sammy danced out of reach, her eyes wild and her mouth set in a stubborn line. "No," she said, clutching the cards to her chest like a talisman. "I'll figure it out myself."

Sadie lunged for her, a growl of frustration tearing from her throat. "Give me those," she repeated, her voice rising to a shout. "You don't know anything about those cards!"

They grappled for a moment, a tangle of limbs and flying cards. And then, with a sickening lurch, Sadie felt the box tumble from the bunk, its contents scattering across the floor like leaves in a gale.

"Now look what you did," she spat, scrambling to gather up the precious artifacts.

But Sammy was already on her knees, pawing through the jumble with a kind of manic intensity. "Use them," she pleaded, her voice raw and ragged. "Tell me, please."

Sadie shook her head, her jaw clenched so tight she thought her teeth might crack. "I'm not telling you anything," she gritted out, snatching the box out of Sammy's hands.

But the younger woman was not so easily deterred. She made another grab for the box, her fingers scrabbling against the polished wood.

"Then I'll use what's in here," she said, a note of triumph creeping into her voice.

Sadie felt a surge of panic, hot and bright and all-consuming. The box was her sanctuary, her one small corner of privacy in a world that sought to strip her bare. To have Sammy pawing through its contents, to have her secrets laid out for all the world to see...it was a violation, a desecration of the highest order.

"Put that down now," she snarled, her voice low and deadly. "I told you not to touch that."

But Sammy just shook her head, a fevered light dancing in her eyes. "Do a spell," she demanded, thrusting the box back into Sadie's hands. "Read the cards or something. I need to know!"

Sadie felt something snap inside her, a final, fragile thread of control. She lunged for Sammy with a howl of rage, her fingers clawing at the younger woman's face and hair.

"Give it to me right now," she screamed, punctuating each word with a sharp, stinging blow. "Stop it, Sammy! Let go!"

They tumbled to the floor in a flurry of flailing limbs and flying curses, the box trapped between their straining bodies. Sadie could feel the hard edges of it digging into her ribs, could hear the sickening crack of wood as Sammy's elbow connected with its polished surface.

And then, suddenly, Paige was there, her face a mask of shock and disgust as she took in the scene before her.

"What is going on in here?" she demanded, her voice sharp with disapproval.

Sammy scrambled to her feet, her chest heaving and her eyes wild. "Sadie is about to read the cards," she panted, pointing a shaking finger at the scattered deck. "Do a spell, or tell me something."

Sadie clutched the box tighter to her chest, a low, warning growl building in the back of her throat. "Give me the box," she spat, her voice thick with fury.

But Paige just shook her head, her lip curling in revulsion. "I told you I didn't want that witchcraft mess in my room," she snapped, her eyes flashing with righteous anger.

Sammy rounded on her, her face flushed with indignation. "It ain't just your room," she shot back, her voice rising to a shout. "She knows what I need to do about Otis, and she needs to tell me!"

Paige's gaze flicked to Sadie, cold and assessing. "Give her the box," she said slowly, each word dripping with disdain.

But Sammy was not to be swayed. "Just tell me," she pleaded, turning back to Sadie with desperation in her eyes. "Please."

Paige let out a sharp, humorless bark of laughter. "That mess is evil," she said, her voice dripping with contempt. "She practices it, so that makes her evil. If you get involved in it, that makes you evil too."

The words hit Sadie like a sledgehammer, stealing the breath from her lungs. She felt something break inside her, some final, fragile barrier between herself and the darkness that always sought to claim her.

"I'm not evil," she whispered, her voice small and broken in the sudden, ringing silence. "You think I wanted to be born this way? You think I want to know the things I know, see the things I see?"

She lifted her head, her eyes blazing with a fierce, defiant light. "Well, I don't," she spat, her voice rising to a shout. "I never asked for this, any of it. But it's part of me, as much as the blood in my veins and the breath in my lungs. And I can't change it, no matter how much I might want to."

Paige's face twisted with disgust, her eyes hard and pitiless. "You've got a choice," she said coldly, each word a tiny, stinging barb. "Don't nobody make you use them cards or do whatever you do with that stuff in that box."

Sammy's head swiveled between them, her eyes wide with shock and confusion. "She sees spirits too," she blurted out, her voice high and thin with fear. "She's seen a spirit here, even seen one in our room."

Paige recoiled as if struck, her hand flying to her throat. "A spirit?" she repeated, her voice trembling with a mix of horror and revulsion. "In our room? A dead person?"

She shook her head, a sharp, disbelieving bark of laughter tearing from her throat. "Now I've really heard it all."

Sammy nodded eagerly, her eyes fever-bright in the dim light of the barracks. "I bet she can even bring somebody back from the dead," she said, a note of wonder creeping into her voice. "I read that hoodoo voodoo people can bring folks back."

Sadie felt a surge of bitter laughter bubbling up in her throat, hot and corrosive as acid. "You can't bring people back from the dead," she said flatly, her voice heavy with weary resignation.

Sammy stared at her, her brow furrowed in confusion. "Well, you act like that's what I'm trying to get you to do," she said slowly, a hint of accusation creeping into her tone. "I just need to know one little favor."

Paige threw up her hands, her face twisted with disgust. "That's it," she spat, her voice trembling with barely contained rage. "I can't be around this anymore."

She spun on her heel and stormed out of the barracks, her footsteps echoing like gunshots in the sudden, ringing silence.

For a moment, no one moved. No one even seemed to breathe. And then Cleopatra's voice cut through the stillness, low and urgent.

"I could hear y'all down the hall," she said, her gaze flicking warily between Sammy and Sadie. "What just happened here?"

But Sadie couldn't answer. Couldn't find the words to explain the tangled web of secrets and lies that had finally, inevitably come unraveled.

All she could do was gather up her cards with shaking hands, stuffing them back into the box with a kind of desperate, clumsy haste. And then she crawled back onto her bunk, curling in on herself like a wounded animal.

Cleopatra noticed the letter, addressed to Otis, that had fallen to the ground in the frenzy. Picking it up, she asked, "Is this Otis's letter? Sammy, how long have you had this?"

She heard Cleopatra's sharp intake of breath, sensed the weight of Sammy's stricken gaze as she snatched Otis's letter from Cleopatra and ran out the room.

And then, as the tears began to fall hot and fast down her cheeks, Sadie buried her face in her pillow and wept.

For the curse that had shadowed her steps since birth, the burden she could never escape. For the love she had lost, the future she would never have.

And for the tiny, flickering spark of hope that had finally, irrevocably been snuffed out, leaving her alone in the darkness with nothing but her grief and her ghosts for company.

CHAPTER 45:
SAMMY

Sammy's heart raced as she hurried across the base towards the mailroom, her mind a whirlwind of guilt and anxiety. She had been carrying Otis's letter for weeks now, the weight of it burning a hole in her pocket and her conscience. Every day, she told herself she would give it to him, that she would finally come clean and face the consequences of her actions.

But every time she saw his warm, trusting smile, every time he looked at her with those deep, soulful eyes...she lost her nerve. How could she bear to hurt him like that? To shatter the fragile, precious thing that had been growing between them?

So she had held onto the letter, telling herself that she was just waiting for the right moment. That she needed more time to figure out what she wanted, to untangle the knot of feelings that twisted in her chest every time she thought of Otis and Vera and the future that hung in the balance.

But now, as she caught sight of him waiting outside the mailroom, his tall, broad-shouldered form leaning casually against the wall, Sammy knew she couldn't put it off any longer. She had to tell him the truth, no matter how much it hurt. She owed him that much.

"There's my girl," Otis called out as she approached, his face splitting into a wide, easy grin.

Sammy felt her heart stutter in her chest, a sudden, sharp ache blooming beneath her ribs. His girl. The words were like a knife to the gut, a reminder of all the ways she had betrayed his trust, his faith in her.

"Hey, Otis," she managed, forcing a smile that felt brittle and false on her lips.

Otis pushed off the wall and ambled towards her, his steps loose and languid. "I got you a surprise," he said, his eyes sparkling with mischief. "Long Johns. You're always saying how cold you are in here, and I found some in town."

He held out a brown paper package, tied up with string. Sammy stared at it for a long moment, her vision blurring with sudden, hot tears.

Long Johns. Such a simple, thoughtful gift, and yet it broke her heart into a million jagged pieces. Because it was a reminder of all the ways Otis cared for her, all the little things he did to make her feel seen and cherished and special.

And she had repaid that care with lies and deceit, with a betrayal so deep and so cruel that she could hardly bear to contemplate it.

The tears began to fall in earnest now, streaking hot and fast down her cheeks. Sammy felt her knees buckle, her body wracked with great, heaving sobs that tore at her throat and made her chest ache.

"Long Johns," she gasped out, her voice thick and choked with emotion. "I don't deserve Long Johns. I'm sorry, Otis. I'm so, so sorry."

And then Otis was there, his arms coming around her in a tight, fierce embrace. He pulled her close, one hand cradling the back of her head as she wept into his chest.

"Shh, it's alright," he murmured, his voice low and soothing in her ear. "Hush now, don't cry. You better get in there 'fore you get in trouble."

He pulled back, his eyes searching her face with a mixture of concern and confusion. "You alright?" he asked softly, his thumb brushing a stray tear from her cheek.

Sammy shook her head, a fresh wave of sobs welling up in her throat. "I'm just sorry," she choked out, her voice raw and ragged with emotion. "Will you ever forgive me? I'm so sorry."

Otis frowned, his brow furrowing in bewilderment. "Whatever it is, you know I forgive you," he said slowly, his voice firm and unwavering. "You're my best friend. I would forgive you for anything."

The words were like a balm to Sammy's battered soul, a glimmer of hope in the darkness that threatened to swallow her whole. But before she could respond, before she could find the courage to tell him the truth, a familiar voice cut through the air like a knife.

"Good, you finally told him about the letter."

Sammy's head snapped up, her heart leaping into her throat. Cleopatra stood a few feet away, her arms crossed over her chest and a knowing, almost accusatory look on her face.

Otis glanced between them, his expression clouding with confusion. "What is she talking about?" he asked slowly, a note of trepidation creeping into his voice.

Cleopatra raised an eyebrow, her gaze boring into Sammy like a laser. "The letter," she said flatly. "From Vera. She gave it to you, right?"

Sammy felt the blood drain from her face, her stomach twisting into knots. This was it. The moment of truth, the reckoning she had been dreading for so long.

She reached into her pocket with trembling fingers, the crumpled envelope feeling like a lead weight in her hand. And then, before she could lose her nerve, she thrust it towards Otis, her eyes squeezing shut against the pain and the shame that threatened to overwhelm her.

"I'm so sorry," she whispered, her voice small and broken in the sudden, ringing silence.

And then she turned and fled, her footsteps echoing like gunshots as she raced towards the mailroom, her vision blurred with tears and her heart shattered into a million jagged pieces.

She didn't look back. Couldn't bear to see the betrayal and the hurt that she knew would be written all over Otis's face. All she could do was run, as fast and as far as her legs would carry her, away from the truth and the consequences of her actions.

But even as she burst through the doors of the mailroom, her chest heaving and her cheeks streaked with tears, Sammy knew that there was no escape. No hiding from the terrible, inescapable reality of what she had done.

She had lied to Otis. Had betrayed his trust and his faith in her, had shattered the fragile, precious thing that had been growing between them. And now, she would have to face the fallout, the wreckage of her own making.

Sammy sank to the floor, her back pressed against the cool, unyielding metal of the mailroom lockers. And there, in the dim, dusty stillness, she wept.

For the love she had lost. For the future she had thrown away. And for the terrible, aching knowledge that she had no one to blame but herself.

Days passed without a single glimpse of Otis. Sammy's heart grew heavier with each moment. Finally, she spotted him walking across the base. Heart in her throat, she raced after him, calling his name. Otis tried to avoid her, but Sammy was determined. She caught up to him, breathless and desperate.

Before she could get a word out, Otis's question cut through her like a knife. "Why did you do it, Sammy?"

She looked at him, heart heavy with regret. "You know why. It was foolish, but you know why."

He sighed. "I wish you would have just gave it to me".

"Me too."

A pause. Then, softly. "She said no."

Sammy's heart leapt with hope. "She did?" She tried to control her excitement. "I mean...she did?"

Otis nodded. "Yeah, she said I'm not the one. That it would be a mistake."

"Oh". Sammy swallowed hard. "So what does that mean for us?"

Otis looked away. "I've got to go."

Panic seized her. "Am I going to hear from you again?" Silence. "Otis, I'm sorry."

His eyes were distant, pained. "I thought I could trust you, Sammy. Guess I was wrong."

"You can trust me, Otis. I swear it!"

But he just kissed her cheek and walked away. "Bye, Sammy".

"Otis, wait!"

He didn't look back. As Sammy watched him go, tears stinging her eyes, the words caught in her throat. "You wouldn't have to ask me a million times to marry you. I'd marry you in a heartbeat."

But it was too late. He was gone. And Sammy was left with nothing but the aching realization of what she had lost.

CHAPTER 46:
PAIGE

Paige sat on her bunk, the worn pages of her Bible cool and familiar beneath her fingertips. She ran her hand over the cracked leather cover, tracing the faded gold lettering with a reverent touch. This book had been her constant companion, her anchor in the storm of war and uncertainty. Its words were a balm to her soul, a reminder of the unshakable truths that had guided her all her life.

But now, as she watched Cleopatra and Sammy burst into the barracks, their voices raised in a heated argument, Paige felt a flicker of unease stirring in her gut. There was a tension in the air, a crackling undercurrent of barely suppressed emotion that set her nerves on edge.

"Sammy, for the hundredth time, I'm sorry," Cleopatra was saying, her voice sharp with exasperation. "I thought you had told him. It's been days. You have to let this go. "

Sammy whirled on her, her face flushed with anger. "Next time, just mind your business," she snapped, her hands balling into fists at her sides.

Cleopatra opened her mouth to retort, but then her gaze fell on Paige, and she stopped short. A strange expression flitted across her face, a mix of surprise and something that might have been pity.

"I thought you might be moved out already," she said quietly, holding out a small stack of envelopes. "Here's your mail. Special delivery."

Paige took the letters with a frown, her brow furrowing in confusion. "I'm still waiting for them to move me," she said slowly, her gaze flicking to Sadie's empty bunk.

As Sadie entered the room, Paige rifled through the envelopes, her heart giving a painful lurch when she saw the familiar handwriting on one of them. "It's from my mother," she murmured, her fingers trembling slightly as she tore open the seal.

Paige's eyes scanned the page, her breath catching in her throat as she read the words that would shatter her world into a million jagged pieces.

"No," she whispered, shaking her head in desperate denial. "No, no, no..."

The letter slipped from her numb fingers, fluttering to the floor like a wounded bird. Paige's legs gave out beneath her, and she sank onto her bunk, her whole body shaking with the force of her grief.

"Paige?" Cleopatra's voice seemed to come from a great distance, muffled and distorted as if by water. "What's wrong?"

But Paige couldn't answer. Couldn't force the words past the lump in her throat, the agonized howl that threatened to tear itself from her chest.

"No," she moaned, rocking back and forth like a child. "No, no, no!"

She barely registered Cleopatra picking up the letter, barely heard the words that spilled from her friend's lips like shards of broken glass.

"My dearest daughter," Cleopatra read, her voice trembling with emotion. "I am so sorry to have to write these words, but the Army has informed us that Joe has been killed."

The world tilted on its axis, the ground dropping away beneath Paige's feet. She saw Joe in her mind's eye, saw him boarding that bus in Durham with his head held high and his uniform crisp and clean. She saw him refusing to move to the back, saw him standing tall and proud in the face of hatred and bigotry.

And then, with a sickening lurch, she saw him lying on the ground, his chest a bloody ruin and his eyes staring sightlessly at the sky. Saw the bus driver standing over him with a smoking gun, his face twisted with rage and hate.

Paige's heart shattered into a million pieces, the pain of it tearing through her like a knife. This couldn't be happening. It had to be a mistake, a cruel joke, a nightmare from which she would surely awaken at any moment.

Joe couldn't be gone. Her beautiful, brave boy, the light of her life, snuffed out like a candle in the wind. No.

Dimly, as if from a great distance, Paige heard Cleopatra's voice falter, heard the catch in her throat as she finished reading the letter. And then, suddenly, Sammy was there, her face a mask of stricken disbelief.

"Paige," Cleopatra whispered, her voice thick with unshed tears. "I am so sorry."

But Paige shook her head, a wild, desperate energy thrumming through her veins. "No," she cried, her voice rising to a keening wail. "No, that's not true. It has to be a mistake. They got the wrong boy. That's not my boy."

Cleopatra reached for her, her eyes shining with sympathy. "Paige--"

But Paige jerked away, her whole body trembling with the force of her denial. "No, it's not him," she insisted, her voice cracking with hysteria. "It's not. Sammy, tell her it's not him."

Sammy stared at her, her face a mask of helpless anguish. "Maybe I should get the Chaplain," she mumbled, her gaze darting away.

Paige surged to her feet, her hands balling into fists at her sides. "I don't need the Chaplain," she snarled, her voice rising to a shout. "I just need you to tell her it's not him. Stop looking at me like that. It's not him. It's not him!"

And then, suddenly, her gaze fell on Sadie. The strange, silent woman who always seemed to lurk at the edges of their little group, her dark eyes glittering with secrets and shadows.

Paige stumbled towards her, her breath coming in ragged gasps. "You," she choked out, her voice thick with desperation. "You tell them. Tell them it's not him."

But Sadie just shook her head, her face a mask of sorrow. "I'm sorry," she whispered, her voice barely audible over the pounding of Paige's heart.

Something snapped inside Paige, some last, fragile thread of sanity. She lunged at Sadie, her fingers clawing at the other woman's shoulders.

"Fix it," she screamed, her voice raw and ragged with grief. "Fix it! Do something. You bring him back!"

Cleopatra tried to pull her away, her voice low and urgent in Paige's ear. "Come on," she murmured, her touch gentle but insistent. "Let's get you to the infirmary. Maybe they can give you something to calm you down."

But Paige wrenched free of her grasp, her eyes wild and unseeing. "I don't need to calm down," she spat, rounding on Sadie once more. "You bring him back. You can do it. Sammy said you bring him back."

Sammy flinched as if struck, her face draining of color. "I was just talking, Paige," she stammered, her voice small and frightened.

But Paige was beyond reason, beyond sense. All she could see was the yawning, aching void that Joe's loss had carved into her soul, the black despair that threatened to swallow her whole.

"You're the Voodoo lady," she snarled, jabbing a finger at Sadie's chest. "The conjure woman, the one with the crazy eyes. You bring him back."

She seized Sadie by the shoulders, shaking her like a rag doll. Cleopatra tried to intervene, her voice rising in alarm.

"Sweetie, you need to stop," she pleaded, her hands fluttering uselessly at Paige's back.

But Paige was beyond hearing, beyond reach. All she could see was the box that peeked out from beneath Sadie's bunk, the strange, carved thing that seemed to pulse with a dark and deadly energy.

"Do a spell," she demanded, her voice rising to a fevered pitch. "Do something. Make this not true. Where's that box?"

She lunged for it, her fingers scrabbling against the rough wood. Sadie jerked upright, her eyes wide and panicked.

"Give me the box," she whispered, her voice trembling with fear.

But Paige was relentless, her grip tightening on the lid. "Do it," she screamed, spittle flying from her lips. "Do your spell. Bring him back!"

Sadie tried to wrench the box away, her face contorted with desperation. "Give it to me!" she cried, her voice rising to a howl.

But Paige was stronger, her grief lending her a manic, impossible strength. With a final, wrenching tug, she tore the lid from the box, scattering its contents across the floor like so much detritus.

Pictures fluttered to the ground, black and white images of a handsome, smiling man in uniform. And there, nestled among them like a viper in the grass, was a crumpled, yellowed envelope, the words "RETURN TO SENDER" stamped across its face in stark, unforgiving letters.

Sammy dropped to her knees, her fingers trembling as she gathered up the photographs. "Pictures?" she whispered, her voice thick with disbelief.

Sadie scrambled forward, her hands shaking as she snatched the photos from Sammy's grasp. "Give me those!" she cried, clutching them to her chest like a talisman.

And then, in a voice so soft and broken that it hardly sounded human, she spoke. "This is my husband," she whispered, her fingers tracing the smiling face that stared up at her from the photographs. "This is my Andrew. He was stationed at Port Chicago. He was loading munitions, and they detonated."

She raised her head, her eyes shining with unshed tears. "I should have told him not to enlist," she said softly, her voice thick with regret. "I should have told him not to go."

But Paige was beyond sympathy, beyond compassion. All she could feel was the white-hot blade of her own grief, the searing, unendurable pain of her loss.

"I need you to bring Joe back," she snarled, her fingers curling into claws.

Sadie shook her head, her face a mask of sorrow. "I can't," she whispered, her voice cracking with emotion. "You know that."

Paige's vision tunneled, the world narrowing to a single, burning point of fury. "Tell me this is a mistake," she screamed, her voice rising to a keening wail. "Tell me it's not true!"

But Sadie's next words drove the breath from her lungs, the blood from her veins. "It's true," she said softly, her eyes haunted and distant. "I've seen him. I've seen him."

She shuddered, her whole body wracked with fine tremors. "I don't want to see him," she whispered, her voice thick with anguish. "I want to see Andrew."

Paige stared at her, her mind reeling with the implications of Sadie's words. "Seen him?" she breathed, her voice thin and thready with shock.

And then, suddenly, Sadie was reaching for the photograph that lay on Paige's bunk. The picture of Joe, smiling and whole and so painfully, impossibly alive.

"He's been here," Sadie murmured, her fingers brushing over the glossy surface with a reverent touch. "For a while now. I'm sorry. He just wants to say goodbye."

She raised her head, her eyes shining with a terrible, knowing light. "It's not fair," she whispered, her voice thick with bitterness. "Why do you get to say goodbye, when I don't?"

Something snapped inside Paige, some last, fragile thread of restraint. With a howl of anguish, she snatched the photograph from Sadie's grasp, clutching it to her chest like a lifeline.

"You don't know what you're talking about," she snarled, her voice rising to a scream. "It's not Joe. Please, don't let it be Joe."

And then, with a strength born of desperation, she shoved Sadie away, sending her sprawling to the floor in a tangle of limbs.

Dimly, as if from a great distance, Paige felt Cleopatra and Sammy's arms come around her, felt the warmth of their embrace as they tried to hold her together, to keep her from flying apart at the seams.

But it was too late. The dam had broken, the floodgates had opened, and there was nothing left but the howling, empty void of her grief.

Paige sagged into their arms, her whole body wracked with great, heaving sobs. And as the world dissolved into a blur of tears and anguish, she barely registered the sound of Sadie's footsteps, barely heard the slam of the barracks door as the other woman fled into the night.

All she could do was cling to the shattered remnants of her heart and pray for the oblivion of sleep to claim her at last.

But even in the depths of her despair, Paige knew that there would be no peace for her. No rest, no solace, no balm for the wound that Joe's loss had carved into her soul.

There was only the endless, aching emptiness, the yawning chasm of a life that would never be whole again.

And in that moment, Paige knew that she would have given anything, everything, just to hear her son's voice one last time. Just to hold him in her arms and tell him that she loved him, that she was proud of him, that he was her heart and her soul and her reason for being.

But it was too late. Joe was gone, and all that remained was the shattered wreckage of a mother's broken heart.

And so Paige wept, and the world wept with her, and the night stretched on into a bleak and endless darkness that knew no end.

CHAPTER 47:
SADIE

Sadie stumbled through the darkness, her vision blurred by the hot, stinging tears that streamed down her cheeks. She didn't know where she was going, didn't care. All she knew was that she had to get away, had to escape.

Witch. Hoodoo woman. Crazy eyes.

The words echoed in her mind, each one a tiny, stinging barb that lodged itself deep in her heart. She had tried so hard to fit in, to be just another soldier, another cog in the great, grinding machine of war. But no matter what she did, no matter how hard she tried, she could never escape the curse that had shadowed her steps since birth.

And now, with Paige's anguished screams still ringing in her ears and the image of Joe's ghost seared into her mind's eye, Sadie knew that she could no longer bear the weight of her own strangeness. Could no longer endure the crushing isolation, the constant, gnawing ache of being an outsider in her own skin.

She had to leave. Had to get as far away from this place, these people, as she possibly could.

And so she ran. Ran until her lungs burned and her legs trembled, until the neat rows of barracks and supply sheds gave way to the wild, tangled undergrowth of the forest that bordered the base.

She didn't know how long she stumbled through the darkness, her breath coming in ragged gasps and her heart pounding a frantic tattoo against her ribs. Time seemed to blur and warp around her, the minutes stretching into hours, the hours into an eternity of misery and despair.

But finally, as the first pale fingers of dawn began to creep across the sky, Sadie found herself standing before Major Dixon's door.

She hesitated for a moment, her hand hovering over the heavy brass knob. She knew she had no right to be here, no right to barge in on the Major's private domain in the middle of the night. But something deep inside her, some desperate, clawing need, propelled her forward.

And so, with a shaking hand and a heart full of trepidation, Sadie pushed open the door and stepped inside.

The office was dimly lit, the only illumination coming from a single lamp on the Major's desk. But even in the half-light, Sadie could see that the room was not empty. Major Dixon sat behind her desk, her face drawn and her eyes shadowed with exhaustion. And clustered around her, their expressions grim and their voices low, were a handful of other officers.

For a moment, Sadie simply stood there, frozen in place by the weight of their collective gaze. She knew she must look a fright, with her tear-stained cheeks and her wild, tangled hair. Knew that she had no business interrupting their meeting, no right to demand their attention or their time.

But then, from somewhere deep inside her, a small, stubborn spark of courage flared to life. A flicker of determination, of sheer, bullheaded resolve that refused to be extinguished by the doubts and fears that clamored at the edges of her mind.

She had come this far. Had risked everything, put everything on the line, for the chance to speak her truth. And she would be damned if she let anything, even her own crippling self-doubt, stand in her way now.

And so, with a deep, steadying breath, Sadie stepped forward into the pool of lamplight. Cleared her throat, her voice rough and ragged with emotion.

"Excuse me," she said softly, her words almost lost in the hushed stillness of the room. "I need to talk to Major Dixon."

The officers turned as one to stare at her, their expressions ranging from surprise to outright hostility. Captain Carter frowned down at her, her brow furrowed in disapproval.

"Private, this area is for officers only," she said. "What are you doing here at this time of night?"

Sadie swallowed hard, forcing herself to meet her gaze. "I need to speak to Major Dixon," she repeated, her voice firmer now, more insistent.

The captain's frown deepened, her eyes flashing with irritation. "There is a chain of command," she snapped, jabbing a finger towards the door. "And you need to follow it."

But Sadie couldn't back down. Not now, not when everything she had ever believed in, everything she had ever fought for, hung in the balance.

"Major Dixon," she said, her voice rising in desperation. "I need you to send me home."

The room fell silent, the officers exchanging startled glances. The Captain opened her mouth to speak. But before she could get a word out, Sadie pushed on, the words tumbling from her lips in a frantic, breathless rush.

"Please," she begged, her voice cracking with emotion. "I can't stay here any longer. Coming here was a mistake."

Major Dixon leaned forward in her chair, her eyes searching Sadie's face with a mix of concern and confusion. "Private Lewis," she said slowly, her voice low and measured. "I can't just let you out of the WAC and send you home. You know it doesn't work like that."

She hesitated, her brow furrowing in thought. "You're not thinking clearly," she said gently, her tone almost motherly in its concern. "Maybe we should get you to the infirmary, have them take a look at you."

But Sadie shook her head, a wild, desperate energy thrumming through her veins. "I thought you would understand," she whispered, her voice small and broken in the stillness. "I thought you, of all people, would see why I can't stay. Why I don't belong here."

And then, before anyone could stop her, she turned on her heel and fled, her footsteps echoing like gunshots in the sudden, ringing silence.

She ran blindly through the base, her vision blurred by tears and her breath coming in ragged gasps. She didn't know where she was going, didn't care. All she knew was that she had to get away, had to put as much distance as possible between herself and the accusing eyes of the officers, the pitying gaze of Major Dixon.

And so she ran. Ran until her lungs burned and her legs gave out, until she collapsed in a heap on the cold, damp earth of the forest floor.

There, in the shadow of the towering pines, Sadie finally let herself break. Let the sobs come, great, heaving things that tore at her throat and made her chest ache with the force of her grief.

She wept for Andrew, for the love she had lost and the future she would never have. For the curse that had stolen everything from her, that had marked her as an outcast and a pariah from the moment she drew her first breath.

And she wept for herself. For the scared, lonely little girl who had never quite fit in, who had always known that she was different, that she would never be like the other children who laughed and played in the dusty streets of her hometown.

She had tried so hard to be normal. Had buried her gifts, her strange and terrible powers, deep inside herself, had hidden them away like shameful secrets. But in the end, it hadn't mattered. In the end, the truth had come out, as it always did.

And now, here she was. Alone and adrift in a world that had no place for her, that looked upon her with fear and revulsion and called her monster.

But even as the despair threatened to swallow her whole, even as the blackness closed in around her like a shroud, Sadie felt a small, stubborn flicker of defiance kindling in her chest. A tiny, feeble spark of hope, of sheer, bullheaded determination that refused to be extinguished.

She was not a monster. She was not evil, or cursed, or damned. She was just a woman, a soldier, a human being who had been given a burden she had never asked for and a power she could not control.

CHAPTER 48:
MAJOR DIXON

Major Clarissa Dixon sat at her desk, her brow furrowed in concentration as she pored over the stack of reports and requisition forms that seemed to multiply every time she turned her back. The weight of command hung heavy on her shoulders, a constant, nagging pressure that never quite let up, even in the rare moments of quiet like this one.

She knew she should be used to it by now, the endless parade of paperwork and personnel issues, the constant, simmering tension that came with being the highest-ranking Negro officer in the European Theater. But some days, the burden felt almost too much to bear, the expectations and the scrutiny and the sheer, grinding exhaustion of it all threatening to crush her beneath their weight.

A soft knock at the door startled her out of her reverie, and she looked up to see Captain Carter standing in the doorway, her face grim and her shoulders tense.

"She's AWOL," the captain said without preamble, her voice tight with worry. "We need to report it."

Major Dixon felt a flicker of unease stirring in her gut, a cold, creeping dread that she couldn't quite shake. She knew exactly who Carter was talking about, knew the face that swam before her mind's eye like a half-remembered dream.

Private Sadie Lewis. The strange, silent woman who always seemed to hover at the edges of things, her dark eyes glittering with secrets and shadows. The one who had come to her in the dead of night, her face streaked with tears and her voice raw with desperate, clawing need.

"No," Major Dixon said slowly, shaking her head. "Don't do that. I'll handle it."

She hesitated, a sudden, sharp pang of guilt twisting in her chest. "We should have taken her to the infirmary last night," she murmured, almost to herself.

Captain Carter frowned, her brow furrowing in confusion. "But the process is--" she began, her voice rising in protest.

But Major Dixon cut her off with a sharp, decisive gesture. "I said I'll handle it," she repeated, her tone brooking no argument.

For a moment, Captain Carter simply stared at her, something like doubt flickering in her eyes. But then, with a crisp nod and a murmured "Yes, Major," she turned on her heel and strode out of the office, leaving Major Dixon alone with her thoughts.

She sat there for a long moment, her mind awhirl with memories and unanswered questions. She thought of Private Lewis's face, the haunted, hunted look in her eyes as she had pleaded for release, for the chance to escape the demons that dogged her every step. Thought of the way the woman's thin, trembling frame had seemed to vibrate with a kind of manic, desperate energy, as if she might fly apart at any moment.

Major Dixon had seen that look before, had felt the echoes of that same desperate, clawing need in her own heart. She knew what it was like to be an outsider, to feel the weight of other people's fear and mistrust pressing down on you from all sides. To walk through the world wearing a mask, hiding the truth of who you were behind a carefully cultivated facade of strength and competence.

And so, even as her rational mind insisted that she follow protocol, that she report the Private's absence and let the chips fall where they may, something deeper, something instinctive, held her back. Something that whispered that there was more to Sadie Lewis than met the eye, that the woman's strange, unsettling gifts might just be the key to unlocking the secrets that haunted them all.

With a heavy sigh, Major Dixon pushed herself to her feet, her mind made up. She would find Private Lewis, would do whatever it took to bring her back into the fold. And then, together, they would find a way to make sense of all that seemed to close in around them like a noose, tightening with every passing day.

But first, she had a stop to make. A duty to perform, a debt to pay to a woman who had already lost more than any mother should ever have to bear.

The infirmary was quiet when Major Dixon arrived, the halls echoing with the soft, muffled sounds of sleep and slow, steady breathing. She made her way to the private room at the end of the corridor, her heart heavy with the weight of the news she carried.

Paige Thomas lay in the narrow bed, her face pale and drawn against the stark white of the pillowcase. She stared blankly at the wall, her eyes glassy and unfocused, as if she were seeing something far beyond the confines of the little room.

Major Dixon hesitated for a moment, suddenly unsure of her welcome. But then, with a deep, steadying breath, she stepped forward, her voice low and gentle in the stillness.

"I'm so sorry to hear about your son," she murmured, her throat tight with emotion. "I wanted to come and pay my respects. He was a hero. He didn't deserve to die that way. No one does."

Paige said nothing, gave no sign that she had even heard the words. But Major Dixon pressed on, her voice growing stronger, more insistent.

"If there is anything that I can do," she said softly, "or anything you need, please don't hesitate to reach out."

At that, Paige finally looked up, her gaze meeting Major Dixon's for the briefest of moments. She gave a small, jerky nod, her lips pressed together in a thin, bloodless line.

Major Dixon hesitated again, torn between the desire to offer comfort and the knowledge that there were no words, no platitudes, that could ever ease the ache of a mother's grief. But there was something else, too, a nagging sense of unease that tugged at the edges of her mind, a mystery that demanded to be solved.

"I'm sorry to worry you with this," she said slowly, choosing her words with care. "But I'm trying to locate your bunkmate, Sadie Lewis. Do you have any idea where she might be? It is urgent that we locate her immediately."

For a long, tense moment, Paige simply stared at her, her eyes dark and inscrutable in the dim light of the infirmary. But then, just as Major Dixon was about to give up, to turn and leave the grieving woman to her solitude, Paige spoke.

"The stables," she whispered, her voice rough and ragged with unshed tears. "Check the stables."

Major Dixon felt a sudden, sharp thrill of excitement, a flicker of hope kindling in her chest. She gave Paige's hand a quick, grateful squeeze, murmuring a soft "thank you" before turning and striding out of the room, her steps quick and purposeful.

She found Captain Carter waiting for her in the hallway, her face tense with worry. Together, they made their way across the base, the weak winter sunlight filtering through the clouds above like a pale, watery promise.

The stables were dark and silent when they arrived, the air thick with the musty scent of hay and horse. Major Dixon shivered in the chill, her breath misting in the air before her like a ghost.

"She can't have been in here all night," Captain Carter murmured, her voice low and doubtful.

But Major Dixon just shook her head, a sudden, inexplicable certainty settling over her like a mantle. "Thomas said to check here," she said firmly, her gaze sweeping the shadowed corners of the building.

They searched for a long moment, their footsteps echoing loudly in the stillness. But there was no sign of Sadie Lewis, no trace of the haunted, desperate woman who had come to Major Dixon in the dead of night, pleading for release.

"Well, she's obviously not here," Captain Carter said at last, her voice heavy with defeat.

They turned to leave, their shoulders slumped and their hearts heavy with disappointment. But just as they reached the door, something caught Major Dixon's eye. A flicker of movement in the shadows, a huddled shape tucked away in the farthest corner of the stable.

Her heart in her throat, Major Dixon ran to the figure's side, her breath catching in her chest as she took in the sight before her. It was Sadie Lewis, her thin frame curled in on itself like a child, her skin pale and waxy in the dim light. She was shivering violently, her lips tinged with blue and her eyes glassy and unfocused.

"Go get help!" Major Dixon barked, her voice sharp with fear and urgency.

Captain Carter hesitated for a moment, her eyes wide with shock. "My God," she whispered, her voice trembling.

"Now!" Major Dixon snapped, her tone brooking no argument.

Captain Carter turned and ran, her footsteps echoing like gunshots in the sudden, ringing silence. Major Dixon barely noticed her go, all her attention focused on the woman before her.

With shaking hands, she stripped off her coat and wrapped it around Sadie's shoulders, pulling the shivering woman close against her chest. She could feel the cold seeping into her bones, the icy bite of the wind cutting through her uniform like a knife. But she didn't care, couldn't bring herself to care about anything but the fragile, broken creature in her arms.

"Lewis," she murmured, her voice low and urgent. "What are you doing out here? What were you thinking?"

Sadie's eyes fluttered open, her gaze hazy and unfocused. "My...my grandmother said it was...a gift," she whispered, her voice thin and thready. "But...it's a curse. I...can't help...anyone. Andrew..."

Her eyes slid closed again, her body going limp and still in Major Dixon's arms. Panic surged through Major Dixon's veins, hot and bright and all-consuming. She gave Sadie a gentle shake, her voice rising in desperation.

"That's not true," she insisted, her words tumbling out in a frantic, breathless rush. "You helped me. You helped me."

She pulled Sadie closer, feeling the faint, thready flutter of the other woman's heartbeat against her own. "Hey," she whispered, her voice cracking with emotion. "Stay with me now. Don't you dare give up on me, Lewis. Don't you dare."

But Sadie was fading fast, her breaths growing shallow and labored. Major Dixon felt a surge of helpless rage, a bitter, aching fury at the cruelty of a world that would take a woman like Sadie Lewis and break her, crush her beneath the weight of its fear and ignorance.

She had failed her, Major Dixon realized with a sudden, sickening lurch. Had let her suffer in silence, had turned a blind eye to the pain and the darkness that had eaten away at her soul like a cancer. And now, it might be too late, the damage too deep and too irreparable to ever be undone.

But even as the despair threatened to swallow her whole, even as the blackness closed in around her like a shroud, Major Dixon felt a small, stubborn flicker of hope kindling in her chest. A tiny, feeble spark of determination, of sheer, bullheaded resolve that refused to be extinguished.

She would not let Sadie Lewis die. Would not let the narrow minds and spiteful tongues of the world claim another victim, snuff out another bright and shining light.

She would fight for her, would claw and scrape and beg and borrow for the chance to bring her back from the brink. Would move heaven and earth and every stubborn, bureaucratic obstacle in her path to get her the help she needed, the care and compassion she so desperately deserved.

It was a vow, a promise, a solemn oath sworn in the stillness of the stables, with nothing but the cold and the shadows to bear witness. And as she cradled Sadie's limp, unresponsive form against her chest, Major Dixon felt a fierce, unshakable conviction settle over her like a mantle.

She would not fail her. Not again. Not ever.

Even if it meant facing down the demons that lurked in the darkest corners of her own mind, the fears and doubts that whispered that she was not enough, that she would never be enough.

She would be strong. For Sadie, for herself, for all the bright and shining souls who had been broken on the wheel of this cruel and uncaring world.

And together, they would find a way back to the light.

CHAPTER 49:
SADIE

Weeks later, Sadie stood at attention, her eyes fixed straight ahead as Major Dixon addressed the battalion. The early morning sun glinted off the Major's expertly polished buttons, turning her into a beacon of strength and authority against the pale English sky.

"You're working your fingers raw every day," Major Dixon began, her voice ringing out clear and strong across the assembled ranks, "freezing in a cold warehouse, only to be beat down by the negative press back home."

Sadie felt a flicker of recognition at the words, a pang of empathy that thrummed through her like a plucked string. She knew all too well the bitter sting of rejection, the soul-deep weariness that came from pouring yourself out day after day for a world that seemed determined to grind you into the dust.

"You feel uncertain with President Roosevelt's passing," the Major continued, her gaze sweeping over the sea of upturned faces. "You question your decision to come halfway around the world for a country that does not value you. You ask yourself, why should I care about the morale of soldiers, the majority of whom don't give a damn about me?"

A murmur rippled through the crowd at that, a low, uneasy rustle of agreement and discontent. Sadie felt it too, the simmering resentment, the gnawing sense of futility that threatened to eat her up inside. What was the point of it all, really? What difference could they possibly make, one small battalion of Negro women in a vast, uncaring machine of war?

But then Major Dixon's voice softened, her eyes growing distant and reflective. "I know you are thinking and feeling these things," she murmured, "because I am thinking and feeling them too."

And as she spoke, Sadie felt something shift inside her, a subtle realignment of perspective. She looked around at her fellow soldiers, really looked at them for perhaps the first time. And what she saw took her breath away.

They were beautiful, these women. Flawed and fragile and perfectly, impossibly human. Each face was a story, a tapestry woven of joy and sorrow, triumph and despair. And yet, beneath it all, there was a core of strength, a stubborn, unshakable resolve that glowed like an ember in the depths of their eyes.

"For every White soldier that stops to thank me in the street for getting the mail moving again," Major Dixon said wryly, "there are five more who cross to the other side so they won't have to salute me. For every step of progress I think we make, there's a new hotel in London built 'just for us'."

Sadie nodded to herself, a bitter smile tugging at the corners of her mouth. It was the same old story, the same tired dance of one step forward, two steps back. But somehow, hearing it from the Major's lips, it didn't feel quite so hopeless anymore. Somehow, it felt like a challenge, a gauntlet thrown down at their feet.

"When these thoughts creep into my mind," Major Dixon continued, her voice growing stronger, more insistent, "I remember I am here because of divine providence. I am here because this is where I am supposed to be."

She paused, her gaze sweeping over the battalion once more. "I gathered you here today to tell you that's why you are here too.

You are exactly where you are supposed to be. I see something in every single one of you."

Sadie felt a lump rise in her throat, a sudden, sharp ache blooming behind her breastbone. She had spent so long running from herself, so long trying to bury the strangeness, the otherness that set her apart. But here, in this moment, she felt seen. Felt valued, not in spite of her differences, but because of them.

"We've got to help each other," Major Dixon urged, her eyes blazing with fierce conviction. "We've got to take an interest in each other. Because if we don't, no one else will. It's up to us to believe in us. It's up to us to find that magic we each possess."

Magic. The word sent a shiver down Sadie's spine, a crackle of electricity that danced across her skin like static. She had always thought of her abilities as a curse, a burden she was doomed to carry alone. But maybe, just maybe, there was power in them too. Maybe there was a way to turn them to the light, to use them for something greater than herself.

"Now we have a month left to meet our goal here," Major Dixon said briskly, her tone sharpening with resolve. "Yes, it was an ambitious goal, but I set it because I believe in you. If you are looking for something to still have faith in, have faith in yourselves. Have faith in each other. Have faith in the six triple eight."

She raised her chin, her eyes flashing with a fierce, defiant light. "That's all we need," she declared, her voice ringing out like a clarion call.

And as Sadie stood there, her spine straight and her heart full to bursting, she felt something kindle deep inside her. The weeks in the infirmary in the past. A spark, a tiny flame of hope and purpose that burned bright against the darkness.

She would not let it go out. Not now, not ever. She would tend it, nurture it, fan it to a blaze that would light her way through whatever trials lay ahead.

Because Major Dixon was right. They had each other. They had the Six Triple Eight. And that was enough. It had to be.

The days that followed passed in a blur of activity, a whirlwind of sorting and stamping and loading that left Sadie's fingers numb and her mind spinning. But through it all, she clung to that tiny spark, that stubborn ember of determination that Major Dixon had ignited in her heart.

She watched it catch and spread, watched it blaze to life in the eyes of her fellow soldiers as they bent to their task with renewed vigor. Saw it in the set of Cleopatra's jaw as she organized morale-boosting events and performances, in the fierce, protective way Sammy hovered over Paige as she emerged from her fog of grief.

And slowly, impossibly, the piles began to shrink. The towering stacks of letters and packages that had once seemed so insurmountable gradually dwindled, day by backbreaking day, until the warehouse echoed with empty space and the taste of victory hung sweet in the air.

When Major Dixon strode in on that final day, her face alight with quiet pride, Sadie felt her heart swell to bursting. They had done it. They had achieved the impossible, had proven to the world and to themselves just what Negro women were capable of.

But even as she basked in the warmth of that triumph, Sadie couldn't quite shake the shadow that lingered at the edges of her mind. Couldn't forget the cold, dank darkness of the stables, the aching emptiness that had threatened to swallow her whole.

She found herself seeking out Cleopatra in the quiet moments between shifts, drawn to the other woman's steady warmth and unfailing compassion. And when Cleo suggested a small, private ritual to honor their lost loved ones, Sadie knew she could not refuse.

They gathered in the barracks one evening, just the four of them - Sadie, Cleo, Sammy, and Paige. Sadie's heart clenched at the sight of Paige's drawn, haggard face, the dark circles that shadowed her eyes. But she knew, too, the strength that lay beneath, the unbreakable core of iron that had carried Paige through the darkest nights of her grief.

Cleo lit two candles, the flames casting a soft, flickering glow over their solemn faces. "This is for Andrew," she murmured, touching one wick with reverent fingers. Then, with a nod to Paige, "And this is for Joe."

Sadie swallowed hard, her throat suddenly tight and aching. She had never dared to hope for this, for a chance to lay her burdens down among women who understood, who knew the shape and weight of loss like a second skin.

But as Paige began to speak, her voice rough and halting, Sadie felt something loosen inside her, a hard, tight knot of grief and guilt and longing that she had carried for so long, she had almost forgotten it was there.

"He was the best son anyone could ever ask for," Paige whispered, her eyes bright with unshed tears.

Sadie reached out, laying a tentative hand on the other woman's arm. "I thought joining might bring me closer to Andrew," she said softly, the words like ashes on her tongue. "He was my everything."

Paige turned to her then, her gaze searching, almost desperate. "Joe," she breathed, the name a broken prayer. "Is he still--"

"I haven't seen him," Sadie said gently, sensing the unspoken question. "I think...I think he's at peace now, Paige."

Something in Paige's face crumpled at that, a sudden, painful hope blooming in the depths of her eyes. "And Andrew?" she asked, her voice small and fragile as a bird. "Have you seen--"

Sadie shook her head, a sad, rueful smile tugging at her lips. "I haven't seen anyone," she murmured. "Not since that night."

And then, to her shock, Paige was leaning into her, slender arms coming up to wrap around Sadie's waist in a fierce, desperate embrace. Sadie stiffened for a moment, every instinct screaming at her to pull away, to retreat back behind the walls she had built so high and so strong.

But some deeper impulse held her fast, some part of her that had been starving for this, for the simple, human comfort of touch and connection. And so she let herself sink into Paige's arms, let herself be held and known and understood in a way she had never dared to imagine.

Beside them, Sammy and Cleo joined the embrace, their own faces wet with tears of sorrow and solidarity. And as they clung to each other in the candlelit dimness of the barracks, Sadie felt something shift inside her, a tiny, crucial piece of herself slotting back into place.

She was not alone. She had never been alone, even in her darkest, most desperate hours. And now, with these women by her side, she knew she never would be again.

The day of their departure dawned bright and clear, the English Channel glittering like a ribbon of diamonds beneath the pale winter sun. Sadie stood on the dock with her sisters, her eyes fixed on the horizon as she waited to board the ship that would carry them to their next great adventure.

Beside her, Sammy bounced on her toes, a ball of barely-contained excitement and nervous energy. "I don't know if I can get on this boat," she moaned, clutching dramatically at her stomach.

Sadie huffed out a laugh, reaching into her pocket to pull out a battered tin of ginger candies. "Here," she said, pressing one into Sammy's palm with a wry grin. "This will help."

Sammy beamed at her, popping the candy into her mouth with a grateful sigh. "You're a lifesaver," she mumbled around the sweet.

"So are you," Sadie said softly, meaning it with every fiber of her being.

They shuffled forward in line, the ship looming larger with every step. But just as they neared the gangplank, a voice rang out over the clamor of the crowd, high and urgent and achingly familiar.

"Sammy!" it cried, the sound of it sending a jolt of recognition through Sadie's chest. "Sammy, wait!"

Sammy whirled around, her eyes widening with shock and joy. "Otis?" she breathed, her voice trembling with disbelief. "Is that really you?"

And then he was there, pushing his way through the throng with single-minded determination, his face split in a grin so wide it looked almost painful. He skidded to a stop in front of Sammy, his chest heaving and his eyes bright with unshed tears.

"I can't let you leave like this," he panted, reaching out to take her hands in his. "Not without telling you...not without making sure you know..."

He dropped to one knee, his gaze never leaving Sammy's stunned, radiant face. "Sammy Love Bonnet," he said, his voice ringing out clear and strong. "Will you do me the honor of being my wife?"

Sammy let out a sound somewhere between a laugh and a sob, her head bobbing up and down in ecstatic agreement. "Yes," she gasped, tugging Otis to his feet and throwing her arms around his neck. "Yes, yes, a thousand times yes!"

They crashed together in a fierce, passionate kiss, their joy so bright and infectious that Sadie could almost taste it on the air. Beside her, Cleo and Paige exchanged misty smiles, their eyes soft with vicarious delight.

"I told you that you were going to love Europe," Sadie murmured, nudging Sammy with an elbow as the newly-engaged couple finally came up for air.

Sammy just grinned, her cheeks flushed and her eyes sparkling with incandescent happiness. She opened her mouth to reply, but before she could get a word out, the ship's whistle pierced the air, sharp and insistent.

"Don't miss the boat, Sammy!" Cleo called over her shoulder, already moving towards the gangplank with Paige in tow.

Sammy hesitated, torn between her desire to stay wrapped in Otis's arms and her duty to her sisters. But Sadie just smiled, giving her a gentle push towards the ship.

"Go on," she said softly, her heart full to bursting with affection and pride. "I'll catch up."

Sammy flashed her a grateful grin, pressing one last, quick kiss to Otis's cheek before turning to race up the gangplank, her skirt flapping in the brisk sea breeze. Sadie watched her go, a bittersweet ache blooming behind her breastbone.

She was happy for Sammy, truly she was. But she couldn't help the tiny, selfish part of herself that envied her friend's easy joy, the simple certainty of her love and her future. What would it be like, she wondered, to be so sure of one's place in the world? To know, deep in your bones, that you were exactly where you were meant to be?

"Sadie Lewis?"

The voice startled her out of her reverie, low and unfamiliar and somehow, inexplicably, filled with warmth. Sadie turned, her brow furrowing in confusion as she took in the stranger standing before her.

He was tall and broad-shouldered, with dark, earnest eyes that seemed to see straight into her soul. There was something achingly familiar about the set of his jaw, the curve of his mouth.

"Yes?" she said slowly, hating the tremor of uncertainty in her voice.

Nathan smiled, a small, almost shy thing that made Sadie's heart skip a beat. "You're a hard woman to reach," he said ruefully, rubbing the back of his neck with one hand. "I'm Nathan. I'm...I was a friend of Andrew's."

Sadie felt the breath leave her lungs in a rush, her knees going weak and watery beneath her. Andrew. The name was like a key turning in a rusted lock, a door swinging open onto a room she had long since sealed away.

"I don't understand," she whispered, her voice cracking on the edges. "How...why are you here?"

Nathan's face softened, his eyes filling with a strange, aching tenderness. "I've been trying to catch up to you for months," he said quietly, reaching into his pocket to pull out a battered envelope. "To give you this. It's...it's the last letter Andrew wrote to you, before he died."

Sadie stared at the envelope, her vision blurring with sudden, hot tears. She had never dared to hope for this, never allowed herself to imagine that there might be some final piece of Andrew out there, some tangible reminder of the love they had shared.

"I know I could have just mailed it," Nathan continued, his voice rough with emotion. "But it was important to me to give it to you in person. I needed to know for sure that you got it. That you...that you had a chance to say goodbye."

Goodbye. The word hit Sadie like a punch to the gut, stealing the breath from her lungs. She had never gotten to say goodbye to Andrew, not really. Had never had the chance to tell him one last time how much she loved him, how deeply and irrevocably he had changed her life.

But now, with this letter in her hands...maybe she finally could.

"Thank you," she breathed, her fingers trembling as she reached out to take the envelope from Nathan's grasp. "I don't...I don't know what to say."

Nathan just smiled, a sad, understanding thing that made Sadie's heart ache. "You don't have to say anything," he murmured, his hand brushing hers for the briefest of moments. "Just...just read it. And know that Andrew loved you, more than anything in this world."

Sadie nodded, too choked with emotion to speak. She clutched the letter to her chest, feeling the crinkle of the paper beneath her fingertips, the weight of Andrew's words lying heavy against her heart.

She opened her mouth to thank Nathan again, to ask him the thousand questions that suddenly burned on her tongue. But before she could utter a word, Sammy was there, grabbing her arm and tugging her towards the ship with breathless urgency.

"Come on!" she cried, her eyes wide and her cheeks flushed with excitement. "We can't miss the boat!" She grinned, her face nearly splitting with the force of her joy. "We've got a wedding to plan!"

Sadie let herself be pulled along, too stunned and overwhelmed to resist. She glanced back over her shoulder, her gaze locking with Nathan's for one final, charged moment.

"If you have questions," he called after her, his voice nearly lost in the clamor of the crowd, "you can write to me. My information is in there." He hesitated, his eyes softening with something that might have been longing. "I hope you do."

And then he was gone, swallowed up by the sea of bodies as Sadie was swept up the gangplank and onto the deck of the ship. She stood at the railing, her fingers clutching the worn wood as she watched the shoreline recede, the tiny figure of Nathan growing smaller and smaller until he was nothing more than a speck on the horizon.

But even as the distance between them grew, Sadie felt a strange sense of peace settling over her, a quiet certainty that this was not the end of their story. That somehow, in some way she could not yet fathom, their paths would cross again.

She reached into her bag, her fingers brushing against the smooth, polished surface of Andrew's box. The familiar weight of it was a comfort, a tether to the past and the love she had lost. But it no longer felt like a shackle, a burden she was doomed to carry alone.

For the first time in longer than she could remember, Sadie felt a flicker of something that might have been hope kindling in her chest. A sense that maybe, just maybe, there was a future for her beyond the darkness and the pain. A chance for healing, for growth, for a love that could weather any storm.

She looked out over the water, watching the sun paint the waves in shades of gold and crimson. And as the sky slowly deepened to a velvety black, the stars blossoming like flowers in the endless expanse of the night, Sadie felt a smile tugging at the corners of her mouth.

She was not the same woman she had been when she first set foot on this journey. The war, the Six Triple Eight, the unbreakable bonds of sisterhood she had forged in the crucible of hardship and heartache...they had all left their mark on her, had shaped and molded her into someone stronger, someone braver, someone more wholly and authentically herself.

And now, as she stood on the cusp of a new beginning, a new chapter in the story of her life, Sadie knew that she was ready. Ready to face whatever challenges and triumphs lay ahead, secure in the knowledge that she had the strength and the courage to meet them head-on.

She was not alone. Not anymore. She had her sisters, her comrades-in-arms, the women who had seen her through the darkest nights of her soul and emerged on the other side, battered but unbroken.

And she had herself. Her gifts, her scars, the strange and terrible beauty that made her who she was. The magic that flowed through her veins like stardust, like the promise of a brighter tomorrow.

Sadie closed her eyes, letting the salt spray wash over her face like a baptism. And as the ship carried her onwards, towards the great, unknowable future that stretched out before her like a blank page waiting to be written, she felt a sense of calm settling deep in her bones.

She was exactly where she was meant to be. Exactly who she was meant to be. And come what may, she knew that she would face it with her head held high and her heart open wide.

For she was Sadie Lewis, daughter of magic and steel. And she was finally, finally coming home to herself.

As if on cue, the soft scuff of footsteps sounded behind her, the warmth of familiar presences drawing near. Sadie turned, a smile already blooming on her face as she took in the sight of her dearest friends, her sisters in all but blood.

Cleopatra grinned, a mischievous glint in her eye as she raised a battered camera to her face. "Smile!" she called, her voice bright with laughter.

Sadie rolled her eyes fondly, but obliged, feeling the stretch of her cheeks as her smile widened into something true and real and utterly unguarded. The shutter clicked, immortalizing the moment, and Cleo lowered the camera with a satisfied nod.

"A new hobby?" Sadie asked, arching a playful eyebrow.

Cleo shrugged, her eyes soft with some unspoken emotion. "Something like that," she murmured, her gaze drifting out over the darkening sea.

Paige and Sammy joined them then, their arms linking with Sadie's and Cleo's as they stood together at the railing, four silhouettes against the vast, glittering expanse of the sky.

No words were needed. No grand speeches or tearful confessions. They simply stood there, shoulder to shoulder and heart to heart, basking in the quiet miracle of each other's presence.

They had walked through fire together, had seen the very best and worst that humanity had to offer. Had loved and lost and grieved and raged, had clung to each other through the long, dark night of war and separation.

For they were the Six Triple Eight. The finest, fiercest, most unbreakable women the world had ever seen. And whatever lay ahead, whatever trials and triumphs and impossible choices the future held in store...they would face it together.

Always and forever, come what may.

Sadie leaned her head on Cleo's shoulder, feeling the steady thrum of her heartbeat beneath her cheek. And as the last sliver of sunlight slipped beneath the horizon, painting the world in shades of velvet and shadow, she let her eyes drift closed, a profound sense of peace settling over her like a mantle.

She was home. Not the physical place, the bustling streets and cramped tenements of her youth. But the deeper, truer home that lived in the hearts of the ones she loved, the unshakable certainty of belonging that came from being seen and known and cherished for all that she was.

And as the ship sailed on into the endless, starlit night, Sadie knew that she would carry that feeling with her always. A talisman against the darkness, a reminder of the love and the light that had brought her through the valley of the shadow and out the other side, stronger and surer and more wholly herself than she had ever been before.

For she was Sadie Lewis. Daughter of magic, sister of steel. And she knew, with a bone-deep certainty that could never be shaken, that her story was only just beginning.

THE END

About the Author

Mary McCallum *is a writer, actress, director, librettist, and producer with a passion for telling untold stories. She has written several award-winning stage plays and films. She strives to use her voice to amplify the stories of forgotten heroes, spark dialogue on vital issues, and empower artists. For more information on "Six Triple Eight" the stage play or screenplay, email sistastyleproductions@gmail.com or visit her website at www.themarymccallum.com*

Made in the USA
Middletown, DE
29 May 2025